OTHER BOOKS BY CAROLE GIFT PAGE

FICTION
PAGE

Heartland Memories Series
The House on Honeysuckle Lane
Home to Willowbrook
The Hope of Herrick House

Harlequin Steeple Hill
In Search of Her Own
Decidedly Married

DISCARD

STORMS OVER WILLOWBROOK

STORMS OVER WILLOWBROOK

CAROLE GIFT PAGE

A JANET THOMA BOOK

THOMAS NELSON PUBLISHERS
Nashville
Printed in the United States of America

Published in Nashville, Tennessee, by Thomas Nelson, Inc., Publishers.

Library of Congress Cataloging-in-Publication Data

Page, Carole Gift.
    Storms over Willowbrook / Carole Gift Page.
       p.   cm. — (Heartland memories ; bk. 4)
    ISBN 0-7852-7671-8
    I. Title. II. Series: Page, Carole Gift. Heartland memories ; bk. 4.
PS3566.A3326S7
813'.54—dc21
                                         98–5803
                                             CIP

Printed in the United States of America

1 2 3 4 5 QPK 02 01 00 99 98

For my father,
Aldon Gift,
who played saxophone and clarinet with the Big Bands.
Daddy, I love you more than words can say.

Chicago, June 1951

When the phone call came—the call that would change Alice Marie's life forever—she had less than five minutes before airtime when she would step in front of the television camera and say something resplendent about Mott's Apple Juice. With Mott's as her show's newest sponsor, she didn't dare flub her lines like she had yesterday or the powers-that-be at WBKB would have her head.

"Four minutes, thirty seconds," Rudy, her producer, clucked, hovering like an insufferable mother hen. He was a wiry, freckled redhead, agile as an eel and witty as Milton Berle. "Remember, Doll, smile big and show those pearly whites."

She inspected her lipstick in the rosy, blinding glare of her dressing room mirror and rubbed her tongue over her teeth. "Don't worry, Rudy, I'll grin like a Cheshire cat."

"Forget the cat, Doll Baby! It's that sultry Mona Lisa smile viewers eat up."

She straightened the off-the-shoulder neckline of her blue shantung sheath. "You're a darling, Rudy. I promise, I'll get it right." She snatched the bottle of juice from his hands and trilled her lines. "From the first sparkling sip, you know here's something really different! Tangy Mott's Apple Juice is so delightful with meals—so joyously refreshing in-between!"

"You got me sold, Kiddo."

"Rudy, you rascal, you'd buy an ice box from an Eskimo!"

"You betcha—if she had your eyes and your gams!"

Julia picked just that moment to poke her head in the door. "A phone call for you, Miss Reed."

"Julia, please! Can't you see—?"

"A man—he says it's important."

Alice Marie returned a withering glance. "Sure, they always say it's important. I'm on in four minutes, Julia. Tell him to call back after the show!"

Julia wrung her hands, her plain face looking dismal. "He sounded urgent, Miss Reed."

"My show comes first, Julia, not some pest on the phone." Time for a new assistant. Someone with backbone and grit. Julia was a patsy for anyone with a sob story.

Julia tugged at her starched white collar. "He says—"

Alice Marie's stomach knotted. Surely she'd have an ulcer before she was thirty-five. "For heaven's sake, Julia, I haven't even greeted today's guest!"

The fabulous—and very late—Dinah Shore had just arrived and was being rushed into makeup, her tardiness sending everyone from Rudy down to the cameramen into near hysterics. Dinah wasn't the first guest to arrive just before the cameras rolled, thanks to Chicago's sooty, jam-packed, bumper-to-bumper noonday traffic.

Why was it that just before airtime the entire universe teetered on the edge of chaos? Every day at this time Alice Marie vowed to quit television and go back on the road with the big bands. Maybe she would if the bands were still big.

Since the war the sound and texture of bands had changed. Old-time, two-beat, small-band jazz was making a comeback under the name of "Dixieland." Sure, great band leaders like Stan Kenton were resisting the tide, but plenty of traditionalists were now playing in the fifty-year-old New Orleans style.

These days it was a man's world and most of the girl singers had traded the road for a husband, a house, and a couple of kids. Not Alice Marie, of course. Fame had tasted too good to surrender for an anonymous white cottage in the suburbs. Besides, when it came to husbands and lovers, she was the queen of misfortune.

But what did it matter? The Alice Marie Show was putting her on the map, establishing her reputation in a bold new medium that was attracting some of the biggest stars in radio and Hollywood. She loved the excitement of stepping before the camera each day, knowing she was connecting at that exact moment with thousands of people in countless cities across the country.

Somehow she always managed to pull things together and put on a good show. Some of Chicago's most hard-nosed critics had given Alice Marie rave reviews. Half of Chicago's television viewers set aside their noon hour to watch the Alice Marie Show, and now affiliates everywhere were picking up the half-hour program. Network chiefs predicted the show would go nationwide in the fall when the long-awaited transcontinental relays were opened for TV's first coast-to-coast telecasts.

Julia was still waiting in the doorway like a scolded child, her pale lips parted beseechingly.

"I told you, Julia, I'm not taking any phone calls. The show's about to start, and I'm juggling a thousand crises. I don't care if it's a matter of life or death."

The magic words. Julia's gray eyes widened behind her wire-rimmed spectacles. "He—he did say it's a matter of life and death, Miss Reed."

Alice Marie's heart lurched. *Maybe something's happened to Mama!* "All right, I'll take it," she said, heading out the door with a backward glance at Rudy. "Be a doll and take care of Miss Shore! Tell her our duet will be after her first number. And make sure the orchestra knows the order of her songs."

He gave her a thumbs up. "Will do. Three minutes, Kiddo, and you're on!"

Her stacked heels clicked on the polished hardwood floor as she dashed for the fingerprint-smudged wall phone just outside Studio C. As she picked up the receiver she realized she was still holding the bottle of Mott's apple juice. She juggled it with the receiver, pushed back her shoulder-length blonde pageboy, and finally managed a breathless hello.

A voice from the past assailed her like a chill night wind. "Hello, Allie-girl."

She froze. "C-Cary?"

"It's me, baby."

She held her hand over the mouthpiece until she caught her breath. Her heart pumping with excitement and dread, she closed her eyes and steeled herself.

"You there, Alice Marie?"

"Yes, I'm here."

"I saw you on the television, Allie. Man alive, I was flabbergasted, seeing you on that little screen, natural as life. You looked gorgeous, Allie, just like always."

"Why are you calling, Cary? After all this time! What's wrong?"

"Plenty. Nothing's right without you, baby."

She had heard that deep, familiar voice—the voice of the man she loved and hated with equal intensity—a thousand times over the past eight years. On the radio—*the Stardust Ballroom brings you the mellow tunes of Cary Rose and the Starlighters!* On his albums singing soulfully, "Because of You" and "I'll Never Smile Again." And, worst of all, his voice echoing always like a death knell in the deepest recesses of her heart.

"You shouldn't be calling, Cary." Her tongue felt dry and thick. Could he hear the nervousness in her voice? "We have nothing to say to each other."

"Sure we do, Allie. You're my wife."

The iciness in her veins turned to lava. "Your wife? That was a long time ago, Cary Rose. Go back to whatever hole you crawled out of. I've got a show to do!"

"Wait, Allie!"

"Cary, just—just drop dead!" She was about to hang up when she heard something different—a note of desperation—in his voice.

"Listen, baby. That's just what I'm doing. I'm dying. I'm in the hospital on the corner of Madison and Grand Avenue. I've gotta see you once more before I . . ."

No! He was playing on her sympathies the way he always did! She slammed down the receiver and in fury swung the bottle of apple juice against the wall. Thank heaven the bottle didn't break. How would she explain a shattered bottle to the sponsor?

She looked around and saw Rudy striding smoothly toward her with Dinah Shore on his arm. Dinah, dressed in a white, summery dress with puffed sleeves and a cinched waist, flashed the smile she was famous for. Alice Marie extended her arms in a welcoming gesture. "Dinah, thank you for coming. You look lovely!"

The phone was ringing again as they left Studio C and crossed the cavernous building to Studio A. At exactly noon they walked in graceful, synchronous steps onto the sprawling stage while the orchestra struck up the familiar theme song, "Got a Date with an Angel." The center camera moved in for a close-up as Alice Marie stepped under the hot, vivid glare of a dozen blinding lights. She opened her arms wide, fingers splayed, as if eager to embrace every faceless, nameless fan ensconced in his living room armchair. There was no time to think of a husband who had deserted her so many years ago. She had a show to do.

After greeting her viewers, she introduced Dinah with lavish praise. Dinah sang her poignant, melancholy hit, "I'll Walk Alone." Then, like carefree school girls, the two women linked arms and sang a bright, fast-paced version of, "Ac-cent-tchu-ate the Positive."

After the Mott's commercial, the two sat on the velvet rose sofa and chatted like old friends. Forget that tens of thousands of strangers watched, pretending they were part of this intimate little soiree.

Maybe even Cary was watching. He had said, *I saw you on the television, Allie. . . .*

She pushed the thought away and flashed a radiant smile at Dinah. She asked all the right questions and kept her smile in place as Dinah talked about her husband, George Montgomery, her three-year-old daughter Melissa Ann, and her radio days singing with Harry James' orchestra. "I was fortunate to be on radio," Dinah said, beaming. "I had to go out only one evening a week. All my rehearsals and program conferences were at home so I could be with Missy when she was a baby."

"Obviously motherhood agrees with you," said Alice Marie, her smile rivaling Dinah's. Which hospital had Cary mentioned? The corner of Madison and something. Surely he wasn't really dying! Cary Rose had always been larger than life—vibrant, exuberant, spontaneous, unpredictable.

Dinah shook her shiny, russet curls. "You'll have to stop me, Alice Marie, or I'll rave on about Missy all day."

"No, go on, Dinah. Your fans want to hear every word."

"You're sure? Wonderful! You know, of course, George and I hoped and prayed for a baby for three years. He even built her cradle himself. He loves building things. He made her a Welsh cupboard for her toys and a huge merry-go-round horse. In fact, our friends, the Alan Ladds and Fred MacMurrays, asked him to build pieces for them too."

"How fascinating," said Alice Marie. Her lips were growing tight and dry against her teeth. Her smile felt forced, brittle.

Surely she had dreamed Cary's phone call. Even Cary wouldn't intrude on her life again in such a prosaic way. A phone call from some hospital? No! He was one to announce his arrival with trumpets and white stallions. He did everything in a big way—just the way he had callously trampled her heart, her pride.

Dinah was still prating on about George and Missy. "That spring I had a feeling I might be expecting. I went to the doctor's and—it was so amazing!—the next day I actually heard the news on Walter Winchell's show!"

"I've read a lot of things in Winchell's column," said Alice Marie, summoning a faint chuckle, "but a baby announcement?"

Dinah nodded, her perfect white teeth gleaming between glossy red lips. "Somehow he found out, because when I went back for the test results, my doctor just smiled and said, 'Well, we can't let Winchell down, can we?'"

Alice Marie straightened her back and turned to face the right camera. "And we can't let our sponsors down, can we, Dinah? It's time to do a commercial for Richard Hudnut Enriched Creme Shampoo. *See lustrous, natural 'lovelights' in your hair tonight. The egg makes it extra gentle!*"

Somehow Alice Marie made it through the last ten minutes of her show, closing with the ironic, bittersweet song, "You Made Me Love You," before her mind succumbed entirely to thoughts of Cary. Why was he intruding on her life again? Was he really dying? Would she run to him now—recklessly, heedlessly—the way she had so long ago when she was about to marry another man?

To this day she couldn't be sure Knowl Herrick had forgiven her for leaving him at the altar. Surely he had. He was happily married now to her sister Annie. But had Annie ever forgiven her for nearly stealing Knowl back again when Cary ran off with another woman?

The questions that had lain dormant for years were suddenly resurrecting themselves like phantoms rising from a graveyard. There were no answers, only more questions.

But with the show over, she could indulge herself and let the questions flow freely.

Predictably, after a show Alice Marie felt exhilarated, exhausted, hungry, weak, distracted, edgy. She would thank her guest, her staff, and crew, then head for wardrobe to select tomorrow's outfit while Julia followed with Alice Marie's favorite repast—an icy cold ginger ale and a chicken salad sandwich with lots of mayonnaise.

But today Alice Marie wasn't hungry and didn't care a whit what she wore tomorrow. Without a word to Rudy, Julia, or even Dinah herself, she slipped out of the studio and caught a taxi home. Familiar route. Up Michigan Avenue through the River North District, across the Chicago River, east on Ohio, north on Lakeshore Drive to the familiar high-rise overlooking Lake Michigan.

This was her regular routine, yet today everything seemed amiss and out of kilter. If she was about to suffer nervous prostration, she wanted to be alone. Even as she entered the spacious lobby, with its ornamental 1890s *Art Nouveau* style, and took the elevator to the tenth floor, she felt out of sync with her surroundings.

It was Cary, of course, she acknowledged as she strode down the carpeted hall to her apartment. He had disturbed the fragile balance of her universe. She had worked so hard to create a life without him, he had ceased to exist for her. She had actually begun to believe he might be dead. How often had she told herself that he must have drunk himself to death, or plunged his speeding car over some precipice, or partied himself into oblivion? She turned her key in the lock with a nervous urgency, as if being pursued. Fool! No one was following her, except the ghosts of the past.

She shut the door behind her and turned the dead bolt lock. But locks couldn't shut out memories. Or pain. She leaned against the wall and gazed around the high-ceilinged room as if it might have changed too. Thank heaven, her furnishings were reassuringly familiar—the pale blue velvet sofa and love seat, her Venetian chair and writing desk, the gray marble fireplace, her Monet prints in their ornate frames, and the lovely mosaic of braided rugs and Oriental carpet stretching from wall to wall. A sigh of relief escaped her lips. Everything was as she had left it this morning. This place had nothing to do with Cary. What had she thought—that Cary had somehow invaded her home as well as her heart?

He had said he was in the hospital.

He said he was dying.

For the first time in several years Alice Marie wished she had a bottle of Scotch in her cupboard, or some wine. Anything to take the edge off her nerves. Even a cigarette! Was she really that desperate? She hated the stinking things.

She kicked off her platform heels, padded to the kitchen in her stockinged feet, and put on the kettle. A cup of tea might be soothing. Swell! Who did she sound like now? Her mother! Anna Reed—bless her—always solved the world's ills with a steaming cup of tea. She never would have allowed an ounce of liquor to pass her lips—or anyone else's, if she could help it—but don't let anyone take away her chamomile tea.

Alice Marie removed a delicate Wedgwood cup and saucer from the cherry wood hutch, made her tea, and set it on the table. Usually when she arrived home after a show, she stripped off her dress, slip, garter belt and hose, and shrugged into her terry cloth robe, then stretched out on her four-poster bed for a nap. But not today. She was too agitated, too unsettled.

She crossed the dining room and opened the drapes to golden, diffused sunlight spangling over shimmering, diamond-studded waters. Folded her arms. Inhaled deeply. She loved this view of Lake Michigan. It was the reason she had chosen this apartment—a luxury even on her generous income.

Finally she sat down and sipped her tea, savoring its warmth even on this warm, tiptoeing-toward-summer day. She felt surprisingly comforted—an indulgence she rarely allowed herself these days. Comfort was something she associated with Mama, with home—with sweet, stultifying Willowbrook.

After all this time the memories of home were still vivid. When she closed her eyes she saw lace curtains framing a familiar window and smelled the ripe sweetness of gardenias in a porcelain vase. And in her mind—surely it wasn't real; she was still in her Chicago apartment after all—but in the darkness behind her lids she saw a wisp of movement, like the flutter of a moth's wings, and she felt a caress, ever so slight, on her head—the cool, gentle touch of her mother's palm on her hair—the way her mother used to brush back her long golden locks at bedtime and whisper, "Alice Marie, God colored your hair with His glorious sunshine."

Just the thought of Mama calmed her. Now with her emotions in control, she must decide what to do next. If she could, she would erase Cary's call from her consciousness, but that was out of the question. In a handful of words he had resurrected himself. He was real and alive. She had no choice but to pursue this new, unexpected pathway wherever it led.

Steeling herself, she flipped through the phone book and found the number of the hospital then dialed with trembling fingers. She would at least find out if Cary was there.

"I'm sorry, Ma'am," came the nurse's frosty reply to her inquiry. "We're not allowed to give out information about patients over the phone."

"But you do have a patient there named Cary Rose," Alice Marie persisted.

"Yes, Ma'am, we do."

"Please tell me how he is. Is his condition serious?"

"Ma'am, are you family?"

The question stunned Alice Marie. What was she to Cary—this man she had not seen for so many years? "I'm his wife," she announced, the words feeling strange, terrifying on her lips.

The anonymous voice on the other end of the line seemed equally startled. "His wife? Why didn't you say so, Mrs. Rose? Your husband is resting now, but I'll tell him you called."

"Wait! How is he? Tell me, please."

"I'm sorry. If you'll give me your number, I'll ask his doctor to call you."

Alice Marie felt her palm grow damp against the receiver. "That won't be necessary," she said with sudden resolve. "I'll be there. I—I'm leaving now. I'm coming to the hospital to see my husband myself."

The clock on the gray hospital wall was round and flat and as large as a serving platter, its numbers coal-black and sharp. Alice Marie noticed if she stared at the clock for a certain length of time that its solid white mass gave way to a slight slipping, hardly perceptible, but evident nonetheless, as if the flat sphere were melting, detaching itself from its static perch. The image brought to mind Salvador Dali's startling painting, "Persistence of Memory," with its bizarre, draping clock looking like someone's laundry hung out to dry.

She had seen the painting years ago in a gallery or museum in New York or Chicago or San Francisco when she was traveling with Cary's band. Dali's images had touched a deep place in her, a place she rarely traveled—she who was often accused of being shallow and who preferred to make her way through life with as few emotional entanglements as possible.

But the painting had stirred something deep and primal, as had Cary's phone call, unearthing memories that were still fresh and pungent now, years later, coming back to her in this hospital waiting room.

She knew if she walked twenty paces down the hall and entered Cary's room she could never turn back. The years without Cary would be erased in a single glance, and she would be his again, bound to him, the two of them sewn together once more like pieces of the same fabric. She had tried so hard to snip him from her life, remnant by painful remnant, until there was nothing left. How could she face him again and risk everything? How could she not?

The air stirred slightly. Alice Marie looked up to see the nurse approaching. The woman's solid, pear-shaped body moved sluggishly under her ill-fitting and heavily starched uniform. "Goodness, I'm sorry, Mrs. Rose, leaving you in the waiting room like this. The doctor is still with your husband." Her solemn eyes were inscrutable, her pale jowls heavy as kneaded dough. "But, lands, it shouldn't be long now. You hold tight, and I'll let you know the minute Mr. Rose can see you."

Alice Marie murmured a distracted, "Thank you."

Get up, run away, she told herself. *Take a taxi home.* It wasn't too late to flee, to pretend she'd never heard Cary's voice today. Forget Cary Rose existed. Soak in a hot tub until her mind was pleasantly numbed into slumber. Forget the summer he hired that pretty singer from Tallahassee to take Alice Marie's place in the band, and later in his bed.

It was the summer Papa died—1943. Just days after catching Cary with his young paramour, Alice Marie—stunned, enraged, and heartbroken—went home to Willowbrook to bury her father and comfort her mother. She ended up staying a year, hoping desperately that Cary would call or write and beg her to come back. He never did.

"Mrs. Rose?" The nurse again—what was it, five minutes, ten?—hovering, smelling of the same lavender soap Mama used, her breathing a bit ragged now. "Excuse me, Mrs. Rose. What a busy day! Too busy. The doctor's moved on to another patient. Your husband can see you now."

Alice Marie straightened, her hand moving to the back of her neck, damp under her rolled pageboy. "Thank you."

The nurse remained, tapping her pen on an official-looking pad. "Mrs. Rose? I don't mean to keep you—"

"What is it? Something about Cary—?"

"Lands, no. It's just something niggling at me. I gotta ask. Are you that lady on that television show—Alice Marie?"

Alice Marie stood up and wearily met the nurse's gaze. "Um, . . . yes, I am."

The thickset woman beamed. "I thought so! Would it be asking too much? My daughter loves your program! I've got a paper right here—a prescription pad—if you could sign it—I just know she'd love having your autograph."

Alice Marie took the pad and pen with a resigned sigh. "What's her name—your daughter?"

"Phyllis. Phyllis Badgley."

Alice Marie scribbled "Best wishes to Phyllis" and signed her name.

The nurse clasped the autograph to her ample bosom. "Thank you, Alice—uh, Mrs. Rose. I'll take good care of your husband. I promise!"

Alice Marie turned and took several tentative steps down the hall, then stopped, panic tightening the lining of her throat. She inhaled sharply against the constricting membranes. The nurse was watching, waiting, looking puzzled, so Alice Marie squared her shoulders and marched on down the hall and into the semi-dark room.

She shrank back. The air smelled medicinal, unpleasantly antiseptic. Cary Rose had always smelled of Old Spice, Lucky Strikes, and Bay Rum.

As her eyes adjusted to the shadows, she realized she had made a dreadful mistake. The frail, wasted man in the bed wasn't her lively, bursting-with-energy Cary Rose. This was a stranger, someone gravely ill, not Cary! She pivoted abruptly and headed out of the room, hoping she hadn't disturbed the poor ailing soul.

"Allie! Allie-girl, is that you?"

It was Cary's voice—raspy, but unmistakably his. She spun around and stared at the man. For the love of heaven! Beneath the jaundiced skin and sunken cheekbones, it was Cary's face. The same lean, angular features deepened by nearly a decade of years—the generously chiseled nose, square chin, and crinkly black eyes hugged by bushy brows. His curly black hair was feathered with gray at the temples; his prominent white teeth flashed from pallid lips.

"Alice Marie?" His reedy fingers made a beckoning gesture.

She approached the elevated bed. Her heart should have been pounding like a kettle drum, but her breathing had slowed, and her heart rate with it. She was moving in slow motion, her blue sheath brushing the starched white linens, her fingertips barely touching Cary's. As their eyes met, he smiled that smile—wide, beaming, the laugh lines traversing his nose to his chin. "I knew you'd come, Allie."

"You said—you were dying." She said the words almost accusingly.

He nodded. "Almost did. Real close call."

She shook her head. "Why did you call me?"

His shadowed gaze was riveting. "I couldn't check out without looking into those big blue peepers of yours one more time."

She looked away. "I shouldn't have come. I swore I never would. I swore I'd make you come to me."

"I have, Allie. I swallowed my pride. I called you. Do you know how many weeks it took me to get back my strength so I could walk out to that phone in the hallway?"

"You've been here—in this hospital—for weeks?"

"Since the last of April. Been through two surgeries to sew up my liver and who knows what all. It was touch and go for days. Doctors still don't know if the operations will take. One nasty infection and I could keel over tomorrow, Allie. Now you understand why I had to see you?"

Alice Marie lowered herself into the chair by Cary's bed. She felt faint. She couldn't digest Cary's words. He had almost died? Could still die?

Not the Cary Rose she knew. He had smooth-talked his way out of every calamity and misadventure life had thrown at him. If anyone had the luck of the Irish, it was Cary. He always said so. *With a Jewish papa and an Irish mama, I've got God and the leprechauns on my side!*

"How did you find me?" she asked.

He handed her a yellowed, dog-eared newspaper clipping from *The Chicago Sun Times,* dated August 16, 1950. She smoothed out the wrinkles and scanned the words.

Attention, fans of that bright new medium, television!
A fresh face has appeared on the Chicago horizon—
Alice Marie, a blonde charmer with a voice to match
belting out the best of Big Band melodies
on a show aptly titled, "Alice Marie."
Folks hankering for the good old days of radio
should take a gander at this gal. With the
girl-next-door beauty of Doris Day and the
knock-'em-dead voice of Peggy Lee,
Alice Marie will carve a stunning and unforgettable
niche in Chicago's swank entertainment scene.
Catch her show daily on WBKB at twelve noon
and sample a delectable program that will give
that king of radio, Arthur Godfrey, a run for his money.

She handed the article back to him. "This was published almost a year ago. You're just now finding me?"

He managed a crooked grin. "A buddy sent the column to me in Korea. Figured I might wanna look you up again."

"Korea? You fought in Korea? Is that how you were hurt?"

"Nah. I didn't fight. But lots of guys were going over, some drafted, some enlisting—vets who were still trying to get the big war out of their heads, you know? The band was losing guys right and left to the armed forces. So I figured, if you can't beat 'em, join 'em."

"Join them? How?"

"Easy. I packed up the band and we went to Korea to entertain the troops. Only, we saw more action than I wanted." He fingered the bed sheet, twisting a corner around his index finger, a gesture she remembered with a pang of affection. "For a while we traveled with the Eighth Army, from the United Nations beachhead at Pusan to Seoul, then all the way to the North Korean capital at Pyongyang. Can you imagine? I played my saxophone while bombs lit up the night sky like a meteor shower.

Even got a standing ovation from the commander, Lieutenant General Matthew Ridgway. What a guy won't do for a gig, huh?"

"You could have been killed."

"I came home without a scratch. Luck of the Irish. Came to Chicago just after Christmas."

"Looking for me?"

"Mainly. Truth is, we got some good bookings here. Edgewater Beach, the Aragon, Nob Hill, the Blue Note, and the Grand Terrace ballroom. Remember when we played there during the war, Allie? It was like old times. No kidding. I still got Sid Vance on trumpet and Charlie Williams on trombone. Remember how they ribbed us, called us the little love-birds, because we were always necking in the back of Sid's Rambler wagon?"

Alice Marie's expression remained stony. She wasn't about to encourage Cary's sentimental musings. "You still haven't told me how you were hurt."

"Oh, yeah. Funny thing. All those close calls in Korea, and what does me in? I was crossing the street in front of the Marshall Field warehouse. A car comes careening around the corner and mows me down, just like that. I never saw him coming. And I swear, Allie, I wasn't drinking. I gave that up years ago. So, here I am—I wake up in the intensive care unit hooked up to all these tubes, and the doctor's ready to call in a priest or a rabbi, he doesn't know which. I saved him the trouble. I lived."

She sat forward slightly. "Why did you call me, Cary?"

He shrugged. "Okay, I get it. You're still sore about me running out on you. Right?"

She clenched her fingers and released the words with a hard, bitter edge. "Sore? That doesn't begin to describe how I feel. You left me. I thought you were dead. For years I wanted you to die. But after eight years I could finally wake up in the morning and not wonder where you were. I finally got the image of you and *her* out of my mind. And now you suddenly waltz back into my life and act like you've just been away on a little vacation?"

"It's not like that, Allie. I'm not asking a thing of you. I just wanted to see you one more time." He stretched his hand toward her. "I've always loved you, Allie. Always."

Her voice broke with rancor. "Even when you were with her?"

"You mean Gloria? That was over in a few months. Sweetheart, that girl couldn't hold a candle to you. I would've dropped her like a hot potato if you hadn't run home to Mama."

"My dad died, Cary. I went home for his funeral."

"Must have been the longest funeral on record. You never came back to the band. It was like you just dropped off the face of the earth."

The blood rose in her cheeks. "You never asked me back. You were with *her*!"

He was still twisting the sheet. Perspiration beaded on his upper lip. "All right, I was a jerk. But if you'd given me one little hint that you wanted me back, Allie. One call, one letter!"

"I didn't know where to find you! The band had moved on. I didn't know your itinerary. You could have been in Timbuktu!"

His shadowed eyes narrowed. Were tears glistening? "Sounds like we were both done in by our stupidity and pride."

She shook her head. "It was more than stupidity, and a whole lot more than pride. You betrayed me, Cary. When I think of all you put me through, that woman was the last straw."

His hand clasped hers, trembling, urgent. His touch was still electric. "Come on, Allie. It wasn't so bad. We had lots of good times. We were good together. Real good. I've never met another woman like you."

Hot tears stung her eyes. "You mean, a woman you could cheat on and slap around whenever the mood struck?"

His shaggy brows furrowed over wounded eyes. "Aw, Allie-girl, don't dredge up the old stuff. That's not me anymore. I'd never lay a hand on that gorgeous face."

"But you did. More than once."

"Okay. A coupla times in the early days, when I was falling-down drunk. We were both kids then. I had a temper, and you knew just what to say to make me see red. But I've mellowed, sweetheart. I don't touch the hard stuff. Look at me. I'm not the same man."

She pulled her hand away and stood up. "I—I shouldn't have come. I can't think straight when you talk to me."

He struggled to sit up, his lean, muscled arms gripping the side rails. "Don't go, Allie. Stay a few more minutes. For old time's sake. Just sit and talk to me like you used to."

She reached in her pocketbook for a hanky and blew her nose. "There's nothing to talk about, Cary, nothing either of us can say to erase all the pain between us, the years we've lost. It's too late."

He sank back against his pillow, his dark eyes crinkling the way they always did when he wanted to convince her of something. That look was magnetic, seductive as a siren song. "Come on, Baby. I'm not asking you to take me back. Just keep me company. Tell me about your show. I hear you've booked some top names—Artie Shaw, and Tex Beneke and the Modernaires. I read it in the trades—you had Kay Kyser, right? And Vaughn Monroe?"

With a despairing sigh she sat back down, knowing it was already too late to leave. Cary had her right where he wanted her. "Yes, we've had some great talent. Just last month Woody Herman was on."

"Oh, yeah, I always liked Woody. They don't come any better."

"And Dick Haymes and Helen O'Connell," she went on listlessly. Where was her steel will now, her pride, the callous indifference her family so often accused her of showing? Why couldn't she just walk out on Cary the way he had walked out on her? "And Martha Tilton's scheduled for tomorrow's show," she heard herself saying, as if it mattered anymore.

"I'm real proud of you, Allie. You've hit the big time. You've got it made, Sweetheart. Your dreams came true after all."

"Did they?" Absently she massaged her finger where her wedding ring had been so long ago. "What do you know about my dreams, Cary? Or anything else about me, for that matter?"

He grinned, the lines deepening in his face. "I know you couldn't wait to get away from that little Indiana town and that straitlaced family of yours so you could make a name for yourself in the big city. And you did it, Baby. What do they think of you now—your mama and your sister and that fancy husband of hers you almost married?"

Alice Marie bit her lower lip and looked away, her gaze straying to the utilitarian windows with their cheap, mustard-yellow curtains so typical of hospitals. "Honestly, Cary, I don't know what they think of me, and I really don't care."

"What did you tell them—about us?"

Her tone hardened. "I told Mama we got divorced."

"Divorced? No!"

"I didn't have the heart to tell her I couldn't even find you to serve divorce papers."

Cary grabbed hold of the bed rails. "But we're not divorced, Allie. The next time you go home, you tell your mama you're still my wife."

She stared down at the linoleum floor—a patchwork of pale, ugly marbled red and gray squares. "I haven't been home in years, Cary."

He sounded surprised. "But you must write or phone once in awhile."

"Sure. At Christmas. And birthdays. I always send Mama something expensive and pretty. Her favorite perfume. A print from the Art Institute. I scribble off an occasional postcard. Believe me, that's as much as they want to hear from me."

Cary chuckled faintly. "Well, I was afraid you might have gone home and hooked that fella, Knowl Herrick, for yourself by now."

She bristled. "Don't make jokes, Cary."

"I'm not. I hear the ol' boy's got his own publishing house and even a few titles on the *New York Times* best-seller list. He must be rolling in dough."

"I wouldn't know. I'm the last person Knowl would confide in."

Cary shrugged. "I remember—it's all coming back to me—the bad blood between you and your family. But time has a way of working things out, Allie. Live and let live, you know?"

Alice Marie shook her head. Just thinking about home and Knowl and her sister Annie tied her stomach in knots. She and Annie had never talked about that dreadful time, but it remained between them, dark and palpable as a malignancy. "I did something that can't be forgiven, Cary."

He looked at her. "Nothing can't be forgiven."

"This can't. It hasn't been. It won't ever be."

"What? Tell me."

She folded her arms in a protective gesture across her chest and mindlessly rubbed one elbow. She paused and then said sharply, "When you left me years ago, I was so—so distraught, I went home and tried to break up my sister's marriage. . . . I tried to seduce Knowl."

"And?"

"I think he was tempted for a time, but he never weakened. He sent me away. I think he hates me to this day."

"What a fool!" said Cary under his breath.

Alice Marie's voice broke with a sudden rush of emotion. "No, Cary, Knowl's the strongest, most honorable man I've ever known."

"Sure. The man's a regular saint."

Alice Marie bristled. "The truth is, Cary—and I never thought I'd have a chance to tell you this to your face—what you did to me . . . what you did twisted something inside me, turned me so mean and spiteful, I wanted to hurt someone the way you hurt me. I wanted to prove I could make someone love me again. But what I did—I nearly destroyed someone I loved. I drove my sister from her own home. I lied, convinced her that her husband wanted me. I even convinced myself."

Cary fingered the corner of his sheet. "I didn't know, Babe. I'm sorry."

Alice Marie's voice tightened. "My sister Annie—she was devastated. She left Knowl and was gone for nearly two years before she learned the affair was all a lie. Annie and I—we were never close, but after that . . . well, let's just say, it's not something a woman forgives easily."

"Have you ever asked her?"

Alice Marie managed a disdainful little chuckle. "My pride won't let me. Why should she forgive me? I haven't forgiven myself. And I haven't forgiven you, Cary."

When he didn't respond, except for a tightened muscle along his gaunt jawline, she went on, her voice high and breathy. "The irony is, Cary, I know now I never really wanted Knowl Herrick. Okay, maybe I wanted him, but I never loved him. I loved the way he treated me. Like a queen. He put me on a pedestal. No one else ever made me feel that special."

"Sure they did!" Cary protested. "*I* did, didn't I, Babe, in the good days?"

"You made me feel a lot of things, but never special."

"Listen, Allie, you would have been bored in a minute with Knowl Herrick. You need a man with fire and sizzle. A man like me."

"I had a man like you," she said dryly, "and he fizzled out, like water on a firecracker."

With a deep groan Cary shifted his torso in the large bed, stretching out his legs under the nubby, olive-green blanket. The effort seemed to sap his energy. "Allie, my girl," he sighed, "if I could change the past, I would. But all I've got is today, this very minute, and, God willing, a handful of tomorrows. And, Sweetie, forgiven or not, all I wanna do is spend them with you. Whaddaya say?"

Alice Marie told herself she would never go back to the hospital to see Cary, that he could rot there for all she cared. She told herself this the very next afternoon, after her show, as she hailed a taxi to take her to the hospital. She told herself this every day for the next two weeks as she walked the hospital corridor to Cary's room.

But a part of her simply wasn't listening. A part of her insisted on overruling every commonsense argument she had about Cary. He was bad news. He didn't deserve a second chance. Her life was finally on track; Cary Rose would only derail her!

She knew all the arguments; they swirled in her head night and day. But her heart didn't care. Her heart was still Cary's.

If she wasn't careful, it would be just like the old days. Whenever she was near him she felt the familiar yearning; she had never been able to resist him, his kiss, his touch. She had always melted in his arms; she felt herself disappear as he became the only thing in her life.

She couldn't let that happen again; no matter how she felt she must keep Cary Rose at arm's length.

When Alice Marie entered Cary's hospital room on the last Saturday of June, he was sitting on the bed in a brown silk robe with a tie sash, clean-shaven, his curly black hair neatly combed. He flashed his wide, toothy smile. "Babe, my fever's finally gone. The doc says I can go home— if I had a home to go to."

"You can't come home with me." The words were out before she had time to think, a defensive, visceral reaction.

"Did I even ask?"

"You were thinking about it. It just wouldn't work, Cary. There's no future for us, you know that. We're like oil and water."

"Come on, Gorgeous. Once upon a time, we were a pretty good mix. Better than gin and tonic, hotter than Dixieland and Bourbon Street."

She sat down in the chair by his bed. "You're a scream, Cary. A real comedian. They should put *you* on television."

He reached for her hand, intertwining their fingers. "You're still my wife, Allie. For better or worse."

"All I've seen is worse."

His fingers tightened around hers. "For richer or poorer, in sickness and in health."

She extricated her fingers, one by one. "I must be sick to even listen to this."

"It'd just be till I was back on my feet, Sweetheart."

She sat back and crossed her legs, smoothing her skirt over her knees. "I just have a one-bedroom apartment, Cary."

"I could sleep on the couch, Babe."

"What about your old place—where were you staying when the car hit you?"

"The Drake Hotel. Our band was scheduled to open at the Aragon. The boys and I were making big bucks. But since my accident, the band's broken up."

"It doesn't sound like they were very loyal to you."

"What could they do? The doc told them I was dying. He already had me six feet under. So Arnie Shavers—remember him, the lanky guy with the wild Harpo Marx hair?—he took over as band leader until the rest of our scheduled bookings were played out. But poor ol' Arnie didn't want all the headaches of leading an orchestra, so they disbanded a few weeks ago."

Alice Marie nodded. "Arnie could never fill your shoes."

Cary smiled. "Thanks, Sweetheart. Actually, Arnie paid me a visit just the other day. Told me two of my drummers joined Duke Ellington and my sax players went with Woody Herman. Lucky stiffs, huh? My girl singer—Dolores Wayne, a real fine blonde chick—joined a combo; and my pal Buddy Baker, the best trumpet man in the business, teamed up with Ray Robbins."

"But you can get them back, can't you, when you're well? Or you'll find even better musicians. I know you, Cary—the way you can pull together a band. You'll come up with a swell outfit again."

He pulled at a raveling on the hem of his robe. "Sure, I guess I could do it again, but I don't think I will."

"Why not? The band is your whole life."

He looked at her, and some of the old fire had gone out of his eyes. "It's a different world out there now, Babe. It used to be kids would travel a hundred miles to hear a swinging band on a one-nighter. No more. You know how it is. With be-bop and all, big bands have it tough today. You gotta hit on a record first and get fire hot; then they'll open the doors to you."

Alice Marie nodded. "That's why I'm doing television."

"Smart gal." Cary heaved a sigh, his bristly brows hugging his ebony eyes. "So, anyway, now that I'm a little down on my luck, I'm looking for a friendly place to hang my hat."

Alice Marie felt her guard go up. "My heart bleeds for you, Cary, but I just can't—"

"You'd be safe with me, Sweets. I wouldn't lay a hand on you, I promise. Besides, the doc says no strenuous activity. I'm as harmless as a kitten."

"Don't you mean a tomcat?"

Cary's voice took on a new desperation as he waved his hand around the cramped, shadowed room. "I swear I'm going stir-crazy in this place, Allie. They wake you in the middle of the night to give you a sleeping pill and again at dawn and stick a thermometer in your mouth. They feed you pabulum three times a day. I'm dying for a juicy steak. The doc won't spring me from this joint unless I got someone to play nursemaid. Just let me come to your place and recuperate for a few weeks, and I'll be out of your life forever."

She felt herself weakening. He did make sense in a certain obscure way. Where else could he go? And she was still his wife, even if in name only.

"I'll talk to your doctor," she said at last. "If he says you're well enough to go home, I guess we can try it for a few weeks. But you're sleeping on the couch, and that's final. This is no second honeymoon."

He seized both her hands in his. "You won't be sorry, Baby. I promise!"

On Sunday, the first day of July, Cary was released from the hospital and, against her better judgment, Alice Marie took him home to her apartment. She put his duffel bag of belongings in the front hall closet and tossed a pile of sheets, blankets, towels, and a pillow on the sofa. "This should be all you'll need for now," she told him. "There's soap and toothpaste in the bathroom. If you need any toiletries, make a list and I'll pick them up after my show tomorrow."

He hung his coat and derby on the hatrack. "Don't go to any trouble, Babe. I can run down to the corner grocery. There is a corner grocery somewhere around here, isn't there?"

"Six blocks. The doctor told you to take it easy, Cary. You're not out of the woods yet. You could have a relapse."

He looked around, his gaze taking in the marble fireplace, the velvet sofas, Monet prints, and Oriental carpets. "A guy could get used to a place like this."

"Don't get too comfortable, Cary. This is temporary, remember?"

He tweaked her cheek. "You won't let me forget."

When Alice Marie rose at seven the next morning, she tiptoed quietly down the hall to the kitchen, lest she wake Cary. To her surprise, he was already at the stove in his robe and slippers, scrambling eggs in an iron skillet. "Good morning," he crooned. "The coffee's on, and take a gander at the bagels and cream cheese on the table."

Sure enough, the table was already set with china, silver, linen napkins, neatly folded, and a glass of orange juice beside each plate. "Cary, you did this?"

"It wasn't little gremlins, Doll. Sit down. The coffee's hot and black, the way you always liked it."

"You remembered."

He handed her a steaming cup. "You'd be surprised at all I remember about you. About us."

"Cary—"

"Don't worry, Allie, I'll be good. But you can't keep a guy from thinking. Wishing. Hoping."

She sipped her coffee and steered the conversation to a safer topic. "I'm amazed. I never knew you to get up before noon."

He spooned a mound of scrambled eggs on each plate and sat down across from her. "That hospital wrecked my whole routine. On the road we always had breakfast at lunchtime and lunch at dinnertime and supper at midnight. Now, with those nurses waking me at six every morning, I'm wide awake soon as the sun comes up."

"Good for you, Cary. Maybe you'll become a normal person yet."

He chuckled. "Don't count on it. I'm a gypsy at heart. On the road I never saw the sunrise unless I caught a glimpse of it before I collapsed into bed after a night of playing. Or partying."

"Don't remind me," she cautioned, her tone hard-edged. She sampled the eggs. Not bad. Cary had obviously learned a few skills during their years apart.

"What are you hankering for for dinner, Doll? Spaghetti? Chop suey? Beef stew?"

She looked at him in astonishment. "Don't tell me I'm married to a culinary genius and didn't even know it."

"I learned to cook in self-defense. Too many lousy meals at too many dives and beaneries across the country. It's amazing what you can do with a hot plate and a little imagination."

Alice Marie washed her eggs down with her last swallow of coffee. "Well, I've got a modern electric stove complete with double oven, and there should be something suitable to fix in the pantry or freezer, so surprise me."

When Alice Marie arrived home from the studio late that afternoon, her apartment was filled with delicious aromas. She found Cary where she had left him that morning—in the kitchen. He was dressed in a white polo shirt, navy slacks, and black loafers. He was a handsome man who wore his clothes with a casual sophistication, although at the moment he was frying lamb chops and stirring a pot of boiling rice.

He glanced around briefly, then turned his attention back to the stove. "Swell! You're home just in time, Allie. Would you put the mint jelly on the table and pour the iced tea? I would've got wine, but you know what it does to me, and I promised to be good."

"It does what it does because you don't know when to stop."

"You know me so well." He put the rice and chops on the table, disappeared into the living room for a moment, and was back lighting the white tapered candles before she had even kicked off her heels and stretched her sore feet. From the record player in the other room came the romantic strains of Glenn Miller's "Moonlight Serenade."

"Cary, you didn't have to go to all this trouble."

"No trouble, Babe. What am I gonna do—sit around this place all day twiddling my thumbs?"

She sat down and unfolded her napkin. "The doctor says you're supposed to rest. No exertion whatsoever. Now I happen to know I didn't have lamb chops in the house. That means you—"

"Took a little jaunt to the corner grocery."

"Six blocks away!"

"Six and a half actually, but who's counting?" His olive-black eyes twinkled. "Don't worry. I shooed the dogs away and rested on six fire hydrants on the way home."

She gave him her sternest look. "No more of this, Cary. Do you understand? *I'm* supposed to be taking care of *you*."

He winked at her. "Okay. You can tuck me in, if you like."

She made a face at him. "Sure, Cary. When cows fly."

In spite of Alice Marie's cautioning, Cary continued to serve sumptuous breakfasts at sunrise and delectable candlelight dinners when she arrived home from the studio. He kept the apartment spotless, polished the silver, and ran errands, walking blocks to the post office or dry cleaners. She worried about the dark circles under his eyes and his increasing weight loss. But no matter how much she chided him, he would shrug and tell her, "Stop fussing. You're becoming a *noodge*, a nag. I'm fine. I have to keep busy."

Sometimes she thought she noticed him grimace with pain, but whenever she asked him about it, he dismissed her concern with one of his silly little jokes.

"What would your doctor say if he saw all you were doing?" she challenged one evening in mid-July. They were sitting together on the sofa, in their robes, sipping their final cup of coffee for the night. The melodic ballad "Stairway to the Stars" spun out from a 78-rpm record on the player.

Cary reached over and touched her hair. "Doc would tell me, 'After all these years God has given you a chance to win back your wife. Don't waste a minute of it!'"

She shook off his touch. "Please, Cary, don't—"

"I won't, Babe. It's just—I need you. I never stopped loving you."

"It's too late," she argued, her words as fleeting as air.

"That's where you're wrong, Allie. It's never too late when you love somebody. Love is timeless, eternal." He drew her into his arms as she had known he would, and as she had yearned for him to. Gently he kissed her lips, her eyelids, her hair. This moment was inevitable, written in the winds of destiny. She was powerless to resist. Every inch of her being told her she was his—yesterday, today, always.

"I'm still your husband and you're still my wife," he whispered against her ear. They kissed again, with passionate abandon, unaware of the finished song and the needle scratching over and over in the record's circling groove.

After a while—it could have been seconds, minutes, or hours, she had lost all track of time—Cary swept her up in his arms. He held her close to his chest and nuzzled her head with his chin. "I'll never leave you again, Alice Marie," he promised, his voice husky with emotion. "Not tonight. Not ever." He kissed her again, soundly, decisively, then with a sure stride carried her into the bedroom and nudged the door shut with his foot.

The days of summer slipped by in a lovely, pastel haze. Alice Marie had never been happier; Cary had never been more attentive. It was the second honeymoon she had always dreamed of. She even telephoned her mother, Anna Reed, in Willowbrook and rhapsodized, "Mama, you'll never guess what's happened. Cary Rose and I are back together! We've never been more in love!"

Anna Reed sounded incredulous. "You mean you remarried that gallivanting scalawag?"

"No, Mama, we were never divorced. I—I fibbed about that. I've always been his wife. Only now I'm truly his wife—forever, Mama, just the way you always said marriage should be."

Her mother's tone remained skeptical. "Don't you dare let that man break your heart again, Alice Marie."

"I won't, Mama. Please, be happy for me."

On the second Saturday of August, Alice Marie woke at seven as usual, stretched languidly, and reached across the bed for her sleeping husband. At her touch he always woke with a snort and pulled her into his arms for a morning kiss. But today he only groaned and weakly squeezed her hand. The heat radiating from his palm startled her. She leaned up on one elbow and felt his forehead and looked into his face. His eyes were glazed and he was flushed, burning with fever.

"Oh, Cary, no!" she cried.

"Call the doc, Baby," he rasped.

Half an hour later an ambulance arrived and whisked Cary off to the hospital. Alice Marie rode along, kneeling beside the steel gurney, holding her husband's hand. "Please be okay, Darling," she whispered over and over against his ear.

Cary's physician—a stocky, balding man with pale gray eyes—met them in the emergency room. After checking Cary, he told Alice Marie, "We'll be prepping your husband for surgery and taking him up as soon as an operating room is free. An hour or two at most."

"What's wrong with him?" she wailed.

He peered at her over rimless spectacles. "He has an infection, but our immediate problem is internal bleeding. We've got to go in and get that under control. Beyond that his liver may be failing."

Alice Marie shook her head. Was she hearing right? "His liver?"

"Yes, Mrs. Rose. Have you noticed his yellow coloring lately? His skin is jaundiced."

"His coloring? No, I've worried about the dark circles under his eyes, but Cary's always had olive skin. You never mentioned—"

"It's evident his liver isn't doing its job. Has he complained of pain?"

"Pain? No, not in so many words. But sometimes I wondered. Why? I don't understand." Tears blurred her vision. "You released him from the hospital. You said he was well!"

The physician's expression remained infuriatingly stoic. "No, Mrs. Rose. I released Cary because we had done everything we could for him.

The accident caused severe internal injuries. We did the best we could to patch him up, but there's only so much that medicine can do. Cary's liver wasn't functioning at capacity. He knew he was living on borrowed time."

Alice Marie brushed tears from her eyelids. "He knew?"

"He knew he was walking around with a damaged liver. That's why I cautioned him to take it easy, don't overdo. I told him his liver could last weeks, months, maybe even years, if he was lucky."

She fished in her pocketbook for a tissue. "He never told me. I thought he was fine."

"Evidently that's what he wanted you to believe."

She dabbed at her eyes. "I've got to see him, please, before he goes to surgery."

"Of course. Right this way." He led her to a small cubicle at the far end of the emergency room. As she approached Cary's bed, an attendant closed the curtain around them.

"Cary?" She leaned over and put her hand on his forehead. His skin did have a yellow cast. Why hadn't she noticed it before? "Cary, I'm right here, Baby. How are you feeling?"

He looked up at her with glazed eyes. He started to speak, then moved his tongue over his dry lips. "I'm sorry, Babe," he said huskily. "I thought for sure I could beat this thing. The luck of the Irish, you know?"

She clasped his hand. "You will beat it, Darling. Don't give up now. You'll be on the mend before you know it."

"I'd never give up, Doll, but this time it's not up to me."

"It is, Cary. You can fight your way back. You're too stubborn to let anything take you down."

"Sorry, Allie." His eyes teared as he searched her face. "I've used up all my luck. These weeks with you—the best ever—a dream come true. What more can I ask for?"

"More time, Cary." She bent close to his face and laid her head on his brow. "Ask for more time!"

He shook his head. "I've run out of time, Allie."

"No, Cary, don't! Don't say it!"

He reached for her hand and pressed her fingers against his lips. "One more thing, Babe. One thing I gotta do."

"What, Darling?"

"With all the carousing I've done, I—I haven't scored many points with the Man upstairs. Help me, Allie. I gotta make peace with my Maker."

She stared at him, a sour taste in her throat. "You're not going to die, Cary. I won't let you! You're not going to leave me again!"

"Just in case, Babe."

"You mean you want me to call someone—a minister?"

"Naw. I don't wanna do 'the priest or the rabbi—which will it be?' routine. Just say a little prayer for me, okay?"

Her pulse raced. "I can't, Cary. I—I've never prayed."

"Sure you have. Everybody prays sometime."

"Not me," she said in a small, broken voice. "I've made a point of never asking God for anything."

"For the love of Pete!"

"You know why, Cary. My family—they're religious. I've told you how they are. I couldn't stomach it. All my life we had to be in church every Sunday. I used to put my hands over my ears and tell myself stories in my head so I wouldn't have to listen." She ran her fingers through his curly hair with a distracted nervousness. "I'm sorry, Sweetheart. I don't know the first thing about God. I never even learned a Bible verse. The only time I was happy in church was when I was singing. All I know of God is the songs I sang as a child."

Cary's eyes took on a solemn urgency. "Then sing to me, Allie. Sing the hymns you sang as a girl."

"Here? Right now?"

His lips twisted into a sardonic smile. "Yes, now. I may have to miss the show next week."

She searched her memory. What hymns did she know? She had sung for countless weddings and funerals over the years, starting with her Grandfather Reed's funeral when she was only fifteen. Self-consciously, her voice verging on a whisper, she sang, "Rock of Ages." When she had sung all the verses she could recall, she stopped and waited, hoping Cary was satisfied.

He squeezed her hand. "Did anyone ever tell you you sing like an angel?"

"Yes. Often." A little smile escaped her lips. "Those were the only times anyone ever called me an angel."

"Sing some more. You remind me of my mama. She sang to me, 'Ave Maria,' when I was no bigger than a button. Sing it for me."

She sang it haltingly, unsure of the words, then scoured her mind for traces of other bygone melodies. "Jesus Loves Me," the chorus she sang in church when she was only three. "Amazing Grace." She tried them, one by one, in a light, tentative voice that grew stronger and surer with each stanza—"Nearer, My God, to Thee," "O Love that Wilt Not Let Me Go."

Amazing that they were all still there, those moldering hymns, buried in a dusky crevice of her consciousness. Amazing how her own emotions soared with the music—a mixture of anguish, hope, and supplication. Oddly, the singing became worship—she, who claimed no faith at all. She felt God in the singing—or perhaps not God, but a presence nonetheless, strong, unshakable. She sensed a hush around her and realized that people nearby were listening. It didn't matter; only Cary mattered; only this moment. She sang on in her lilting, bell-clear soprano.

Cary's hand tightened around hers. "Allie, my girl, how can you sing so gloriously about a God you can't even talk to?"

It was a startling question. She thought a moment. "Because my voice is the only thing about me that's good enough for God. Maybe that's—"

A nurse pulled open the curtain and peeked inside, flashing a sympathetic smile. "Excuse me, Mrs. Rose. I'm sorry, but it's time to go. The attendants are ready to take your husband to surgery."

With effort, Cary lifted his head off the bed. "Please, I know you gotta do the Florence Nightingale bit, but just give us one more minute. Go count aspirins or tongue depressors for awhile, okay?"

With a sigh she relented. "A minute, Mr. Rose. No more."

Alice Marie wound her arms around Cary's neck; he wrapped his arms around her. "I'll say a prayer," she whispered, choking back a sob.

"Me too." He rolled his eyes upward and murmured, "Jesus, from one Jewish son to another, can You give me a hand here? I know Your Papa parted the Red Sea. Has He got something left for me? I'd be mighty grateful."

Alice Marie's last glimpse of Cary was of his wink and his grin as he mouthed the words, "Love you, Babe!" He looked weary and weak, but also happy, confident, and resolute. They could have been wheeling him off to play opening night at the Hollywood Palladium, with his name in lights and the promise of glowing reviews in *Variety*. She could imagine him now—her Cary on top, hitting the big time, ready to give the performance of his life. Cary at his best, the Cary she had fallen in love with, the quirky, indomitable man she would carry in her heart for the rest of her life.

Less than two hours later Cary's surgeon emerged from the white double doors of the operating suite, still wearing his surgical gown, traces of blood—Cary's blood?—on the olive-green fabric.

Alice Marie read the news in his eyes.

"No!" she screamed before he said a word.

He stretched out a hand to her, but she pushed it away.

"No, don't say it! Don't tell me!"

He stepped forward again. "I'm sorry, Mrs. Rose." He spoke in the same funereal monotone he must have used a hundred times before when the patient died. "A blood clot hit his heart. There was nothing we could—"

She clutched his blood-spattered gown in her fists. "No! He can't die! He promised not to leave me again! He promised!"

That evening Alice Marie telephoned her mother in Willowbrook. "Mama?" she said, her lips trembling against the mouthpiece.

"Alice Marie? Is that you? What's wrong, Honey?"

A sob tore at her throat. "Mama, it's Cary!"

"Merciful heavens, did that man leave you again?"

Another sob. "Yes, Mama."

"Oh, Alice Marie, I was afraid this would happen. You never should have gone to the hospital to see him. That man can't be trusted. Tell me what happened. Where'd he go this time?"

Alice Marie wept freely now. "He's dead, Mama. Cary's dead!"

There was a long minute of silence before her mother spoke again. "Alice Marie," she said in her gentle, familiar, take-charge voice, "I don't know what happened, and I don't need to know. You just come home. Do you hear me? Right now. You go pack up your things and come home. I'll get the rosebud room ready. Remember how you loved that room as a little girl? We'll all be here waiting for you. It'll be okay, Honey. God help us, we'll get through this together!"

Willowbrook, Indiana, August 1951

All the way home on the train Alice Marie kept asking herself what in the world she was doing, running home to Mama after all these years like a nose-bloodied, scaredy-cat kid. She had to be crazy.

She was crazy. Crazy with grief. She had buried Cary, the love of her life. Actually, his body had been shipped home to his family in Ohio for burial. His parents were dead, but he had a brother, a sister, and a handful of nieces and nephews Alice Marie had never met. They hadn't seen him in ten years and didn't sound too excited about having him shipped home to them in a box, but where else was Cary, who had lived his life like a nomad, going to rest in peace?

Crazy. Life was crazy. Death, craziest of all! With Cary gone, the whole depressing world was wacky, and Alice Marie was ready to wash her hands of the whole stupid mess.

To prove her point, the day Cary died she walked away from her television show. Just like that. Without a second thought. From the hospital she phoned Rudy and told him to find someone to take her place for the next few weeks. "I'm no good to anyone right now, Rudy," she told him between sobs. "I—I need to get away and clear my head. Maybe you can get Patti Page or Rosemary Clooney to step in for a while. Or maybe bring Dinah Shore back on. She's got that new album with RCA. Maybe she'd love some extra television exposure right now." Still sobbing. "Yes, I know I'm breaking my contract. Yes, Rudy, I know what the sponsors will say." More sobs. "I can't help it! My husband just died, and I'm dying inside right along with him. Do the best you can, and I'll be forever grateful. Thanks, Rudy, you're a godsend!"

The next day, after the necessary arrangements had been made for Cary, Alice Marie gave Julia the keys to her apartment and asked her to find someone to sublet it for a couple of months. When Julia asked who on earth she should rent to, Alice Marie shot back, "For crying out loud, Julia, I don't care who you get, as long as it's not Al Capone or some Nazi war criminal!"

That settled, she emptied out her refrigerator, dumping the contents of milk bottles and mayonnaise jars down the drain and throwing away all leftovers—the week-old lamb chops, half a cherry pie, a dried-out salmon loaf, even the chicken cacciatore Cary had made two nights ago.

She tossed a few clothes into a suitcase (forget her Dior and Schiaparelli originals; Willowbrook had no fashion sense). She made one concession—her traveling outfit—a fitted jacket and skirt of houndstooth check and her white felt derby. She grabbed her hatbox and cosmetics bag, caught a taxi to Chicago's sprawling, jungle-maze, steaming hothouse of a station, and boarded the afternoon train for Indiana. Now, here she was watching out the window as the whistle blew and the passenger car shuddered from side to side and back and forth, nearly rattling her teeth loose. When she was sure she could tolerate no more jouncing, the train finally wheezed to a lurching, clattering stop beside the familiar old red-brick station.

Willowbrook. Her birthplace. She had spent a lifetime trying to get away from this place. Now she was back. Someone somewhere had to be playing an immense practical joke!

Knowl Herrick was waiting for her at the depot—straight-arrow, true-blue Knowl, her sister's husband, the man Alice Marie had left at the altar to run away with Cary. He looked more handsome and sophisticated than she remembered. His tousled brown hair held a touch of gray; he seemed taller, more broad shouldered and muscular than the lanky youth she recalled. But his hazel-brown eyes hadn't changed; they were as riveting and intense as ever behind his wire-rimmed glasses.

As she stepped off the train and approached Knowl, her high heels clacking on the cobblestone, she thought about how he had doted on her since childhood. And while her fondness for him had always been a bit self-serving, she had shamelessly encouraged his adoration anyway. She had liked the idea of him loving her, liked the sense of security it gave her. It was like having extra change in your pocket so you could call home in an emergency. But these days Knowl Herrick probably felt little more than pity and contempt for her.

As she expected, he greeted her now with polite reserve, offering a brief embrace that kept her at arm's length. "Hello, Alice Marie." There was an awkward pause. "Listen, I want you to know. I was sorry to hear about Cary."

This was it?—his entire conversational repertory delivered in their first fifteen seconds together? Sure enough, he remained silent as he collected her things and walked her to his waiting car—a shiny new, black Hudson Hornet.

As they drove over the familiar streets of Willowbrook, Alice Marie made a stab at conversation. "How's Mama? How's Annie? How's your sweet little Maggie? She must be about four now, isn't she? I bet she looks just like you."

Knowl shook his head. "Actually, she's the spitting image of Annie."

"Oh, poor little thing!" The words were out before Alice Marie could catch herself. She cringed, knowing how catty she sounded. She hadn't meant it; it was a stupid thing to say. Why, why did her family always bring out the worst in her?

Knowl didn't take the comment well at all. A tendon tightened along his sturdy jawline and his knuckles blanched on the steering wheel. "Alice Marie," he said sharply, "your mother may want you here—"

"She does! She said so!"

"But if you've come home to make trouble, I'll turn this car around and drive you right back to the station."

Her own anger flared. "Go ahead! Turn around. I should have known. It was a mistake for me to come home!"

He slowed the vehicle but made no effort to turn around. He kept his gaze on the road. "I had hoped you'd changed, but obviously you haven't."

"Is this why you met me at the depot alone—so you could put me in my place after all these years?"

"I want answers, Alice Marie. What do you expect to find here in Willowbrook?"

"I don't know." Tears sprang to her eyes. She looked out the window so he wouldn't notice. She would smile and put on a happy face even if it killed her. She would never let Knowl Herrick see her grief.

"We're all the same here," he went on, with a note of defensiveness. "We're the same people we always were. If you couldn't get along with us then, what makes you think it'll work now?"

She gave him a look of deep contrition. "I'm sorry, Knowl. I don't know what made me say such a horrible thing about Annie. But you know how we were, growing up, always at odds with each other. She was goody two shoes and could do no wrong; I was always in trouble and could do no right. I guess the old childish jealousy slipped out."

"You're not a child anymore," said Knowl.

"I know that. It's just—I've been so distraught since Cary died. I'm not myself."

He tossed her a cynical glance. "Really? I think you're exactly yourself." He paused for a long moment. "About Cary—"

She held her breath. Knowl had never talked to her about Cary.

"Your mother tells us you two never got a divorce. I don't know why you lied about it, or what kind of game you two were playing, but I hope you have no more surprises up your sleeve."

"I don't know why I lied, Knowl. Pride maybe."

"Well, just so you know. Annie and I, and little Maggie and your mother—we get along very well together. Life is peaceful here on Honeysuckle Lane. We want it to stay that way."

"It will, Knowl, I promise." She tucked a loose strand of hair into the chignon at the back of her neck. "I just came home to—to pull myself together. I won't stay long."

He looked at her with a glimmer of sympathy. "It's not that we don't want to help you, Alice Marie. We all feel bad about your loss."

"Thank you." She smiled inwardly. Yes, the old Knowl was still there, buried under the feigned coldness and indifference. He acted aloof because he was afraid to let his defenses down. Even now, with his indignation flaring, she knew he still cared about her.

"Just so you'll know," he went on quietly, "I've never stopped praying for you."

She gazed down at her white-gloved hands, uncertain how to respond. She would have felt flattered, even secretly pleased, if he'd said, *I never stopped thinking of you . . . I never stopped loving you. . . .* But she didn't want someone feeling obligated to pray for her. That implied she was lacking something that prayers might supply. She wanted to tell Knowl she was perfectly capable of managing her life without anyone's prayers, but since Cary's death she knew that wasn't true. She wasn't managing well at all. The day he died Cary had asked her to pray for him, and she hadn't even managed a few parting words on his behalf to the Almighty.

"Did you hear me, Alice Marie? I said—"

"Yes, I heard you, Knowl."

His tone softened. "Your mother hopes you'll sing in church like you used to."

She looked earnestly at him. "But you don't think I should, do you?"

"I know the people would love to hear you again."

"And old Reverend Henry? He's still alive, isn't he?"

"Yes, but he's retired. Todd Marshall is pastor now. He married my half-sister, Bethany Rose."

"I know. I received invitations to Bethany's wedding as well as your sister Catherine's to that editor, Robert Wayne. I would have come home, but the band was playing in Palm Beach, or Boston, or Missoula, Montana. I forget where now. I sent something to each of them—a silver tea set or serving tray, something silver."

"Your mother had hoped you'd come home for the weddings."

Alice Marie emitted a dry chuckle. "She's the only one, then, isn't she, Knowl? It's obvious the rest of you weren't waiting on pins and needles for me to come back." She met his gaze. "You've made that perfectly clear in the few minutes we've been together."

He turned the wheel a little too sharply. She swayed toward him, but caught herself before their shoulders touched.

He gave her a long, searching look before turning his eyes back to the road. "Maybe I'm being too harsh on you, Alice Marie. If I am, I'm sorry."

"Since when?"

"I just felt I had to let you know where things stand. I can't have Annie worried about the two of us living under the same roof again."

"It's always poor little Annie, isn't it?"

"Stop it. I won't have you playing your coy little games. With all that's happened to both of us in these intervening years, I hope we're past the childish flirtations. If I encouraged you—and I realize in some subconscious way I may have—I apologize."

"Then you don't hate me?" she ventured.

The stern lines in his forehead relaxed. "Hate you? No, Alice Marie. I care about you, like a brother for his sister. But you must know this—I love Annie with all my heart, and I pray to God I never hurt her again."

"You won't, Knowl," she assured him. "If you do, it won't be because of me, I promise."

They were already turning onto Honeysuckle Lane, the tires making that familiar bumping sound on the cobbled street. She gazed with mixed feelings—nostalgia, excitement, dread—at the fine old Victorian estates with their winding driveways and manicured lawns surrounded by lush green hedges and wrought-iron fences. Everything was as she remembered it—the sprawling porches, the quaint cupolas, the fancy terraces and vine-covered trellises.

Her heart lurched as her childhood home came into view—the vintage dusty rose mansion on the corner, surrounded by towering oaks and a profusion of satin-pink and ruby-red rose bushes. It looked just as it had in her memories and her dreams, with its steep shingled roof, stained glass windows, and the timeworn wraparound porch with its ornamental gables.

"Remember when we were kids and sat on the porch swing for hours telling ghost stories?" she mused as Knowl pulled up the winding drive.

He smiled. "Your brother Chip could tell tales that would curl the hair on a bat. What an imagination he had!"

"And what an adventurer he was! Wasn't he, Knowl? So daring. Remember when he led us on a wild goose chase through the woods? He was sure a pirate had buried treasure there."

Knowl parked and turned off the engine. "How could I forget? He found some monstrosity of a box—"

"Oh, my heavens! It was filled with wasps, and they chased us all the way home!"

"But Chip went back the next day and kept looking for treasure."

"He never gave up," said Alice Marie. "He was the bravest man I ever knew."

Knowl opened his door, but made no effort to get out. "That's what made Chip such a good soldier."

Alice Marie felt a fullness in her throat. "It's always the good who die young," she murmured. The stark, baleful words of the radio announcer ten years ago still tolled in her mind: *Ladies and gentlemen—this is incredible—God have mercy—Pearl Harbor has been attacked!*

"Chip was the best, no doubt about it," said Knowl. "He was my best friend. And I still miss him."

"So do I," said Alice Marie. "Why is it, Knowl? Why!" Her voice came out uneven, a mixture of irony and lament. "I'm always losing the men in my life—Chip, Papa, you, Cary—"

He gave her a solemn glance, his lips tightening into a thin, hard line. It was an odd expression, partly sympathy, partly anger, or perhaps neither of those, but something else altogether. Abruptly he climbed out of the vehicle, came around and opened her door, and offered his hand. When she had stepped out, he reached in for her hat box and valise, then escorted her up the porch to the paneled mahogany door.

He didn't have to knock. The door flew open and there was Mama moving toward Alice Marie with open arms. "Oh, my beautiful girl," she cried, a pink blush in her lined, porcelain face and her shiny golden hair twined in a wreath of silver. "Thank God, you're home where you belong!"

"Oh, Mama! I've missed you! I wanted Cary—I wanted him to know you! But now he's gone!"

"There, there, Daughter. Don't talk about it now."

"I need to talk about him, Mama."

"We'll talk later, Sweetheart. Just think happy thoughts now. You're home!"

Alice Marie remained in her mother's embrace until she spotted her younger sister from the corner of her eye. Annie was approaching with a small girl in tow. She had to be four-year-old Maggie, a sweet little wren of a child, who, as Knowl had pointed out, looked exactly like Annie, with russet-brown hair and enormous gray-green eyes in an elfin face.

The two sisters embraced and Annie said with what seemed utter sincerity, "It's so good to have you home again, Alice Marie. You look as beautiful as ever." Alice Marie cringed a little. Why was Annie being so insufferably nice when Alice Marie had once tried to steal her husband? But then Annie had a way of making Alice Marie feel guilty even when she hadn't done a thing.

They stepped apart, hands still clasped. Annie's expression clouded. "I was so sorry to hear about Cary. I can't imagine how hard it must be for you, finding him after all this time and then losing him again so suddenly."

Alice Marie nodded. "Life does have a way of kicking you in the teeth, doesn't it? But I'll be okay after a little rest and some of Mama's home cooking."

"Mama keeps all of us going," Annie agreed. She put her hands on Maggie's shoulders and urged her forward. "Sweetheart, this is your Aunt Alice Marie. She's Mommy's sister."

Alice Marie bent down and took Maggie's hand. "You can call me Aunt Allie, if you'd like. My favorite people call me Allie."

Annie smiled quizzically. "Really? I never heard anyone call you that."

"It was Cary's pet name for me." She crossed the marble foyer and gazed into the spacious living room. Grandfather Reed's handiwork was still evident in the delicate rose wallpaper accented by gleaming cherry wood moldings and ornate beadwork. It was all the same, as if she had just left yesterday—the Queen Anne chairs and flowered love seat, the shiny brass lamps, the graceful mahogany tables and plant stands, the ornate paintings of lush landscapes and vivid bouquets.

She paused by the kitchen door and breathed in the tantalizing aromas. "Oh, Mama, you're cooking a pot of your fresh green beans with bacon and onions! You remembered!"

"That it's your favorite? Of course. I hope you're hungry. I've got a huge platter of fried chicken and whipped potatoes with gravy. And fresh peach cobbler for dessert."

Alice Marie gave her mother an impulsive hug. "Oh, Mama, I should have come home years ago!"

"You're home now, Daughter. That's what counts." She clasped Alice Marie's hand and looked her squarely in the eyes. "We'll just have a quiet dinner tonight, dear. I didn't want the whole family here overwhelming you on your first night home. Tomorrow or the next day we'll have a big family dinner, if you're up to it."

"Don't set a place for me, Mother Reed," said Knowl. "I need to get back to work. Editorial is deciding on some manuscripts in the morning, and—"

"Son, that publishing house of yours can wait until you've had a good hot meal," said Mama. "You'll think better with some food in your stomach."

Knowl glanced from Annie to Alice Marie and relented with a little shrug. "If you insist, Mother Reed. I'll phone Robert and tell him to hold down the fort until I get there."

Mama turned back to Alice Marie. "Dear, if you'd like to rest before dinner, just go on upstairs. Knowl will bring your things up. You'll have the rosebud room, of course."

Alice Marie smiled wanly. "I've come full circle, haven't I, Mama? That was my room when I was a little girl. Mine . . . and Annie's. Now, after all these years, it's mine again."

"That room has been a favorite of the women in this house," said Annie. "It was Catherine's when she lived here. And Knowl's sister, Bethany Rose, had it when she stayed with us. There's something comforting, almost healing, about that room."

Alice Marie flashed a tight little smile at Annie. "Then it's just the place for me right now, isn't it?"

Alice Marie's first few days at home seemed peculiar at best. She didn't feel exactly like *Alice in Wonderland*—a sane, sensible young woman thrown among a bizarre assortment of odd, unlikely creatures. But *Alice Marie in Willowbrook* stirred a variety of emotions, many of them long buried and best forgotten.

While Alice Marie, the sophisticated television personality, had acquired a certain amount of fame, here on Honeysuckle Lane the trappings of success seemed inconsequential. In these walls—decades old and suffused with memories—Alice Marie was a child again, her mother's favorite. Everyone knew that, although Alice Marie was convinced such favor was bestowed only because she looked and sang like an angel.

All of her life, from the time she was a three year old crooning "Jesus Loves Me" in church revival services, she had felt compelled to perform—to look the prettiest and sing the sweetest—in order to win the adulation of others. It was an indisputable fact of life: Alice Marie, brittle and abrasive in temperament, had to *do* wonderful, impressive things to win people's love, while Annie needed only to *be* her own sweet, natural self, and everyone adored her.

Of course, Alice Marie's anonymity didn't last long. Word got around Willowbrook soon enough that the Chicago television star was in town. A reporter and photographer with the *Willowbrook News* came out and interviewed her and took pictures, and a front-page story appeared in the newspaper the next day. Alice Marie had considered avoiding reporters, but she knew they'd write something anyway—half-truths, ugly rumors, or outright lies. And they'd dig up garish old snapshots she hated, maybe even her high school yearbook photo, where she looked like Goldilocks with tightly coiled curls shooting out from her head like bed springs. It was better that she tell them what she wanted them to know and that she pose for pictures in an outfit and hairdo she considered flattering.

As soon as the article appeared, the phone calls began. People Alice Marie had met in passing sometime in her life—or maybe never even met at all—supposed childhood acquaintances, grade school classmates, and high school beaus she had no desire to see again all phoned and fawned over her like long-lost relatives. They wanted to have lunch with her, or wanted her to meet their Great-Uncle Hubert or dear Aunt Gladys who had never missed her television show; they wanted her to sing for their YMCA social, or their PTA meeting, or their annual Elk's club dance.

Finally, Mama announced that she would take all the phone calls and tell folks her daughter was resting and would call back at some future time that suited her. Besides, the other families on the party line were getting exasperated. So the only calls Mama allowed Alice Marie to take were from her producer, Rudy. He phoned every other day wanting to know when Alice Marie was coming back to Chicago.

"I'm doing my best to keep things going, Doll Baby," he told her one morning with a faint note of hysteria in his voice, "but I'm no miracle worker. Or maybe I am. I got some hot names to spell you. Sarah Vaughan, Peggy Lee, Connie Haines. And I lined up Jo Stafford and Margaret Whiting for the next couple of weeks. But the network guys say if you don't come back soon, they're gonna rename the show and sue you for breach of contract."

"I'm sorry, Rudy," she told him for the umpteenth time. "I need more time. Another week maybe. I promise, when I get back I'll be better than ever. I just need to get that old vim and vigor back again." She didn't tell him she couldn't face living in her old apartment without Cary there, that she couldn't imagine doing her show without Cary to go home to.

In Willowbrook it was almost as if Cary never existed, as if she had magically traversed her adult life, and gone back to her childhood, where someone else—her own devoted mother—took care of her and made decisions for her. As long as Alice Marie remained in this dreamlike limbo, the pain over losing Cary seemed less searing. How ironic that the home she had fled so long ago now provided the very consolation she longed for.

But while Alice Marie buried her grief under a numbing, bittersweet inertia, September crept in with scorching days and humid, restless nights, bringing to Honeysuckle Lane a word whispered on the lips of townspeople all summer long.

The word struck terror in even the bravest hearts.

Polio.

It's come to our neighborhood, Anna, just as I feared it would! Heaven help us, the Ratcliffes over on Pinefield—their boy Harlan—a mite of a boy, hardly seven—his parents had to drive him all the way to that children's hospital in Indianapolis. The doctor feared complications—encephalitis, I think it was, as if polio isn't bad enough!"

Gertrude Payne, who lived around the corner in the Tudor-style house on Maypole Drive, stopped to catch her breath, her nostrils flaring and her three chins rippling with an intensity that vibrated through her corpulent frame. She pulled a hanky from the flowered bodice of her housedress and mopped her upper lip, then pressed her frosty lemonade glass against her rouge-powdered cheek. "Oh, this helps, Anna. Your lemonade is delightful!" She looked over at Alice Marie on the parlor love seat. "This heat is the worst we've had in years, don't you think so, dear? We've gotten Chicago's sweltering weather; it happens like clockwork every September. But this year it's a killer, the way polio thrives on hot, humid summers."

Anna reached for the ceramic pitcher on the cherry wood table. "More lemonade, Gertie? Alice Marie?"

"No thanks, Mama. I'm fine."

Gertrude held out her glass. "Just half, Anna, and maybe a couple more of those divine molasses cookies of yours."

Anna handed her the platter. "I say the heat has to break sooner or later. You know how Indiana summers are. One minute it's too hot to sleep at night, and the next thing you know the leaves are turning orange and gold and the sweet smell of bonfires is in the air."

"I declare, it won't come too soon for me." Gertie swallowed the last of her lemonade and puckered her lips at the tartness.

Alice Marie turned her glass between her palms, savoring the coldness. "I didn't realize polio had hit Willowbrook so hard this year, Mrs. Payne."

"Your mama didn't tell you? Everyone in town knows somebody who's been crippled by polio. In June four people died right here in our own county. I know of half a dozen who are in iron lungs even as we speak, poor souls."

"It's a dreadful disease," Mama agreed.

"First thing this summer they closed the community swimming pools— the water itself was suspect—and they canceled scores of local events. Even closed the movie houses. People were too afraid to venture out, what with the way polio spreads like the plague in crowded places." Mrs. Payne rushed on, fanning herself with her hanky. "Mothers are so afraid they keep their children indoors, won't even let them play in the sprinklers outside. Rapid chilling could cause the disease, you know. How could you not know about the polio scare in Willowbrook, Alice Marie?"

"I—I don't know." The truth was she had been wearing blinders since Cary's death, seeing only her own pain, but she wasn't about to admit such a thing to the likes of Gertrude Payne. "No one mentioned polio to me," she went on, trying not to sound defensive. "Annie keeps Maggie close to home, but I assumed it's because she's so young."

"I didn't tell Alice Marie about the polio scare," said Mama, taking the blame the way she always did. "She's been home only a couple of weeks, and she's had enough on her mind with her husband's passing."

"Of course she has," Gertie agreed, her tone sweet as honey. "Dear me, it slipped my mind you're a grieving widow, Alice Marie. What a shame no one in town ever got to meet your husband. A fine man he was, I'm sure, in spite of everything."

Alice Marie felt her skin bristle. "Yes, he was the most charming, talented man I ever knew, no matter what anyone says—"

"Now, about the Ratcliffes," said Mama, carefully diverting the conversation. "Is there anything we can do to help while they're in Indianapolis with Harlan? Who's taking care of their girls?"

"I hear they sent the daughters to stay with relatives in Detroit—brave souls!" said Gertie. "I'd be afraid to take those girls in, the way polio spreads like wildfire through a family."

"Most cases are light," said Mama. "Not much worse than the flu. Weakness, achy muscles, headache, and fever for a few days. Most folks get better and pick up their lives where they left off."

"But nobody knows who'll be the lucky ones or who'll end up paralyzed and in an iron lung—or laid out in a coffin. That's what's so terrifying."

Mama stood and picked up the cookie tray. "Land sakes, Gertie, I don't mean to hurry you, but if I don't get my beef roast in the oven, I won't have dinner on the table when Knowl and Annie get home."

Gertie made no effort to move. "I know Knowl's off working at his publishing house, but where's Annie these days?"

Mama set Gertie's empty lemonade glass on the tray. "Oh, Annie works at Herrick House off and on, editing manuscripts and reading the things folks send in. You'd be amazed how many people want to get a book published."

Gertie folded her arms across her ample middle. She looked like she was settling in for the duration. "I'd say Herrick House is making quite a name for itself, Anna. You must be real proud, having your family involved in such a grand enterprise."

"I am, Gertie."

"And Annie's friend Catherine and her husband, Robert—they're so involved too. Catherine showed me some of the book covers she's painted. They're lovely!"

"Yes, Cath is a fine artist. Now, Gertie, I really must—"

"Anna, Dear, it just came to my mind—I have a cousin—Stella's son Henry in Fort Wayne—and he's written a real fine book. He collects postage stamps from around the world, and he's written down the history of every last stamp. Oh, the research he's done. Any editor would be eager to publish his book. I'm sure he would give your son-in-law Knowl the first opportunity to read it."

Mama set her tray down. "That's wonderfully generous of you, Dear, but I make it a point not to tell my son-in-law what he should or shouldn't publish. But if Henry sends his book in, I'm sure the folks at Herrick House will give it a fair reading."

"Mama's right," said Alice Marie, handing Gertie her pocketbook. "If there's one thing I can say about Knowl, he's a fair man."

Gertie smiled faintly. "I guess you'd know, wouldn't you, Alice Marie? You almost married him. I was there, you know, at your wedding—what would have been your wedding. But I guess all things work out for the best, don't they, Dear? Knowl and your sister Annie are obviously a match made in heaven."

Alice Marie breathed a sigh of annoyance. "I suppose some people see it that way."

"Oh, yes, dear, you could have done a whole lot worse than marrying Knowl Herrick. Goodness, not that I'm suggesting anything bad about your poor dead husband—what was his name?"

"Cary. Cary Rose."

"A Jewish man, wasn't he?"

"His father was Jewish, his mother Catholic," Alice Marie said through clenched teeth. Was this woman never going to leave and give them some peace and quiet?

"Well, goodness gracious," Gertie rushed on, wiping her face again with her hanky, "I may be old-fashioned, but I think we'd all be better off marrying our own kind. Look at the trouble the Jews got this world into—a whole world war none of us wanted."

"Nonsense, Gertie!" said Mama, her voice rising in a way Alice Marie seldom heard. "That's like saying the victim is guilty for the crime committed against him."

Gertie tucked her hanky back down the front of her cotton housedress. "I didn't mean it that way, Anna. The Jews are fine people. They're just different from us, that's all I'm saying."

"The way I see it, the Jews are God's chosen people," Mama declared. "The rest of us got adopted in, rather by default, wouldn't you agree?"

"I really never thought about it that way, Anna."

"I suppose you think the Methodists are God's chosen people."

Gertie raised her three chins. "He could do worse."

Alice Marie touched Gertie's elbow. "Let me see you to the door while Mama gets started on her roast, Mrs. Payne."

After Gertie had gone, Alice Marie joined her mother in the kitchen, sat down at the large oak table, and began peeling a bowl of potatoes. "I don't know how you stand that woman, Mama. She sets my teeth on edge, the way she says one thing and means another."

"She's usually quite harmless, Dear. I just let her chatter go right on over my head. But I know she upset you with her remarks about Cary."

"It's not her remarks that hurt me. It's—Cary. Not having him with me. I miss him, Mama. Sometimes I wake up in the morning and think he never came back into my life at all. It was just a dream. I have nothing to prove he even existed. Sometimes I can't even remember his face. I try, but it's gone. I'm losing him a little more every day."

Her mother sat down across from her, her blue eyes glistening. "I know just how you feel, Honey. It was that way for me when I lost your papa."

"You never talk about it, Mama. It seemed you moved on with your life without even skipping a beat."

"Posh! That was an act for you children."

Alice Marie dropped her paring knife into the bowl. "Tell me what it was like, Mama. Losing Papa. I need to know."

Her mother gazed around the room for a long moment, tears glazing her eyes. "Besides losing your brother Chilton, losing Papa was the hardest time of my life. I slept in his pajamas for two weeks because I needed to feel something of him against my skin. For weeks I couldn't cry. The sobs knotted in my chest like a rock. The pressure was unbearable, but I couldn't release it. I thought my heart would explode."

"I feel that way too, Mama. Grieving takes all my energy. I'm exhausted all the time, as if I were doing hard labor. If I could just cry, the pressure would let up and I could breathe normally again."

"And my mind—merciful heavens, Alice Marie—I simply couldn't think straight. I couldn't concentrate on a thing. I'd go to fix myself a cup of tea and forget what I was doing. When people talked to me, it was as if they were speaking from a great distance. I couldn't focus on their words long enough to make sense of what they were saying."

"Yes, that's it exactly."

"I had to get away from this house, because every nook and cranny spoke of Papa. I'd see him coming in doors and sitting in chairs. I'd feel him coming up behind me and touching my hair. I'd walk into a room and smell him there, as if he'd just gone out. He was everywhere and nowhere. Just when I thought I'd caught a glimpse of him, there'd be nothing there. Just empty, silent rooms." Her eyes misted. "That's why I sold the house and moved to Chicago to take care of my ailing sister, Martha. Thank God, Knowl bought back the house for Annie, or we wouldn't be living here today."

Alice Marie wound a potato peeling around her index finger. "I never knew how you felt, Mama. I'm not good at reading people like Annie is. I suppose I'm too self-absorbed."

"You have a right to be, Sweetheart, after all you've been through these past few months."

Alice Marie reached across the table and squeezed her mother's hand. "You give me hope, Mama. You lost your husband and your son, but you're at peace. You're happy. You seem happy. Are you, Mama? Are you truly content with your life?"

The fine lines in her mother's graceful face softened. The afternoon sun suffused her classic features with a golden glow; she could have been the Madonna in a Renaissance painting. "Yes, Dear. God has given me His peace that surpasses our frail understanding. With my family around me, I am very happy."

"I hope I can say that someday," Alice Marie mused aloud. She picked up another potato, then dropped it when the telephone rang in the hallway. "Sit still. I'll get it, Mama."

"No, you're busy with the potatoes. I'll go."

Her mother picked up the phone on the third ring, then called out, "It's for you, Daughter." She put her hand over the mouthpiece as Alice Marie approached. "He says it's the mayor!"

Alice Marie listened for a moment, then replied, "Thank you, Mayor Whitney. I'm terribly flattered, but since my husband's death I haven't accepted any singing engagements. You understand."

Her mother hovered at her elbow. "Alice Marie, what does he want you to do?"

She covered the mouthpiece. "He wants me to sing for the local businessmen at a Chamber of Commerce luncheon at the Brandwynne Hotel, but I can't, Mama. It's too soon."

"You need to do this, Daughter. Healing comes when you do the thing you love. Say yes."

Alice Marie shook her head, but her mother's gaze remained unflinching. At last Alice Marie shrugged and said, "Mayor Whitney, I do have that date available. I suppose I could do a half hour program. I'd need a piano player to accompany me. Do you know any local musicians? The banker's son? No, I don't know him. Oh, he does? What a coincidence. Do you suppose he'd be willing—? You will? Thank you. Then I'll look forward to hearing from you soon."

She hung up the phone and turned to her mother with a grudging smile. "Okay, you got me into this, Mama. I hope I don't regret it."

"It's the mayor, Honey. You can't turn down the mayor! Tell me everything he said."

"You heard."

"Only one side of the conversation!"

"There's not much to tell. He asked me to sing for a businessmen's luncheon next Tuesday, and, thanks to you, I said I would. I know you're right, Mama. It's time for me to start picking up my life again."

"What about this musician he mentioned?"

"A fellow named Dirk Wyman. He's the bank president's son, and he plays piano in his spare time."

"Is he married?"

"I don't know, Mama. But we can ask Knowl. Dirk Wyman is the financial manager for Herrick House Publishers."

Her mother stifled a chuckle. "Well, it's certainly a small world. You say he's the bank president's son? Now if only he's young, handsome, and single."

"No matchmaking, Mama! He's just going to play the piano."

"But sometimes that's how romance begins."

"Romance is the last thing on my mind, Mama!"

"You say that now, but the day will come—"

"Don't talk about someday, Mama. Let me get through one day at a time."

"Still, it won't hurt to ask Knowl about this young man."

At dinner that evening, her mother wasted no time in bringing up Dirk Wyman's name. "What do you think of him, Knowl? Is he a nice fellow? Does he work hard? Is he married?"

Knowl adjusted his glasses and eyed Anna curiously. "What's this sudden interest in one of my employees, Mother Reed? Are you in the market for a beau?"

"Don't be silly. I'm an old lady, too old to endure the foolishness of courting. I'm asking for Alice Marie."

Knowl looked quizzically at her. "You know Dirk Wyman?"

"No. It's just—Mayor Whitney mentioned him to me."

"You know Mayor Whitney?"

"No, I don't, but—" She told him of the mayor's invitation and his suggestion that Dirk Wyman accompany her on the piano.

"I think that's wonderful," said Annie.

"So do I," said Knowl. "Those business meetings could benefit from some musical talent like yours."

"What about this Wyman fellow?" persisted Mama.

"He's a nice chap," said Knowl. "Smart, ambitious, personable. Good background. His father is president of Willowbrook First National."

"Darling," inquired Annie, "didn't they move here from Chicago a few years ago?"

"I think so, Sweetheart. And yes, Mother Reed, Dirk is single."

"I don't care if he has three wives and a dozen children," declared Alice Marie. "He's only playing the piano for me."

There was nowhere else to go with the conversation, so they ate in silence for several moments. Alice Marie picked listlessly at her roast beef and gravy; she had no appetite, hadn't been hungry in weeks.

"Try to eat something, Dear," her mother urged.

"I know, Mama. It's delicious, but—"

"It'll get better with time," said Annie. "I'm glad you're going to sing again. It'll perk up your spirits."

"Annie's right," said Mama. "I hope you'll sing in church again too. No one sings 'Rock of Ages' the way you do."

Alice Marie speared a green bean she had no intention of eating. "Please, Mama, one step at a time, okay?"

Silence again, until Annie broke it. "Mama, you'll never guess who Knowl got a letter from today."

"It must be someone special. You're beaming."

"I'm not sure it's the same man, but everything fits, and how many others would have the same name, so it must be him—"

"I never should have shown her the letter," said Knowl with a wry grin. "She's been like this all day."

"I have not! I'm just excited." Annie's gray-green eyes danced. "You'll see, Mama. It's perfectly understandable."

Mama was smiling now too. "Tell us, Darling, before you jump out of your skin."

"Mama, do you remember the summer before the war when Catherine and I went to the New York World's Fair? Remember me telling you about the Jewish evangelist who witnessed to us? I made my commitment to Christ that day, and I've forever felt indebted to that man. I never dreamed our paths would cross again."

"We don't know that they have," said Knowl patiently. "This could be another man."

"No, I'm positive, Knowl. This is the same Helmut Schwarz I met at the World's Fair."

"Tell us about the letter," urged Mama. "Why did he write you?"

"He has a book he wants published," said Knowl.

"Who doesn't?" mused Alice Marie. "Mrs. Payne's cousin Henry has a book. Wait'll you read it."

"Mrs. Payne?" echoed Knowl. "Who's Mrs. Payne?"

"Our neighbor around the corner," said Mama. "Everyone calls her Gertie. She talks like she eats—constantly. Forget her. About the letter."

"It's a wonderful letter, Mama," said Annie. "So filled with passion and conviction. Just like the man I remember."

"He sounds a bit like a zealot to me," said Knowl. "Out to change the world. I'm not sure his book is right for Herrick House."

"But it is! It's perfect for Herrick House," said Annie.

"Sweetheart, you haven't even seen it."

"Call it writer's intuition."

"That's not how we make decisions in book publishing, Dear."

"But Robert sounded interested," persisted Annie. "He said he found the letter evocative, and he'd like to see the entire manuscript."

Knowl rubbed his chin the way he always did when he feared he was losing an argument. "Schwarz may have found another publisher by now," he said at last. "He said he was contacting a number of publishers around the country. He'll probably go with a prestigious New York house."

"He said he wants a publisher who won't dilute his Christian message," said Annie. "He knows our reputation, Knowl. That's why he wrote us."

"What's his book about?" asked Alice Marie, more out of politeness than genuine interest. She was tiring quickly, and, in spite of nightfall, the muggy Indian summer heat still hung heavy in the air, making it hard to breathe.

"The book is hard to pigeonhole," Knowl was saying. "A modern-day Elijah warning this generation to repent before the Second Coming. He's addressing the issue of Jews dying in the concentration camps while the world looked the other way. Don't ask me how he plans to tie it all together."

Alice Marie shook her head. "Sounds like heavy reading to me."

"That's why I think we'll pass on it," said Knowl.

"No, you don't," Annie protested. "Not until I find out if he's *my* Helmut Schwarz!"

"*Your* Helmut Schwarz?" echoed Alice Marie. "What haven't you told us about this fellow, Annie?"

Annie's face reddened. "That's enough, Alice Marie. Helmut is one of the most memorable men I've ever met. And I'd give up the advance on my next book to meet him again after all these years."

"After two best sellers? Sounds like trouble to me, Knowl," said Alice Marie.

Knowl raised one brow and his voice took on a mildly jesting tone. "And here I thought I was the only memorable man in her life."

"Please don't make light of this, you two," Annie cautioned. "All these years I've thought my Jewish evangelist might be dead. I knew he was going back to Germany to urge his family to leave before Hitler gained greater power. I was afraid he might have been captured and put in the death camps. But now I know he survived and, according to his letter, he worked with the German resistance and rescued many Jews who would have died in the camps."

"He sounds like a wonderful man," said Mama, stealing a glance at Alice Marie. "A truly wonderful man! Tell me, Knowl. Did he mention in his letter? Does he have a wife?"

It wasn't the mayor who phoned Alice Marie the next day, but Dirk Wyman himself, who offered to drive over after work and pick her up for their rehearsal. "We can use the piano at the Brandwynne, if you like," he said in a smooth, take-charge voice. "I checked with the manager and the meeting room will be available this evening. May I pick you up at six?"

Alice Marie had agreed to sing for the mayor's luncheon, but the engagement itself seemed remote, distant, tentative. Now she must deal with this man who had agreed to do her this favor and play while she sang. She couldn't tell him she had no desire to sing, that she had been swept into this commitment by her mother, by her own pride, by the unspoken rule that it wasn't good business to turn down the mayor's invitation. In a heartbeat she considered her alternatives, dismissed them, and said, "Yes, I can be ready at six."

In the hours before Dirk Wyman was due to arrive, she bathed, washed her hair, tried on several outfits and discarded each one, and experimented with her makeup as if she were a teenager getting ready for her first date. Strangely, she felt that same heady sense of expectation and anxiety, the panic and preoccupation with hair that hung too limp, silk hose with crooked seams, and fingernails with chipped fire-engine red polish.

For a long while she stared at herself in the dresser mirror while she brushed a sheen into her rippling, spun-gold hair. Who was this woman who looked back at her with wide, uncertain eyes, a pale, egg-white face, and a full, pouty mouth that had forgotten how to smile? Where was Alice Marie, the confident, brassy television star who with a word or a look sent people scurrying to meet her demands?

"It's this house," she said aloud, in surprise. "It's turned me into a child again—a cowering, helpless baby!" The transformation was unmistakable, she conceded. From the moment she had arrived back on Honeysuckle Lane, she had ceased to be Chicago's popular television personality; the butterfly had been sucked back into its cocoon; she was once again daughter and sister in a family that had always been wary and, yes, critical of her freewheeling ambition and independent spirit. She had unwittingly allowed herself to be pushed back into the conventional, suffocating mold she had spent her lifetime trying to escape. How weak and distracted she must have been to let such a thing happen!

It was Cary, of course, and the whole exhausting, unrelenting process of mourning. How could she be strong and self-confident when the pain was so ravaging? Surely there was some shortcut around grief. Concentrating on her music again might help. Perhaps even an innocent flirtation. Maybe Mama was right. Perhaps Dirk Wyman was the ideal man she had always dreamed of—suave and sophisticated, prosperous and powerful, yet warm and caring. Not weak and flawed like Cary, who had blundered through life with a boyish grin on his face and come out on top in spite of everything.

She wound a golden curl around her finger and held it for a moment. *All right, family of mine, you want to bury Cary, want to pretend he never existed. All right, we'll all bury him, and I'll get on with my life.*

But how did she look to a man? Pretty? Young? Intriguing? She hadn't thought about her looks in weeks, but suddenly she needed to feel attractive. She lined her lips, penciled in her brows, and slipped into a white chiffon blouse and slim, powder-blue skirt. It was decided. She would make a favorable impression on this cheeky piano player, or die trying.

Dirk Wyman arrived at six sharp just as he said he would. Alice Marie's first glimpse told her he was even more imposing than she had anticipated. Tall, urbane, and impeccable in a double-breasted gray flannel suit and swank oxfords, he was as handsome as he was blond. "Alice Marie, I presume?"

She matched his smile. "And you're Dirk Wyman, of course."

"Of course. Part-time pianist and jazz aficionado, at your service." The hint of a self-satisfied smirk played in his smile, as if he knew something the rest of the world had yet to discover. He stepped into the foyer before she thought to bid him enter and looked around as if he contemplated purchasing the estate. "Quite a place you have here," he noted. "Classy, elegant, yet understated. They don't make houses like this anymore."

"It's been in the family for years," she told him, brushing back her flaxen curls. "My Grandfather Reed built it at the turn of the century. In fact, I think he built half the houses in this neighborhood."

"He must have been quite a man."

"He was."

They stood for a moment looking at each other. She sensed that he was appraising her just as she was appraising him, and they both liked what they saw. He had a sturdy face with a full, wide mouth and ruddy complexion, fine blond hair combed neatly to one side, and pale brows and lashes framing narrow blue eyes clear and light as spring water. "Shall we go?" he suggested.

He walked her out to his automobile—a sleek white sports convertible with sparkling chrome and whitewall tires. With a gentlemanly flourish he opened the door for her and held her hand as she stepped inside.

"This is exquisite," she said as she relaxed against the padded seat and ran her hand over the lush black upholstery. "It certainly doesn't fit provincial little Willowbrook."

"It's a Nash-Healey from Britain." He settled into the driver's seat and turned the key in the ignition. "It can do one-twenty-five, but don't worry,

I keep my speed down around town. Get me in the countryside though, and I may let her go."

She smiled at him. "I'm not averse to fast cars."

"It gets pretty breezy. You may need a scarf."

"No, I won't. I like the wind in my hair."

He smiled that inscrutable smile. "What a coincidence. I'd like to see you with the wind in your hair."

They drove toward town in silence, the warm breeze whistling its dissonant music in their ears. Hardly ten minutes had passed when Dirk pulled up beside the Brandwynne, Willowbrook's only luxury hotel—a graceful six-story edifice that blended huge plate glass windows and reinforced concrete into a clean, modern design in the tradition of Frank Lloyd Wright.

"This place reminds me a bit of Chicago," Alice Marie noted as they entered the spacious, marble lobby.

"Does it make you homesick for the big city?" Dirk asked as they approached the check-in desk and got directions.

"I didn't think I was homesick, but maybe I am," she confessed as they walked down a carpeted hallway to a door marked, MAGNOLIA ROOM. "I was never a small-town girl."

He opened the door for her and they entered the empty rose-colored banquet room. "I'm a city boy myself," he said as he walked over to the piano and sat down. "Spent over half my life in Chicago."

"Really? But you have the hint of an accent."

"I was born in Germany," he acknowledged. "My parents came to the States when I was eight." He moved his long, tapered fingers lightly, swiftly over the keys with a practiced grace. "We lived in Chicago until my father accepted the bank president position here in town a few years ago."

"I bet it was quite an adjustment going from life in the bustling city to Willowbrook's bucolic pace."

"Yes, but, believe it or not, I've come to appreciate small-town life. There's something to be said for being a big fish in a little pond."

"As opposed to being a small fish in a big ocean?" Alice Marie ran her hand absently over the gleaming piano. "But I say, why not be a *big* fish in a *big* sea?"

He chuckled. "From what I've heard, that's what you were in Chicago. A lady on her way to the top. Why did you give it up?"

"I didn't give it up. I've just put it on hold for a few weeks. I—I needed a change of scene."

"Then you'll be heading back to Chicago soon?"

"One of these days."

His narrow eyes crinkled warmly. "Then I'm glad Mayor Whitney booked you for our luncheon, Miss Reed. I'd hate to have missed meeting you—and accompanying you on the piano."

"Please, call me Alice Marie. Or Allie," she said recklessly. "My friends call me Allie."

"Allie, it is. I hope you brought the sheet music for your tunes, Allie."

"Yes, Dirk, I did." His name sounded nice on her tongue. She handed him a folder.

He rifled through the pages. "Which numbers do you plan to sing?"

"I haven't decided. You know the audience better than I. What do you think?"

He moved over and patted the space beside him on the mahogany bench. She sat down beside him, and as her arm rested comfortably against his, she felt a pleasant warmth under her skin.

"You can't go wrong with current hits," he told her as he played a familiar tune. "How about 'Hello Young Lovers' and 'Getting to Know You' from that new musical, *The King and I*?"

"Perfect. I'll round out the program with a few Dixieland and jazz numbers and maybe a song or two from *South Pacific*."

"Good call. If you're ready, I'll run through a few scales so you can warm up."

They spent over an hour rehearsing. Dirk, skilled enough to follow her even when she improvised, contributed some nice fills here and there. She relaxed, responding to the music, adding some scats to the jazz tunes, swinging ad-lib stuff, spontaneous and lyrical.

Dirk was a natural. He played the songs in several different keys to see which ones worked best for her. They discussed each song—the tempo she preferred, how many bars of introduction he would give her, and whether he would play an interlude. He was able to transpose the songs right on the spot, so that if the key was too high, he lowered it a couple of steps to accommodate her voice. She found herself growing increasingly impressed with his skills.

Apparently, the feeling was mutual. "You're another Billie Holliday," he told her after a particularly demanding number. "You're *good*!"

"We're good together," she corrected with a smile.

He sat back and rubbed his hands. "Say, Miss Reed—*Allie*—have you had dinner?"

"No, come to think of it, I haven't."

"The hotel has a fine restaurant, the Candlelight Pavilion. It serves the best steaks this side of Chicago. What do you say?"

She smiled. She wasn't hungry, but she was enjoying the company. "All right, Dirk. I think we've earned it."

Alice Marie noted that there were only a few patrons in the formal, dimly lit restaurant. Willowbrook's elite, no doubt. Men in three-piece suits and women in their evening gowns or best Sunday dresses. She and Dirk followed the maitre d' to a round, linen-draped table beside a massive stone fireplace and sat down. The tuxedo-clad waiter placed their linen napkins on their laps and handed them gold-embossed menus, then brought them ice water and took their orders—broiled filet mignon with sautéed mushrooms for Dirk and breast of chicken cutlets almandine for Alice Marie.

"Now I really feel like I'm back in Chicago," she mused, raising her crystal goblet to her lips.

"Let's pretend we are. The night life in Willowbrook leaves much to be desired. But then I'm sure you already know that."

She winced. "To tell the truth, it's been ages since I've thought about the night life anywhere."

"Yes, I suppose your television program consumes most of your time."

She nodded. Strange how her television show seemed like another lifetime. Would she ever go back? Would her producer even want her back?

Dirk was watching her intently. "I hate to admit I haven't seen your show, Allie, but my father has, and he's one of your biggest fans."

"Remind me to send him an autographed photo."

"You can deliver it yourself. You'll meet him when you perform for the Chamber of Commerce luncheon."

"Of course. How could I have forgotten? He's president of Willowbrook First National. He must be a remarkable man."

Dirk nodded. "He's an extraordinary human being. Not only does he work long hours at the bank, he's involved in several charitable functions as well. You'll hear all about it at the luncheon."

"Really? You've stirred my curiosity."

"All right, I'll give you a little preview. Dad has spent lots of money to help the D.P.'s. You know, displaced persons—people who lost their homes, jobs, everything, during the war. Mainly children, but entire families as well. Dad raises money to bring them over from Europe and help them get settled in the States."

"What a generous thing to do."

"It started with my uncle and his family in Germany. They were homeless, destitute, and Dad found a way to bring them over. After that, it seemed there was always someone needing his help. When he had exhausted all his resources, he turned to the community for help. Now he puts on a fund-raiser every spring."

"That must be quite a production."

"It is. Dad usually brings in entertainment from Chicago or Detroit, and people come from all over the state. They love his shows. He's a regular Sid Caesar. No, more like Ed Sullivan. He tries to be funny, but he's not very good at it. But he raises big bucks." He paused and broke into a wide grin. "Hey, it just hit me. Dad should get you for one of his shows. What a draw you'd be—a big Chicago television star! Would you consider it?"

"Oh, Dirk, I don't know. You'd have to talk with my manager." What was she saying? *She* hadn't even talked with her manager!

"Okay, give me his number. I'll pass it on to my dad, and if he's interested, he'll . . ."

Dirk's words fell away as the waiter appeared with their dinners—each a culinary masterpiece artfully arranged on fine china and garnished with delicate sprigs of parsley.

Dirk picked up his knife and fork. "If it tastes as good as it looks, we're in business."

Alice Marie nodded, wishing already that she had ordered only a salad. Since Cary's death she had had no appetite; but she had already decided not to mention Cary Rose to Dirk. The past was gone. Why dredge up painful memories?

"What do you think of the food?" Dirk asked, then answered his own question. "You'd have to go all the way to Chicago to top this cuisine. Right?"

She nodded. Perhaps if she pushed the food around on her plate he would think she was eating. Or better yet, engage him in conversation. "Tell me, Dirk, how did you happen to go to work for Herrick House? Why aren't you playing with some orchestra somewhere instead?"

He speared a morsel of steak and held it poised near his mouth as he spoke. "Actually, I played with several orchestras during college and for a few years afterward, but I got tired of traveling. And there was more money to be made in business, so I moved back home and went to work for my father. When he came to Willowbrook, I followed and became a loan officer with the bank, until your brother-in-law offered me a job I couldn't refuse."

"And you're happy at Herrick House?"

"Sure. It's steady money. Nice people. Challenging work. What more can you ask for?"

She poked at her chicken almandine. "You seem like a man who would thrive on excitement, adventure."

He reached across the table and cupped his hand over hers. His clear blue eyes were riveting. "I am thriving, Allie," he said with a caring, confidential air. "Being here with you tonight—this is an adventure. The first of many, I hope."

7

Singing at the Brandwynne for the Chamber of Commerce luncheon was just what Alice Marie needed. As she held the microphone to her mouth and belted out "How High the Moon," she felt alive for the first time since Cary's death. She was born to sing like this; her voice was strong, clear, flowing smooth, and mellow as cream. She could see the pleasure and approval in the faces of her audience, mainly portly, balding, middle-aged businessmen. But that was fine. Dirk Wyman was close by, comfortably ensconced at the piano, his playing so perfectly in sync with her voice, they could have been twins, anticipating each other's words before they spoke.

She was glad now that the mayor had urged her to perform. Now she knew she was ready to return to Chicago and pick up her television show—and her life—where she had left off. She had found herself again in her music. As long as she was singing, she didn't feel the pain over losing Cary.

After the luncheon, Dirk introduced her to his father, Maxwell Wyman. He was a short, bulky man who wore his navy blue suit well in spite of his girth. Dressed impeccably, he looked every inch the image of a bank president, right down to his gold cufflinks and diamond-studded tie tack. He had obviously been a handsome man in his day, was still handsome for his years. His thinning gray hair framed a thickly jowled face with a distinctive nose and the same pale, spring-water blue eyes Dirk flashed so seductively. There was no doubt they were father and son.

"It's a pleasure to meet you, Miss Reed," he said, taking her hand in both of his and holding firm, as if he had no intention of letting her get away. "I've watched your show on television whenever I've had a banker's holiday." He chuckled as if he had made a joke. "Your music is glorious, my dear. You sing like a nightingale!"

"Thank you, Mr. Wyman," she said in the honey-sweet voice she reserved for her public.

"Max. Max. Call me Max."

She gently removed her hand from his. "Max, then—and Max, I must confess, I couldn't have performed today without your son. He's quite an accomplished musician."

"Yes, he is—and a good judge of talent. I assure you, Miss Reed, he is your fan now just as I am."

"I'm flattered," she said, smiling, feeling warm even in her black georgette dress with its scoop neckline and spaghetti straps. Surely the fierce September heat had invaded even this darkened banquet hall.

"He tells me you might be interested in singing for my fund-raiser for displaced persons next spring," Max Wyman was saying.

"Yes, Dirk mentioned it to me." She brushed her cascading hair back from her face. She was feeling a trifle light-headed. She should have eaten a few bites of the curry chicken, even though she knew better than to eat before singing. Somehow she kept her smile in place and said, "You must be a very generous man to devote so much effort to such a worthy cause."

"Not generous," he scoffed, his face reddening the same way Dirk's did. "You see, Miss Reed, I saw the hardship my brother suffered. Because of the war he and his family were stripped of everything they owned—and I knew if I could spare another human being such misery, I had to do it."

"You have a very kind heart, Mr. Wyman—Max," she replied, casting a furtive glance around the room. Where was a fan to stir the muggy air? Was no one else having a hard time breathing? She heard herself say, "It would be a better world, wouldn't it, if everyone felt that way about helping their fellow man?"

"Indeed! Now, Miss Reed, tell me. Will you do us the honor of performing for our charity benefit next spring?"

"I'll be going back to Chicago soon. Perhaps even sooner than I had anticipated. Next week perhaps. But I suppose I could be persuaded to make a trip home for your charity benefit."

"Wonderful, wonderful!"

"I'll have my manager check my calendar for next spring. Have you—?" She paused. Strange. The room was spinning. She couldn't quite focus on Max Wyman or his son, Dirk, or the other gentlemen crowding around, waiting for a chance to speak to her. What was she about to say? "Have you set a date, Mr. Wyman?" A date for what? she wondered even as she asked the question.

"We've set the date tentatively for April 5th." Max, his blue eyes narrowing, bent close to her. "Are you all right, Miss Reed? You look a bit pale."

"It's a little warm in here," she murmured. Dirk reached toward her, offering his hand. He was saying something, but the words seemed to come at her from a great distance; the sound was wrong, deep and guttural and too slow, like a record played on the wrong speed. The businessmen in their dark, dapper suits surrounded her, pressing in for autographs and handshakes; they were moving in slow motion now, their faces too close, their features oddly distorted. When Alice Marie tried to focus her gaze on them, they coalesced suddenly into massive shadows that obliterated the light.

"Help me," she whispered, extending her hand to Dirk, to Max, to anyone, but it was too late. She felt herself sinking, a rag-doll, knees-to-jelly sensation, dropping, plummeting down a deep tunnel into an oblivion of pure blackness.

"Alice Marie, do you hear me? Alice Marie!"

A rank odor filled her nostrils, causing her to gag. She sat up, choking, her chest heaving with spasms.

"That's enough of the smelling salts," she heard someone say. "She's coming to."

Someone put a glass to her lips. The water was tepid and ran down her chin. Gradually her eyes focused and took in her surroundings. She was in a swank office, lying propped on a pillow on a dark leather couch. Maxwell Wyman and Dirk hovered over her, their foreheads knotted in anxious frowns.

Dirk sat down beside her on the couch. "Are you okay, Allie?"

"Yes," she said, as if that should be evident. Then she realized she had no idea what had happened to her. She looked searchingly at Dirk. "I—I don't know. Am I okay?"

"You fainted," he said, brushing stray wisps of hair back from her face.

"Fainted? Why?"

"I don't know. Perhaps the room was too warm, or you were weak from not eating, or you have a touch of flu. How do you feel now?"

She thought a moment. "A little weak and queasy."

"I asked the chef to bring you a bowl of broth. Are you up to eating?"

She shook her head. "I just want to go home. Please, Dirk, drive me home."

During the next two days both Mama and Annie fussed over Alice Marie, insisting she stay in bed and let them wait on her. They brought her homemade chicken soup and glass after glass of juice—apple, orange, pineapple, and cranberry—until she was sure she had juice pouring out her ears. When they weren't bringing juice they stuck a thermometer in her mouth or felt her forehead or fluffed her pillow. She didn't protest. Something was wrong; she could feel it; her stomach churned with nausea; every muscle in her body felt weak with exhaustion.

"We should call the doctor," Mama said more than once, and each time Alice Marie shook her head. Whatever it was would pass in a day or two and she'd be good as new.

But by the third day, when Alice Marie showed no sign of improvement, her mother declared, "I don't care what you say, Daughter. I'm calling Doc Elrick."

"Doc who? What happened to Dr. Galway?"

"He had a heart attack a year or so ago, so he retired and moved to Florida. Dr. Elrick, from Ann Arbor, took his place. Don't fret. He's a very good doctor. Now, before I call him, would you like some breakfast. Scrambled eggs and toast?"

Alice Marie rolled over and hugged her pillow. "No! Nothing! Please, Mama, just let me sleep! I'm so tired!"

She dozed for a few minutes, then woke to voices outside her half-open door. Mama and Annie were talking in hushed whispers.

"Doesn't it start this way?" Annie was asking. "Don't they say it starts with weakness in the muscles and flu-like symptoms? We've got to face it, Mama. It could be."

"No, I won't think of it! Not Alice Marie. She's so full of life and energy. Surely it wouldn't strike her!"

"We won't know until the doctor checks her, Mama. You've got to call him today, before she gets any worse."

Her mother was weeping now, softly, muffling the sobs. "Merciful heavens, it can't be polio. It can't be!"

Alice Marie leaned up on her elbows, listening, holding her breath lest she miss a word. Did Mama say polio? Surely she didn't think her daughter had polio! It was the flu. It felt like flu. Alice Marie had assumed the illness would be gone before she knew it—here today, gone tomorrow. But a sobering thought gripped her. It had been three days already and she felt no better. This wasn't a twenty-four hour bug.

"Mama!" she called, her shrill voice sounding more panicky than she intended. "Mama, you get that Doc Elrick over here! Mama, you hear me?"

Walter Elrick arrived later that afternoon and lumbered into the room with his tie askew and his little black bag in one beefy hand. "Warm day," he greeted with a wry grimace. He was a big man, portly rather than plump, with a large bald head and features that could have been molded from bread dough. He had no neck; rather, two generous chins that merged unceremoniously with his shoulders. Black marble eyes were couched in fleshy pouches beneath thick, bristly brows that drooped like sagging awnings. "Summer's got to come to an end one of these days," he rasped, opening his worn valise on the bed. "Tell me about yourself, Miss Reed."

She had no idea whether he wanted her life history or a list of her symptoms; she decided on the symptoms. While he checked her in his slow, methodical fashion—the cold stethoscope moving over her chest and back, his fingertips pressing the glands in her neck—she closed her eyes and, fighting self-consciousness, described her fainting spell and the persisting weakness, nausea, and dizziness.

When he had finished his examination, she forced out the words. "Do you think I have polio?"

He sat down beside her on the bed and patted her hand. "I don't know, Miss Reed. It could be many things. Let's not think the worst until we've ruled out the lesser ills, like influenza. It's going around this time of year, you know."

"So is polio," she replied, unwilling to let the subject drop until she was reassured.

"You're right. We've had three new cases here in your neighborhood, but they've all been light, and the patients remained at home. I expect them to be on the mend in a matter of days."

She studied his face, his eyes, trying to read what he wasn't saying. "I've heard that people are staying home because the hospital beds are full. There are no more iron lungs. People are being sent to Indianapolis."

His expression softened. "Yes, that's true. But it's also true that most cases of polio are mild and leave no paralysis."

"But how do you know which cases are which?"

"We take it a day at a time, Miss Reed."

His answer offered little comfort. In a small, anxious voice, she said, "You do think it's polio, don't you?"

"I suspect it is," he conceded, "but I'm going to run some tests. Blood and urine. It could be something else."

"I'm a singer," she told him, tears welling in her eyes. "Polio can paralyze the vocal cords. I've heard that. And then I'd never sing again—never talk. That can't happen to me, Doc Elrick."

"My dear, there's no reason to think—"

"You're not listening to me," she insisted, her tone urgent, accusatory. "The only thing people love about me is my voice. It's the only thing I'm good at. It's what made me a star. People come up to me and ask for my autograph. They watch me on television and write me letters. On the street sometimes they come up and want to touch me, as if I were an angel or a saint or something." She seized his hand, her long, polished nails digging into his porcine flesh. "Do you hear me, Doc Elrick? I'm nothing if I can't sing. I'd rather die than lose my voice."

He gently disengaged her hand from his, then stood up and reached into his medical bag. "Right now, Miss Reed, let's draw some blood and see what that tells us, all right?"

Minutes later, as the doctor packed up his valise, Annie knocked lightly on the open door. "Doc Elrick," she said, her green eyes wide and rimmed with concern, "before you go, would you stop by the nursery and have a look at Maggie? She—she's complaining that her legs hurt."

As the Herrick household geared up to care for their two polio patients, Knowl carried Alice Marie downstairs to the parlor he had transformed into a makeshift hospital room. He had turned the sofa and love seat into beds for Maggie and Alice Marie and had even installed a television set, so they would have something to do while they recuperated. "It'll be easier for Mother Reed to care for you both if you're close at hand," he said as he laid her gently on the sofa. "No running up and down stairs with meals and medicine and what have you."

Not that Doc Elrick was totally convinced they had polio, but the way Alice Marie and little Maggie were lying around weak and listless and complaining of muscle aches, he had to admit polio was the most likely possibility. "Making diagnoses is an imperfect science," he said when he came to check his two patients later that week. "Better to err on the side of caution. Then if it turns out you two just had the flu, well, no harm done."

"If it was flu, it would be gone by now," Alice Marie protested. "Flu never felt like this."

"Well, tomorrow I should have the results back on your tests, young lady, so we'll have a better idea what we're facing." Doc Elrick gave her his usual pat on the hand. "Meanwhile, you and the young one here get plenty of rest, lots of fluids, and a big helping of your mama's homemade chicken soup."

"Can I watch *Time for Beanie*?" asked Maggie from her bed on the love seat? "It's my favorite television show."

Doc Elrick chuckled. "You'll have to fight it out with your Aunt Allie. I'm staying out of it."

"The television is yours, Baby Doll," said Alice Marie, "as long as you let me play my 78s on the record player."

Having a family hovering over her, playing nursemaid, and constantly inquiring about her health was a brand new experience for Alice Marie. Not altogether unpleasant. Often throughout the day and evening, Mama, Annie, and Knowl would appear in the parlor doorway with juice or broth or flowers or fresh custard and ask, "How are our girls doing? Do you need anything? Can we make you more comfortable? Would you like the window open? The television on? An extra blanket? Did you take your medicine?

Alice Marie had never been showered with so much tender loving care. But then even as a child she had rarely been ill and seldom allowed others to know when she needed something. It had been a matter of pride all of her life to let the world believe she could make it on her own just fine, thank you.

But at the moment it felt good to have people fussing over her, acting as if they were truly concerned for her well-being. Perhaps their solicitude was genuine, although Alice Marie had never been convinced anyone loved her for herself, except Mama. And maybe Papa and her brother, Chip, when they were alive.

For most of her life Alice Marie had loftily endured people's complaints about what a vain and selfish girl she was. Why couldn't she be more like her sister, Annie, folks would cluck—sweet, precious Annie, who would gladly give up anything she had for anyone in the world.

Alice Marie usually heard these remarks from relatives at family gatherings during holiday events. To her face they would praise her for her beauty and her marvelous voice, but when they thought she couldn't hear them, they would murmur about her failings with a self-righteous air that wounded her still.

Looking across at Maggie, she recalled the first incident that left her feeling hurt and confused. She was five or six—hardly any older than Maggie—and Mama had urged her to sing at a family Christmas party. Alice Marie wore her fanciest dress with an immense bow holding back her long blonde ringlets. She sang several carols and curtseyed three times while everyone applauded. They loved her! She felt heady with delight.

But afterward, in the kitchen she heard her mother's two maiden aunts talking as they washed dishes. "I declare, that Alice Marie has a voice like an angel," said one.

"But a heart like ice," said the other.

"I have to agree. She's going to grow up to be a vain, prideful young woman if her mama's not careful."

"Such a pity with Annie so sweet. Yes, her mama's going to have her hands full with Alice Marie. That child has a haughty spirit, and a selfish nature to boot. Wouldn't share her Christmas candy with any of the other children. She may be pretty on the outside, but she's not so pretty inside."

From that day on, Alice Marie determined that people would see only the outside and never the inside, lest they discover how ugly she really was at heart. As cutting as her aunts' remarks had been, she eventually learned to steel herself and pretend their words didn't matter. And as she grew up she took an adverse pleasure in behaving in such a scandalous and insolent manner as to prompt such dismayed and dumbfounded responses.

But all of that was behind her now as Alice Marie basked in her family's attention. She even began to believe that the old Alice Marie could change, could become—was it possible?—more like Annie. Kind, considerate, generous, self-sacrificing. It was something to think about at least.

The next morning Doc Elrick arrived bright and early, looking preoccupied even as he greeted Maggie and Alice Marie. "How are my girls today?" he asked, but his usual enthusiasm was missing.

"I'm feeling stronger," said Alice Marie. "I didn't even need help walking down the hall to the bathroom."

"Good." The doctor looked over at Maggie. "Looks like our other patient is asleep. Just as well."

Alice Marie felt a sudden note of alarm. "Why? Is something wrong?"

"It depends." He sat down in a chair beside Alice Marie's makeshift sofa-bed. "Your tests came back, Allie." He called her that now because Maggie did.

"Bad news?" she asked, trying to sound plucky and unconcerned. "Do they prove I have polio?"

"No. If you have polio, it's a very light case."

Alice Marie shook her head, confused. "Then what did the tests show?"

He reached for her hand and squeezed it; a paternal gesture that conveyed genuine compassion. Her heart was racing now. Did she have a terminal illness? Was she dying?

Doc Elrick lowered his head, so that his heavy jowls overlapped his double chins. For an instant he reminded Alice Marie of a walrus—perhaps the walrus from her favorite Lewis Carroll stories—was it *Alice's Adventures in Wonderland* or *Through the Looking Glass?* Yes, she remembered now—"The Walrus and the Carpenter." She loved reciting the rhyme as a child.

> *The sun was shining on the sea,*
> *Shining with all his might:*
> *He did his very best to make*
> *The billows smooth and bright—*
> *And this was odd, because it was*
> *The middle of the night.*

"Alice Marie?"

She blinked and met the physician's kindhearted gaze. "Tell me. Please. I want the truth."

He paused, as if gathering his words. "May I ask you a question first?" When she nodded, he said, "I understand your husband died a couple of months ago."

"Yes, but what does that have to do with—?"

"What I'm about to tell you, Allie, may be a blessing or a curse. Only you can decide how you will feel about this news."

Her mouth felt dry. "Doc Elrick, you're not making any sense. In fact, you're scaring me."

He leaned forward with a confidential air, his hand still holding hers. "There is nothing to be afraid of, Allie. What ails you is the most natural thing in the world. . . . You are going to have a baby."

It took a moment for his words to take hold, and when they did she almost laughed. "A baby? That's impossible. It can't be!"

"I would estimate you to be about three months along," he went on in his perfectly modulated voice. "I expect in a few weeks the exhaustion, nausea, and occasional dizziness will begin to abate."

She stared at him. He wasn't joking. She saw the reality in his eyes. "A baby?" she whispered again, the word sounding foreign on her lips.

"It never occurred to you that you might be expecting?"

"No! I thought I wasn't feeling well because of losing Cary."

He nodded. "The exhaustion and lack of appetite are symptomatic of grief. But I hope that having your husband's child will bring you a measure of consolation."

She stared incredulously at him. "I can't have a baby now, Doc. Don't you see? I'm alone. I have no husband. What would people say?"

"Does it matter?" he asked gently.

She didn't know. She had always lived as if she didn't care what people thought of her, but that was an act, a pretense, a protective gesture so no one would glimpse the real person inside—the prideful girl her aunts called "ugly."

She sat up in bed and pressed her palms against her middle in wonderment. "I never wanted children. I never even thought about it. Cary and I—we never even discussed it, it was so far from our minds."

"I'm sure your family will be very supportive," Doc Elrick assured her. "Your sister, Annie, is one of the most compassionate people I know, and your mother, Anna—"

"I'm not thinking of my family now," she protested. "I—I'm thinking of myself. I'm a woman with a career, not some young girl who's always dreamed of rocking babies and making pablum."

"You'll bring a world of exciting experiences to your child, Allie. That's more than many mothers have to offer their offspring. I think you'll make a fine mother."

"No, don't say it! I can't imagine myself being a mother." She massaged her hands. They felt cold, clammy. She was trying to digest this terrible new truth, but it eluded her. A baby? No! Her mind was veering off somewhere she couldn't follow; she was riding the edge of hysteria. "I won't! You've got to do something, Doc. Make it go away!"

His walrus-jowls sank lower over his round neck. "I'm sorry, Allie. There's nothing anyone can do. You know that. What God has given, no one can take away."

"Did God do this—take my husband and leave me with a baby? Is this God's idea of a joke? It's a kick in the teeth!"

Maggie stirred and rolled over and looked at Alice Marie with sleepy eyes. "Did you call me, Aunt Allie?"

"No, Baby Doll," she said, her eyes filling with tears. "Everything's fine. You go back to sleep, okay?"

Doc Elrick stood up and smoothed his suit jacket over his ample middle. "One more thing," he said, his tone guarded.

"Don't tell me," she said with a note of bitterness. "Twins?"

He cleared his throat. "No, it's the polio I'm concerned about."

She leaned back on her elbows, her satin bed jacket suddenly too warm against her skin. "But you said—you don't even know if I have polio."

"That's true. But I suspect you, like Maggie, have suffered a light case. I've seen countless cases like yours where people show symptoms but aren't ill enough to go to the hospital."

"Then I should be all right, shouldn't I?"

He paused. "We don't know whether polio might affect your baby."

She flinched, as if he had struck her. "Polio could hurt the baby?"

"Polio generally doesn't complicate pregnancy or delivery, but there are cases where an unborn child contracts the disease. I just thought you should be aware of the possibility—"

"What? That I'll have a defective baby? That he might not even survive? Is that what you're saying?"

"No, Allie, I just want you to be—"

"What irony, that God might take me at my word and take my child!"

"Let's not think the worst," Doc urged, patting her hand the way he always did. "Let's just be patient and not despair over what will most likely never occur."

"Are you telling me I won't know if the baby's okay until he's born? I can't live that way," she cried, her arms instinctively cradling her abdomen. "I couldn't stand not knowing what's growing inside me!"

Doc Elrick picked up his valise and plodded to the parlor door. He turned and looked back at her with a kindly smile. "You'd be surprised what amazing things we can do, Allie, when we have no other choice."

Y ou heard me! A baby! I'm going to have a baby!" Alice
Marie's voice rang shrill. It could have been someone else
standing here in the dining room, gripping the mahogany
chair back, staring wildly at her family as they innocently ate their dinner. It had been hours since Doc Elrick had left and everyone had assumed
his visit was routine. It had taken Alice Marie as many hours to work up
the courage to confront her family with the news. "And it's Cary's baby,
in case you're wondering," she added defensively.

Her mother stood up and came quickly to her side. She urged Alice
Marie to sit down. "Darling, of course we know it's Cary's baby. No one
would question such a thing."

"Yes, they will. Wait and see. Some of the old biddies in this town!"

"Alice Marie," exclaimed Annie, "don't even say such a thing!"

"But it's true. Everyone will be talking. You know they will. I'd get on
the train tomorrow and go straight back to Chicago but my producer
won't let me on television if I'm in a family way. It's in my contract that
I won't get pregnant. Don't look at me that way. It's not a dirty word. I
was married. This baby is legitimate. But no one will believe, especially
no one in Willowbrook!"

"It's nobody's business, Darling." Her mother caressed Alice Marie's
shoulder and smoothed her long, tangled curls. "A baby will be very special for you. Now you'll have something of Cary with you forever."

"What did Doc Elrick say?" asked Annie. "Are you well enough to carry a baby? What about the polio?"

Alice Marie's voice quavered. "Doc thinks I've had a light case, just like Maggie. He doesn't think it'll hurt the baby, but he can't be sure."

Annie got up, came around to Alice Marie's chair, and gave her a hug. "We're here for you. Whatever happens we'll take care of you . . . and the baby."

Choking back a sob, Alice Marie returned Annie's embrace. It was the closest she ever remembered feeling to her younger sister. "I don't know anything about having babies, Annie. I never wanted to be a mother like you did. I'll make a lousy mother. I'm all thumbs. I don't even know how to change a diaper."

"You've got two experts in the house," said her mother with a smile. "Annie and I will give you all the help you need."

Alice Marie wiped the moisture from her eyes. "I was going back to Chicago next week. I'll go stir crazy living in Willowbrook for six more months. I'm not about to sit around knitting booties!"

"Maybe I can get you some part-time work at the publishing house," suggested Knowl. "We always need somebody to read the manuscripts that come in over the transom."

She frowned. "Over the what?"

"Transom. The little window over the door—never mind."

"He means unsolicited manuscripts," explained Annie. "What we jokingly call the 'slush pile.'"

"I don't know if I could. I've got too much on my mind to read anything. My mind's spinning like a whirling dervish."

"I understand," said Knowl. "There's no rush."

"Meanwhile, this daughter of mine is going back to bed," said Mama, clasping her shoulders. "I'll bring you and Maggie some hot vegetable beef soup and ginger ale. Everything will look better in the morning."

"I'll go back to bed, Mama, but there's one thing you've got to promise." She looked urgently around the table. "This goes for you, too, Annie. And you, Knowl. You can't tell anyone about the baby. I don't want Dirk to find out, or anyone else at the publishing house. I don't want anyone at church to know, not even Reverend Marshall. Nor any of your neighbors."

"But folks will know eventually," her mother pointed out. "You can't keep a thing like this secret for long. Nature has a way of making sure people know."

"Regardless, Mama, don't any of you utter a word about this to anyone until I'm ready to tell. Not even to Catherine and Robert. Do you hear me? Nobody must know, not a soul outside this room, or I'll pack my bags and be out of here this very day. Promise?"

As the warm, sticky days of September gave way to the chill, invigorating days of October, both Alice Marie and Maggie regained their strength. For them, polio had been—if not kind, at least less ruthless than it had been with others. Maggie was eager to get up and play again, although she tired easily and Annie fretted over every sniffle and sigh. For a week or two Maggie limped slightly, but even that remnant of the dread disease disappeared as she ran and played each day in the colorful, crackling leaves of autumn.

Alice Marie was feeling better too. Her bouts of nausea and dizziness had passed, but now she was concerned with the weight she was gaining. At every meal Mama piled the food high on Alice Marie's plate, insisting that she was eating for two now, and Alice Marie would push the plate away, declaring that she refused to look like a blimp just because she was expecting.

As Alice Marie grew restless for something to do, Knowl started bringing home stacks of unsolicited manuscripts for her to peruse. To everyone's amazement, including Alice Marie's, she discovered that she enjoyed reading these earnest, heartfelt works of aspiring writers; she even enjoyed writing up evaluations of the most promising works for Knowl. At last someone was willing to pay her to express her very vocal and hardheaded opinions. And more often than not, Knowl agreed with her conclusions.

"You've got a good head for editing," Knowl told her one evening as she explained how she would change a promising but obviously flawed project. They were sitting in the parlor going over the manuscripts she had read that day. "I'm serious, Alice Marie. You really have a knack for figuring out not just what's wrong with a manuscript, but also how to fix it. That's rare."

Alice Marie felt her face grow warm with pleasure. "Thank you, Knowl. You don't know what it means to hear you say that."

He winked. "Just don't quote me to Annie," he cautioned. "Sometimes I think she still feels a few jealous twinges where you're concerned."

"She shouldn't. She has everything anyone could ever ask for," mused Alice Marie. "A loving husband, a beautiful home, a darling daughter. She's even a best-selling novelist. Sometimes I'm jealous of her success."

"Whose success?" asked Annie as she entered the parlor with a steaming pot of tea and a tray of oatmeal cookies. She set the tea service and cookies on the coffee table and poured three cups. "What did I miss?" she asked as she handed Knowl a cup, then Alice Marie.

He glanced from sister to sister. "I was just thinking how much you two are alike, at least when it comes to editing. You both have the same keen, observant eye and attention to detail. And you both have a knack for figuring out what's wrong and fixing it."

Annie flashed a generous smile. "Well, dear sister, I'm glad to know we have something more in common."

Alice Marie was about to say, *You mean, something more than Knowl?* But she let the words die on her tongue. No sense in stirring up trouble when life was relatively peaceful lately. "Thank you, Annie," she said instead, with genuine sincerity. "I'm glad we have more in common than we knew too." She noticed Annie fingering a letter in the pocket of her cardigan sweater. "A special letter?" she asked.

Annie's face turned crimson. She slipped her hand over the letter, then seized it and held it up, as if surprised by its presence. "It's nothing really," she said, then said just as quickly, "I don't mean that. It's quite important, actually."

"Who's it from?" asked Knowl, his voice rising.

Annie hesitated just long enough to make Alice Marie wonder what she was trying to hide. "It's from Helmut Schwarz," she said softly. "The Jewish evangelist I met at the World's—"

"I know who he is, Annie." Knowl sounded more than a little curious now; even a trifle suspicious. "How does this fellow happen to be writing you?"

Annie sat down on the love seat beside her husband. "It's not so strange, Darling. You're corresponding with Helm about his book. I thought I would write him too. I still think it's such a coincidence he would write you and want you to publish his book."

"I already told you. He wrote to a dozen houses, Annie. We're just one among many."

"That's why I wanted to let him know of the special bond we share. I knew he wouldn't remember leading me to the Lord all those years ago, so I wanted to remind him. I told him I would love to see him if he ever comes to Willowbrook."

"Is that all," asked Knowl, "or is there more?"

Annie lowered her gaze. "I told him I hoped he would give us the opportunity to publish his manuscript."

Knowl set his cup and saucer down hard on the coffee table and stood up. He removed his glasses and held them up to the light, then cleaned each lens with his linen napkin. Even Alice Marie knew this meant he was angry; he always cleaned his glasses when his anger flared.

"I don't think it was wise for you to go behind my back, Annie, when we're not even in the negotiation stage yet. We're still soliciting critiques of his manuscript. It could be weeks before the editorial committee votes, and here you are making it sound as if we've already made a favorable decision."

"It was just a personal letter," Annie argued, setting her own cup beside Knowl's. "I have a perfect right to write a friendly letter to someone I've been hoping desperately to see again after all these years."

"Desperately?" Knowl repeated coolly.

"You know what I mean. Don't twist my words, Knowl."

"Please, you two," said Alice Marie. "Let's not argue. Just tell us, Annie, what this mystery man of yours had to say."

"Yes," said Knowl. "Read us his letter. Please."

Annie's expression remained dubious, even a bit reluctant, but she removed the letter from its envelope and read aloud in a small, careful voice. When she had finished, Knowl said in astonishment, "He says he's coming to Willowbrook to see you."

"Yes, that's what I was trying to tell you, Darling."

"He's coming all the way from where? New York City? And he says he wants to talk about the book while he's here. I'm not sure we'll even have a decision that soon."

"I'm sure he'll understand."

"I'm not asking him to understand, Annie. I see no reason for him to come here. And frankly—I've told you this before—I think he's something of a zealot. His tone is confrontational. I think the book will be too controversial for our house."

"I don't agree," said Annie.

"Frankly it doesn't matter what either of us thinks. The committee makes the decisions."

"But when you're excited about a book, Knowl, they get excited too. They follow your lead. I'm just asking you to give Helm a chance."

"Don't you see, Annie? So far doubts are all I have about this man."

"Listen, you two," said Alice Marie, more sharply than she intended, "what I want to know is when this fellow is coming to town and where he's staying?"

"Next week," said Annie. "He wants us to pick him up at the depot on Friday night. And he'll be staying here, won't he, Knowl? I couldn't send him off to some dreary hotel."

Alice Marie shook her head ponderously. "This is all we need. Some rabid revolutionary in the house. I can see it now. I'll have to go back to Chicago for some peace and quiet."

"Stop it, Alice Marie," snapped Annie. "Why does everything always have to be about you? I've invited Helmut Schwarz to stay in our home, and I expect you both to treat him like, like . . ."

"Like royalty?" ventured Knowl dryly.

"No. Like an honored guest. It's going to be a wonderful experience. You'll see. You too, Alice Marie. You've never met a man like Helmut Schwarz."

She shrugged. "And I'm not sure I want to."

Two days later a bouquet of red roses arrived for Alice Marie with a card that said simply, "Hope you're feeling better. Fondly, Dirk Wyman."

That evening Dirk phoned and apologized for not calling sooner. "It's not that I've forgotten you, Allie," he said, sounding genuinely apologetic. "Quite the opposite. I've thought often about our evening at the Brandwynne—two evenings if you count our rehearsal and the night you sang—and I can't get you out of my mind. Knowl has told me about your illness, and he says you're better now. I can't believe you had polio—a mild case, thank goodness—it was polio, wasn't it?"

"The doctor couldn't be sure, but my little niece had it too. We think it was polio, but we're both on the mend now."

"Wonderful. Well, I would have paid you a visit, but honestly I don't do well around sick people or hospitals, that sort of thing. I mean, what can you say?" His voice dropped off, as if he realized he was painting himself in a corner. Finally, his tone brightening, he said, "How about dinner tonight at our favorite haunt, the Brandwynne? Considering every other restaurant in town is a bore."

Alice Marie hesitated. She was dying to get out and have some fun again, but what if Dirk took one look at her and guessed she was pregnant? No bachelor in his right mind wanted to squire an expectant mother around town. *He won't know,* her rational self argued back, *and nobody's going to tell him!* "All right, Dirk," she heard herself saying. "I'd love to have dinner with you tonight."

At seven he picked her up in his gleaming Nash-Healey sports car and they headed for the Brandwynne. She wore her fashionable bell-shaped black faille tunic over a just-below-the-knee straight skirt. "You look gorgeous," he told her when they were seated beside a spacious plate glass window overlooking the park.

"And you look very dashing in your tuxedo," she returned.

"No, I'm serious," he said, his gaze appraising her. "I expected you to look pale and thin after your illness, but here you are looking rosy and glowing. If you don't mind me saying, you've even put on a few pounds in all the right places."

She felt her face redden. "Not too many, I hope."

"No," he said approvingly, "I'd say you're just about perfect."

Not for long, she mused ironically. She opened her menu and pretended to study the selections. She hated this feeling that she was keeping a secret from someone she hoped might become more than a friend one day. What was she going to do?—urge him to the altar and then say, *By the way, it's a package deal. Mommy and baby for the price of one!*

"A penny for your thoughts," he said, reaching across the table for her hand.

"It was nothing," she lied. "I was thinking about—about Annie—my sister—about her mysterious stranger."

Dirk smiled blankly. "Excuse me? I'm afraid I'm lost."

Alice Marie's color rose. She was botching it good, rambling on like an idiot. "I mean, I was thinking about the man—the Jewish evangelist from New York—he submitted a manuscript to Herrick House. I just supposed that, working there, you probably knew—"

"Oh, you're speaking of the Helmut Schwarz manuscript," said Dirk with a grin. "You had me for a minute."

"I don't know why I brought it up—"

"Yes, I've read it—parts of it. Knowl asked for my opinion. He realizes that no matter what editorial thinks, if the numbers aren't there financially, it's dead in the water." He paused, his pale blond brows knitting together to form two small knots in his ruddy forehead. "It was very interesting, Allie. An impassioned work, but not at all right for Herrick House. The man's a zealot. Too confrontational."

Strange, thought Alice Marie. *Knowl used the same words.*

"The man's obviously bitter about what happened to the Jews during the war—Hitler and the Nazis, that whole thing—and he wants to blame it on the rest of the world for not stepping in and doing something. Schwarz claims if we don't watch out the same thing will happen again to some other people under some other crazed dictator. You and I both know Hitler was a fluke in the scheme of things—one crazy, demented man in what should have been a civilized world. It won't happen again. We're too smart for that. The world has learned its lesson, right?"

Alice Marie shrugged. Dirk was talking about things—ideas, concepts—that simply didn't enter her mind. "The war is over," she said for want of anything more enlightening to add to the conversation. "Why dredge up the past?"

"My feeling exactly," agreed Dirk, as if she had said exactly the right thing. "And that's just what this Schwarz book would do. It would make people start pointing fingers at one another, innocent people who never intended for anyone to be hurt, who were deceived by Hitler just like the rest of the world."

Alice Marie nodded, as if she understood just what Dirk was saying. She had a feeling they had broached some area of concern he felt ardently about, but she had no desire to pursue it. She looked again at her menu and said, "I think this time I'll try the rack of lamb with mint jelly."

10

On Friday, October 19, while Knowl and Annie drove to the depot to pick up Helmut Schwarz, Alice Marie helped her mother prepare dinner. It would be a royal feast—roast beef, browned potatoes, yams, homemade rolls, fresh fruit salad, and Mama's mouth-watering apple pie. All for Annie's mysterious white knight from the past.

"This is more work than Sunday dinner," Alice Marie groused as she peeled her umpteenth potato. "We should just serve Sir Galahad meat loaf or chipped beef on toast. Something simple and unpretentious."

"Now, Daughter, don't begrudge Annie this important occasion." Her mother lifted the lid to check the roast and a little cloud of steam escaped, filling the kitchen with a tantalizing aroma. "You know your sister wants everything to be just right for her Mr. Schwarz."

"That's the problem, Mama, at least as far as Knowl is concerned. Annie thinks of this man as *her* Mr. Schwarz."

Mama scowled. "If you're suggesting there's any impropriety here, Alice Marie—"

"Of course not, Mama. It's just—why all the fuss for a stranger? Besides, this man wants Herrick House to publish his book. He should be taking all of *us* out to dinner!"

Her mother tucked a stray wisp of hair into the chignon at the nape of her neck and gave Alice Marie her mildly amused, mildly exasperated look. "Are you finished with the potatoes?"

Alice Marie handed her the bowl. "Shall I set the table now, or do you still need help in the kitchen?"

Mama wiped her hands on her apron and took a small plate and glass down from the cupboard. "I'm doing fine with dinner, Dear. I don't want you to get too tired, but would you dish up this plate for Maggie and see that she eats? I'd like to get her fed and off to bed before they get home from the train station."

"Sure, Mama. I guess I'd better get in practice tending to the needs of little ones." Alice Marie had rarely spent time in the company of children, and she still wasn't sure how eager she was to make their acquaintance, but if she was going to start somewhere, it might as well be with little Maggie. The two of them had become pals over their long days of recuperation in the parlor. Alice Marie had even taken to watching an occasional kiddie show and Maggie had developed a taste for big band jazz.

"Sing me a song," Maggie begged as Alice Marie tucked her into bed a half hour later.

"Just a little itsy-bitsy one. It's getting very late." She sat down on the bed and began singing, "On Top of Old Smoky," but Maggie stopped her.

"Sing 'Aba Daba Honeymoon,' about the monkey and the chimp!" Impulsively Alice Marie began tickling Maggie's ribs and under the arms of her cotton nightgown. "That song's for little monkeys, not little girls!"

Maggie giggled and made ape-like gestures with her arms. Alice Marie laughed, thinking how thankful she was that Maggie showed no residual effects from the polio.

"Look, I'm a monkey, Aunt Allie. See?"

"No, you're not. You're a beautiful little girl."

"Not like you," said Maggie solemnly. "My hair's brown. Yours looks like the sunshine. And my eyes are brown, not blue like yours."

Alice Marie pulled the covers up and tucked them under Maggie's chin. "You're beautiful just as you are, dear girl. Just like your mama."

Alice Marie hummed another song, "Beautiful Brown Eyes," until Maggie's eyes closed in slumber. She sat a moment longer watching the child sleep, thinking about the tiny baby growing inside her own body. It didn't seem possible that such a thing was happening, and sometimes she wondered if Doc Elrick didn't just make it all up. A flesh-and-blood baby seemed so remote, so terrifying and miraculous all at once. But like Mama had said, it would mean that something of Cary still existed and would live on and be part of both of them and keep her company in the years to come.

The thought brought tears to her eyes, but she still felt stunned at the idea of some tiny unseen being taking over her body and demanding more and more of her until it finally forced its way into the world. What if she couldn't cope? Could she survive such a monumental upheaval in her life?

The sound of a door opening downstairs and voices in the foyer startled Alice Marie out of her reverie. *They're home. Now I'll get to meet Annie's gallant knight!* She leaned over and gently kissed Maggie's forehead, then stood up and glanced in the dresser mirror long enough to fluff her blonde pageboy and straighten her seersucker jumper.

She made a point of descending the staircase with a slow, rhythmic gait, so that her skirt flounced gracefully around the curve of her legs. Might as well make a good impression on Annie's dinner guest. Like Mama said, maybe he was single. Maybe he was handsome. She patted her tummy. Might as well keep her options open.

As she came down the last few steps, she spotted him in the entryway by the hat rack—a tall, dark, rangy man in a brown suit and camel-colored trench coat. He must have heard her high heels on the marble floor, for he turned and gazed her way, an expression of curiosity animating his angular, deeply etched features. She noticed immediately that he was handsome in a swarthy, brooding, melancholy way. He had the stubble of a beard on his deeply sculpted chin, and his wavy brown hair was combed back from his face and curled unfashionably around his ears. He had a remarkably straight nose, perfectly formed lips, and solemn, low-slung brows that shadowed the most piercingly hypnotic brown eyes she had ever seen.

Annie stepped forward and, taking his arm, said, "Helm, this is my sister, Alice Marie. Alice Marie, I'd like you to meet Helmut Schwarz."

He approached her with a spring in his step and a glint in his eyes and seized both her hands in his long, tapered fingers. "I'm pleased to meet Annie's sister," he said fervently.

Before Alice Marie could reply, Annie, in what seemed an overly possessive gesture, took his arm and led him over to her mother, who had just emerged from the kitchen. "Helm, this is my mother, Anna Reed," Annie said, beaming. "Mama, this is the man I met at the World's Fair twelve years ago who led me to the Lord."

Mama was beaming too. "It's a pleasure to meet you, Mr. Schwarz, or should I say Reverend?"

"Call me Helm, please."

"Yes, Helm it is. Please make yourself at home. Dinner is almost ready. Knowl, show Mr. Schwarz—Helm—where to wash up." Minutes later they were all seated around the table consuming Mama's delectable roast beef and browned potatoes. Helm, of course, was the center of conversation. Both Mama and Annie insisted on knowing everything that had happened to him over the years. From the corner of her eye Alice Marie watched him, intrigued by his energy and vitality, by the passion in his voice, and the graceful, limber way he moved his body and gestured with his hands to punctuate his words. Bit by bit, he related a startling, unforgettable story.

"I was born in Germany. In the twenties, however, when I was just a boy, my parents brought me to America. We lived here for many years, until the war. My father studied for a time at the Rabbinical Seminary of America in New York City, and he prayed every day that I would become a rabbi."

For Pete's sake! mused Alice Marie. *A rabbi no less!*

"But when I was still quite young I went to a tent meeting and heard Billy Sunday preach." He smiled across the table at Alice Marie, but she averted her gaze. She didn't want to hear this.

"I accepted Christ as my Messiah that day," he continued, "and I knew then that I wanted only to preach the Gospel. After college I attended a Christian seminary in New York, much to my father's dismay and, because I had no church in which to preach, I became a street evangelist, preaching the Gospel wherever I could, even at the World's Fair."

"But what happened to you after the fair?" prompted Annie.

"I went back to Germany and worked with the German underground to hide Jewish families and save them from the death camps."

"What happened to your parents?" Annie ventured. "Your relatives in Germany?"

A deep frown creased Helm's forehead. He lapsed into silence and concentrated for a moment on his dinner, spearing several morsels of roast beef. Finally he put his fork down and looked around the table and said, "It's not easy to talk about my family, but that is why I have come here. Someone must tell. Many Jews are ashamed of what happened to them, as if somehow it is their fault. But I will not be ashamed. I will tell everyone who will listen about what happened to my people."

"Tell us, Helm," Annie urged. "We want to know."

"Just before the war," he began gravely, "my parents and I left America and went back to Germany. My grandparents were still there and growing old and needy. And there were the disturbing letters from my aunts and uncles who were already suffering Hitler's persecution. It started with little things—signs in restaurants or stores saying, 'No Jews allowed.' Blasphemies scribbled on my grandfather's home and my uncle's print shop. All Jews were ordered to wear the yellow Star of David on their clothing so that people would know they were Jews. Then someone burned down a synagogue—first one, then another; and eventually most Jewish businesses were forced to close."

"Are you saying even you, being American, were forced to wear the star?" asked Knowl.

Helm shrugged. "No one cares that you are an American Jew. You are a *Jew*. That is all that matters." He took a swallow of ice water and wiped his lips with one long index finger. "At first my parents and I tried to make arrangements to take our family to America, but the immigration laws were very strict and the authorities would allow only a few to go. When my relatives could not get permission, my parents and I decided to stay in Germany."

"Your entire family remained in Germany?" asked Knowl.

"Except for my mother's sister who married a Dutchman and moved to Holland, and her brother who lived in Poland. My father's family remained in Germany."

"What happened then?" asked Annie.

"Entire Jewish families began to disappear. No one knew where they went or what happened to them. I was not content to sit and wait for trouble to come, so I joined with several Christian colleagues and converted Jews. We became part of the German underground and, as Jewish families went into hiding, we placed them with Christian families willing to take them in. Whenever possible we spirited Jews—especially the children—out of the country to safety."

"I've read of such undergrounds," said Knowl. "They were amazingly bold and heroic."

And foolhardy, thought Alice Marie. But she was seeing Helmut Schwarz from a new perspective. He was religious, but he cared about people. Cared enough to die for them. Cared about children.

"We had good success for a time," said Helm. "But as the months passed, fewer countries were safe. As Germany invaded and occupied more of her European neighbors, we heard unthinkable rumors. No one wanted to believe them. What rational man could imagine Nazis rounding up Jews by the thousands and sending them, not to slave labor camps, but to extermination camps to be murdered?"

"Death camps?" Alice Marie said under her breath, as if the significance of the words had just occurred to her.

Again Helm's gaze met hers. "Yes. Death camps. We Jews began to whisper their names with fear and dread—Treblinka, Sobibor, Chelmno, Belzec."

Annie put her hand on Helm's arm. "You don't have to talk about this if it's too painful. Later, if you wish."

He looked starkly at her. "Of course it's painful, and of course I must speak of it. Too many cannot speak. They are dead. Or worse than dead."

He drew in a ragged breath. "It was an appalling time. As evidence of the death camps mounted I tried again to persuade my parents to return to America, but my mother said, 'I will not leave my homeland or my family, and I will not fear my own countrymen. I will stay where I belong, and what will be will be.'"

His voice wavered, husky now. "A few months later—it was early 1944, the first week of February—while I was in Holland transporting Jewish children to a Gentile orphanage, I learned that all of my family in Germany had been taken to a concentration camp in Poland. It was called Auschwitz-Birkenau—an internment camp that Hitler used for Polish prisoners when he invaded Poland in 1939. But what I did not know was that in the intervening years a huge crematorium had been built there—hideous gas chambers where every day the Nazi beasts incinerated thousands—some days as many as eight thousand—innocent men, women, and children."

For several moments a grim silence weighed heavily in the room. No one was eating now. All eyes were on Helm. Alice Marie sat still, her hands in her lap, like a polite, dutiful schoolgirl. She felt queasy. She wanted to excuse herself and get up from the table. She had heard enough for one night of other people's miseries, especially tragedies so vast her mind couldn't begin to comprehend their magnitude. But she knew she didn't dare break the fragile, somber spell of this moment, so she waited, watching Helm. His hands were splayed palms-down on the tablecloth and his mouth twitched as he struggled for control.

At last Mama said softly, "What of your family, Helm?"

He shook his head and took a long moment to gather the words. "I never saw them again, except for my father. It took several years to learn of their fate. Some died at Auschwitz, others at Bergen-Belsen. Others are gone without a trace, vanished from this earth."

"But you say your father survived?" Knowl probed.

"Yes, my father lived. He was spared because the Nazis needed slave labor at nearby Birkenau, where the gas chambers were kept blazing day and night. At the end of January 1945—a bitter Polish winter, it was— he was set free when Russian troops liberated the inmates of Auschwitz." Helm's stony expression softened. "My father was lying in his bunk in sick bay, near death. The Germans had evacuated the camp nine days earlier, taking prisoners who could walk on a forced march to an undisclosed destination. Most of the 58,000 prisoners were killed along the way."

Knowl shook his head. "That many when freedom was so near?"

"Yes," said Helm. "Of the one and one-half million people who passed through Auschwitz, only seven thousand remained when the Russians arrived."

Mama broke in gently. "Is your father still alive?"

Helm managed a twisted smile. "He is alive if living means to exist with a haunted, tortured, broken mind."

"Where is he now?"

"In New York, Mrs. Reed. The two of us share a small apartment in an old neighborhood much like we left behind in Germany. A nurse comes in to check on him every day. He survives. He is a survivor at heart. We are both survivors."

Alice Marie nodded. She could tell that about Helm. His flashing, umber-brown eyes looked like those of a survivor—steely, strong, undaunted. He was a rugged, unbending man who might be physically fatigued but never impoverished in spirit. She liked that quality. It was a trait she valued in herself. Her battles had been far less onerous than his, but she felt an odd kinship with this very vocal, volatile man.

He reminded her of someone.

Was it Cary Rose? Certainly not, and yet . . .

Unquestionably, she had a fondness for survivors.

11

Helm, about your book," said Knowl, taking on a mildly businesslike tone. "I assume you'd like to discuss your manuscript with us tonight. Or, if you prefer to wait until tomorrow?"

"No, tonight is good," said Helm quickly. "This book—perhaps you understand how it is, Annie—this book has become my life. It is my chance to tell the world what I have seen, what my people have lived, and how cruelly they have died. I would give my life to see this book printed for the world to read."

Knowl flashed a kindly smile. "Believe me, Helm, it won't cost you that much. But I do have some concerns."

"What concerns, Knowl?" asked Annie with a note of alarm.

"Maybe this isn't the time to discuss it," he said, gazing around the table. "This is a family dinner, not a conference table. Right, Mother Reed?"

"Don't mind me," said Mama, standing up and brushing her hands on her apron. "I'll just go to the kitchen and get the dessert ready. You young people talk all you please."

"Knowl, what possible concerns could you still have about Helm's manuscript?" Annie persisted.

Slow down, Annie, Alice Marie mused. *You're pushing Knowl too hard.*

"What I need to hear," said Knowl, "is what Helm wants to communicate through this book."

"Have you read my preface?" asked Helm, sounding a trifle impatient. "I've spelled it out quite clearly there."

Knowl raised his hands in protest. "Don't think about your manuscript right now, Helm. Just tell me in your own words what you want people to know; what you want the average American to understand. Tell me as simply and briefly as you can."

Helm's sturdy brow furrowed, his square jaw set with a fierce intensity. "Briefly?"

"Take your time," urged Knowl. "Think about it. What crucial message do you want to leave with your reader?"

Helm's impatience was growing. "Have you read my manuscript?"

"Yes, Helm," said Knowl, "but, to be quite frank, it's not ready to publish. Not yet. Perhaps you're too close to it to have the objectivity you need. Perhaps you need to give it a few more months."

Helm's fist came down hard on the table, jarring the china and silverware with a startling clatter. "No! Enough time has passed already! This book—it's like my family, my child."

"I'm not saying we won't publish it. But it needs work. Think it through, Helm. What's on your heart? Put it in your own words, not in lofty, turgid language you think belongs in a book."

His countenance fell. "Is that what I've done?"

"No," declared Annie. "That's not what Knowl is saying. Is it, Knowl? Tell him you're not criticizing him as a writer."

"Stay out of it, Annie. Let Helm tell us in simple language what he wants to say."

Once again, Helm was silent. Everyone waited. Again, Alice Marie considered excusing herself from the table. But an idea was stirring. She could help this man. But would they let her?

Helm shifted in his chair, then fixed his gaze on each person at the table, one by one. "After the war, when I returned to America, I was shocked by what I saw. People acted as if the war never happened; they were busy buying houses and automobiles and television sets and conversing about their new appliances. Hour after hour people sit watching those little flashing screens, wanting silly clowns like Milton Berle and Arthur Godfrey to make them laugh."

"Maybe after the war we all needed a good laugh," suggested Alice Marie.

"Let him finish," said Knowl.

"Perhaps I anticipated too much," Helm conceded. "I came back expecting to find people changed by the atrocities of war. How could they not be changed, the way the entire world was rocked and altered, its innocence snatched away so grievously? Why was our civilization not still reeling from its impact? Why weren't conversations filled with it?"

"For some, the horrors are still very real," said Annie. "The men who fought will never forget."

"Yes," Helm agreed, "the memories are still keen and tender for those who suffered losses. But for the rest of America the war seems to have happened in the distant past, as if it were another lifetime, another planet. Nothing of the war touches people now; none of their concerns focus on anything remotely connected with the terrible holocaust that has shattered mankind."

"People don't like to remember unhappy times," noted Alice Marie.

"I understand that, but to sweep it all under the rug—that is unforgivable. But then perhaps you see things differently. The war was far away; you were all safe here in Willowbrook."

"No," Alice Marie protested. "The war came to Willowbrook too. My brother Chilton—Chip—died at Pearl Harbor."

"I'm sorry. I didn't know."

"Chip was my best friend," Knowl told him. "I'll never forget him."

"Then you understand, my friends, why we must always remember, no matter how painful it may be."

"Countless families across America will never forget," said Annie.

"But what of the rest of your country? Where is the dialogue dissecting and analyzing what the past decade means to our civilization and to our concept of what it means to be human?" Helm's eyes misted. "How can we have gone so quickly from the horrors of Hitler and the slaughter of millions of people to the bland mindlessness of—of television and Howdy Doody?"

"Your argument is well taken," said Knowl. "You put many of us to shame."

"I don't wish to put your country to shame. It is not my place to be the conscience of America—or even the conscience for this family. But I believe God wants me to present His truth to all who will listen, especially to those who claim to be Christians. I can understand why sinful men would be blind to God's ways, but God's children should have eyes that see and ears that hear His truths."

Annie looked pointedly at Knowl. "That's why a Christian house should publish Helm's book, Dear."

"And we're certainly considering it, Darling, but these things do take time."

"Time is of the essence," said Helm. "Three years ago God brought my people back to their homeland, Israel—an event many thought could never be. In less than fifty years we will ring in a new millennium. God is working in the events of these days to prepare us for our Messiah's return. God has challenged me to bring a wake-up call to His people before it is too late. That is the message I wish to present in my book."

For a full minute no one spoke. In the midst of the silence, Mama emerged from the kitchen with warm apple pie and a bowl of homemade vanilla ice cream. "Dessert is ready," she announced. "Who wants coffee?"

"I'll have a cup," said Knowl. "Helm, how about you? Coffee?"

He waved off the offer.

"Well, pour something in your glass—more water, anything, because I think we have a toast to make."

"A toast?" quizzed Annie. "What for?"

Knowl flashed a congenial smile. "I may be speaking too soon but, Helm, you've done a good job of selling me on the urgency of your message. Mind you, it's not a deal until the committee votes, but if you can put down on paper what you've told us tonight, I'd like to be the one to publish your book."

With an exultant little sigh, Annie raised her water goblet and said, "Let's toast Herrick House's newest author!"

Helm grinned. It was the first time Alice Marie had seen a genuine smile on his face, one that animated his entire countenance. "I am honored, and I will do my best to write my book as you wish," he promised.

"Are you willing to work with a professional writer?" inquired Knowl. "Someone who will help you capture that zeal and fervor on paper?"

"I—I don't know. I never thought of—"

"I'll work with you, Helm," said Annie, her face glowing nearly as much as Helm's. "I'd love to help you with your book."

"I don't think that's a good idea, Annie," said Knowl. "You have your own book deadline coming up, plus galleys to review before they go to press. And there's Maggie. She needs your time. She's still not out of the woods after her bout with polio."

"How can you say that, Knowl? She's running and playing the way she always has."

"Still, she needs your attention."

"You know our daughter always comes first with me." Annie paused, brightening. "But someone else could do the galleys."

"Who? We can't afford extra staff—"

"Don't worry, Knowl. I'll make a schedule and work everything in. I want to do this for Helm."

"Maybe I could help," said Alice Marie offhandedly. "I've got some free time."

Annie looked at her in surprise. "But you're not a writer."

Alice Marie examined one long polished nail. "Knowl said I did a good job on those manuscripts I edited. Didn't I, Knowl?"

"Yes. A fine job, Alice Marie. But Annie's right. Helm will need a seasoned writer." He looked at Helm. "Listen, I'll check my contacts in New York. We may be able to find a local author near your home."

"Perhaps there is another way," suggested Helm. "I have some business in Chicago, urgent business. For some time I have considered moving to Chicago, but I haven't wanted to uproot my father until my plans were firm. If your committee agrees to publish my book, I will bring my father here to Willowbrook to live. He would love a small town."

"Of course!" said Annie. "What a wonderful idea! Willowbrook is just a stone's throw from Chicago."

Helm was still smiling. "That way, I will complete my business and write my book as well."

Annie reached over and patted Knowl's hand. "It's the perfect solution, don't you think so, Darling?"

"I think we should all wait for the committee's decision before making plans."

Annie's hand tightened on Knowl's. "But you know the committee will be enthusiastic if they see your excitement. They have to say yes, Knowl. You'll convince them, I know you will."

Knowl lifted Annie's hand to his lips. "Patience, Darling."

"I do have another concern," said Helm. "Are there apartments to rent in Willowbrook?"

Mama shook her head. "Since the war ended, they're scarce as hen's teeth, as Papa used to say."

"Don't worry, Helm. We'll start looking in the newspaper tomorrow," said Annie. "And until you find something you can stay here with us."

He waved her off. "No, Annie. I couldn't impose on your family's generosity."

"Please, Helm. We'd love to have you and your father stay with us. Wouldn't we, Alice Marie?"

She shrugged and cast Helm a perusing smile. "The more the merrier, I always say."

"Knowl?"

He looked doubtful. "Let's not worry right now about accommodations. When the time's right, I'm sure Helm will find a suitable apartment somewhere in town."

"If you like, I'll help you look for a place, Helm," offered Alice Marie, casting Annie a sidelong glance. *It's like we're children again, vying for the same boy.* "I mean, of course, if Annie's too busy to take you."

"I'm never too busy to help a friend."

Alice Marie tossed Helm a coquettish smile. "Well, in case Knowl keeps Annie too busy at the office, Helm, remember, I'm available."

He matched her smile and nodded. "I'll remember that, Miss Reed."

"Alice Marie," she corrected.

"Of course. Alice Marie." His German brogue gave her name a pleasantly exotic sound.

"Meanwhile, Mr. Schwarz," Mama interjected, "you'll have the guest room upstairs at the end of the hall. I think you should be quite comfortable."

"Thank you, Mrs. Reed. I'm sure I will be." He looked around the table, his mahogany eyes lingering on Alice Marie. "You are good people. I look forward to knowing you better."

So do I! Alice Marie mused silently. It would be nice to have such a handsome man in the house for a few days. A single man at that. At least he hadn't mentioned a wife.

But getting acquainted with Annie's white knight posed a little problem. Annie had nearly lost one man to Alice Marie, so she surely wasn't about to let her Jewish evangelist fall into her older sister's clutches. *For now I'll just have to bide my time and keep my distance,* Alice Marie decided, *but watch out, Annie. You haven't seen anything yet!*

After dessert, while Knowl retreated to his den to make some phone calls, Annie walked Helm around the house and showed him Catherine's oil and watercolor paintings, elaborating on each one in exhausting detail. After the first painting or two, Alice Marie excused herself and went upstairs to bed. She already knew more than she ever wanted to hear about Cath's paintings. Besides, she was too weary to compete for Helm's attentions tonight. *Fiddlesticks! Let Annie have her time with Helm. Knowl will step in soon enough and whisk his bride off to their boudoir.*

Shutting the door behind her, Alice Marie sank down on her comfy feather bed and tried to kick off her two-inch pumps. They wouldn't budge. For crying out loud, her feet were swollen, bulging like overfed piggies over the edge of her too-tight leather shoes! Her ankles were swollen, too, like tree stumps stuffed in silk hose!

Tears of frustration sprang to her eyes. How could she expect to attract Helm, or Dirk, or any other man when her body was swelling like a balloon? Who was she fooling? What man would want a woman expecting a baby, another man's child?

Another thought crept in. She could be carrying a damaged child. Even Doc Elrick couldn't be sure she hadn't had polio during those early weeks of pregnancy. And he couldn't be sure her baby had escaped the disease. What man would want a sickly, crippled baby? It was the last thing on earth Alice Marie wanted. She'd be doing good to take care of a healthy child. Annie was the motherly one, self-sacrificing and generous to a fault; the exact opposite of Alice Marie.

At last she pried off her shoes and wiggled her pinched toes. Relief! She pulled off her seersucker jumper and slipped into her lavender silk nightgown. She looked at her profile in the dresser mirror. Heaven help her, she was starting to show. Drat you, Cary Rose! Before long, everyone would know, and no man would look her way except in pity or disgust.

Tears welled in her eyes, but she bit her lip and refused to let them fall. Silently she railed at her own jumbled, colliding emotions. What was wrong? Usually she could keep her feelings in check; she prided herself in being shrewd, cool-headed, and objective. Maybe it was the lot of expecting mothers to be emotional and weepy, but she wanted no part of it.

She slipped off the bed, pulled on her satin robe, and padded bare-foot to the window. Pulling back the antique-lace curtain, she gazed out at the moon-white cobblestone street flanked by shadowed, bare-limbed oaks and elms. She watched as the crisp October breeze sent whispering whirlwinds of dry leaves skittering over Honeysuckle Lane. Spidery branches creaked outside the window and made scratching noises on the shingled roof. With a leisurely grace, the moon's cold white orb sank behind rising black-gauze clouds, then slipped into view again, its solemn face unchanged.

When they were children, Annie and Alice Marie watched the moon from this same window; Annie made up stories about its sad countenance while Alice Marie imagined herself dancing with a handsome prince in its lovely, mystical moon glow. How could it be the same friendly moon she remembered when the world had changed so drastically?

She shivered and drew her robe tighter around her. Her hands moved instinctively to her abdomen, her palms pressing the sloping roundness. Yes, she wasn't mistaken. Her body was changing, her waist thickening. Any day now others would notice.

She felt a darkness of spirit descending as palpable as the deepening shadows outside her window. It wasn't just the baby, or her grief over Cary, or the prospect of facing the future alone. It was something more, something elusive and intangible.

Perhaps Helmut Schwarz was to blame—he and his depressing dinner table conversation. Why talk about horrors that were past, that one could do nothing to change? Better to forget and go on and try to enjoy life than to wallow in one's miseries. That's what she was trying to do. Blot out the past. Forget that Cary Rose ever existed.

But how could she forget when his child was growing inside her? And even if she could forget, there was a emptiness that went beyond Cary. Living again in the rosebud room stirred something deep—a yearning, a memory, some primitive, wordless need that left her feeling uncertain and vulnerable—a condition she abhorred, she who thrived on being utterly carefree and independent.

Tonight the desolation was more oppressive than ever. Helm's stark accounts had brought the truth home in a way she'd never imagined. How could one laugh and love and be happy in a world where evil was so malignant, so pervasive? How could God let it happen?

The questions nagged her. God, if He existed, had always seemed incidental, a monumental spoilsport. God was behind every galling rule and restriction Mama had ever imposed. And He, surely, was behind the constant guilt that plagued Alice Marie for not measuring up to all that her family expected.

There was a bitter irony here. Why would God frown at Alice Marie's harmless peccadilloes and look the other way while Hitler nearly annihilated an entire race? And not just any race. The Jews, His chosen people. How could Helmut Schwarz still serve a God who had allowed his family to be murdered?

Alice Marie moved her hand over her expanding middle. *A Jewish baby is growing here.* The thought startled her. Hitler's vast bloodbath suddenly seemed disturbingly personal. *He would have hated my child, killed my baby for simply being Jewish.* She shuddered. How would she sleep tonight haunted by such unspeakable ghosts?

She climbed into bed and pulled the comforter up around her shoulders. "Oh, God," she whispered aloud, a despairing prayer without words. "Oh, God," she said again, but no other words came, so she turned her face to the wall and finally ebbed into a restless slumber.

12

ell, Alice Marie, if you aren't a sight for sore eyes!"
Dirk Wyman stood in the doorway in a tan corduroy jacket
and slacks, a leather folio under one arm. "I was hoping
you'd be the one to answer the door."

Alice Marie stared back in surprise. "Did we have a date?"

He sauntered in as if she had invited him. "No, no date, although that's
not a bad idea. Actually, I'm just delivering some contracts and financial
reports to Knowl." He looked at her and winked. "But about that date.
It's a perfect Saturday afternoon, my work is done, and I've got the money,
Honey, if you've got the time."

She glanced down at her knit, lime-green dress with its smocked top
and flowing skirt. Surely he couldn't tell she was expecting, but she felt
self-conscious anyway. She led him into the living room and gestured
toward a chair. "Wait here, Dirk. I'll get Knowl."

He reached for her hand. "You mean, I can't sell you on that date
when I've finished my business with Knowl?"

Her cheeks flushed. "It's not that, Dirk. I'd love to see you sometime.
But I have another commitment today."

He sat down and laid his folio on the coffee table. "Some lucky stiff
beat me to it, huh? That's what I get for dallying."

She smiled. "It's not a date. I'm just helping a friend look for an apartment."

He sat forward, his pale brows rising with interest. "You don't mean Helmut Schwarz, do you?"

"Yes, how did you know?"

"We just finished preparing the contract for his book. I have it here with me, in fact." He patted the folio. "Knowl mentioned that Schwarz would be moving to Willowbrook. Looks like he's not wasting any time."

"He's eager to get settled so he can bring his father out from New York."

Dirk's clear blue eyes searched hers. "I understand he's been staying here with your family."

"Yes. For the past week."

"A strange fellow, isn't he?"

"Strange?"

"Headstrong. Impassioned. An ardent crusader, if I ever saw one."

"I would think those traits will make his book a success."

Dirk nodded. "We're counting on that. If we can just capture his zeal in the pages of his book."

"You sound like you have some doubts."

Dirk fingered the leather strap on his folio. "Why would you think that?"

"You had misgivings about Helm when we talked before."

"Helm, is it? Sounds like you two are hitting it off."

"He's nice enough."

"Yes, I did have misgivings about his book, but Knowl feels it's worth the risk. And with Annie to help with the rewrite—"

"Then it's decided? Annie will be working with Helm?"

"That's what I suggested. Let's hope she can tone him down a bit."

Alice Marie ran her hand over the folds of her skirt. "Let me get Knowl for you." She paused and added in an engaging voice, "And next time, call first, and maybe I'll be free."

He winked. "I'll hold you to that."

She started down the hallway and met Helm striding toward her, shrugging into his trench coat. "I'm ready when you are, Alice Marie."

She nodded toward the living room. "Dirk Wyman is here to see Knowl. He has your contract. You'll want to see him before we go."

Helm brightened. "Indeed I will."

"Go greet him. I'll get Knowl."

"He's in the parlor," said Helm, "playing with Maggie."

Alice Marie entertained Maggie for nearly an hour while the three men conversed in the living room. Finally they emerged, shaking hands and smiling. Little Maggie ran into Knowl's arms and he swung her up on his shoulders. Helm strode directly over to Alice Marie and squeezed her hand. "It's official. I'm under contract with Herrick House. I have until the first of the year to rewrite my book."

"Is that enough time?"

"With Annie's help it should be."

"Of course," she said thickly. "Where would you be without Annie?"

His dark eyes narrowed questioningly. "Will you still go apartment hunting with me? Or is it too late?"

She cast a glance at Dirk. "No, we still have time. I looked through the newspaper and wrote down several addresses."

"Did Knowl say we could use his car?"

She smiled. "As long as I bring it back without a scratch."

Helm turned to Knowl with a grin. "Don't worry, old boy, we'll have your automobile back in one piece, or you can take it out of that generous advance you plan to give me."

As Alice Marie drove to a duplex on the south side of town, she could feel Helm's eyes on her. "You handle the automobile very well," he said, shifting his long legs away from the dashboard. "I don't see many women driving cars."

"I learned in Chicago, where every driver thinks he owns the road."

"They simplify it in New York," he mused. "They take taxicabs everywhere. Or the subway. And if they want to leave town, they take the train."

"Chicago has the 'El,' the elevated railways," she told him.

Helm nodded. "I was there once and got lost in the downtown 'Loop'."

"That's right. You'll be going back. You said you have business there."

"Yes, urgent business." He turned his head to the window and offered no further explanation. After several minutes, he broke his silence with, "Annie tells me you're a singer. She says you were on television in Chicago."

She nodded. "I had my own show. It was a lot of work, but I enjoyed it. What can I say? I'm a ham at heart."

He looked curiously at her. "A ham?"

She laughed. "I like performing. I love the applause."

"Then why did you give it up?"

She paused, carefully choosing her words. "My husband died a few months ago."

"I'm sorry. I didn't know."

"I came home to pick up the pieces of my life."

"I understand. Grieving is a most arduous labor."

She looked at him with a sudden sense of kinship and sympathy. "Yes, you would understand. You've had many more losses to grieve than I have."

"But grief does not deal in numbers. The pain is the same for one or many."

"You express that very well." She pulled up beside a white, clapboard house with a sagging porch and broken shutters. "Here we are—our first address."

"It looks—what would you say?"

"Weather-beaten? Run down? Dilapidated?"

"All of those."

"We can drive on to the next one if you like."

"No. We're here. Let's go in."

A big-boned woman in a flower-print dress showed them the small, cheerless apartment. "It ain't much, I admit," she told them, "but you get what you pays for, and you won't find no better bargain in town."

Alice Marie surveyed the tiny kitchen with its grimy stove, narrow cupboards, and chipped porcelain sink. "Does it come with an icebox?" she asked, wiping a finger over the greasy countertop.

"Icebox is extra," said the woman, crossing her arms in a sullen, impatient gesture. A shiny black cockroach skittered across the floor. With a practiced pounce she squashed it with her scuffed saddle shoe.

"Thank you. We'll get back to you," said Alice Marie as Helm nudged her toward the door.

"Don't wait too long," warned the woman, following them onto the creaking porch. "Someone else will snap this place up in a jiffy."

They walked quickly back to the car and climbed in, hiding their amusement behind tight-lipped smiles. But as Alice Marie pressed her foot on the gas and swerved away from the curb, Helm broke into laughter. It was contagious. Soon they were both laughing so hard she had to pull off to the side of the road until she could compose herself.

"I am not so desperate yet," he said, wiping the moisture from his eyes.

Her eyes were tearing too. "I wonder if the bugs are extra like the icebox."

"Oh, I wouldn't wish to crowd out the little beetles."

More laughter.

"Maybe the next apartment will be better." She pulled back onto the road and headed north. Minutes later she pulled into the driveway of a two-story brownstone with dormer windows and a wraparound porch.

"I like this one," said Helm. "It has character and grace."

"I like it too," she said as they walked up the steps to the door. An elderly woman with silver hair and wire-rimmed spectacles opened the door and smiled warmly as she pulled her shawl around bony arms.

"We've come to see the apartment," Alice Marie told her.

"Oh, yes. It's upstairs. Let me get the key." The woman slipped inside and was back moments later. "Please come with me." They followed her around to a sprawling back yard surrounded by a high, whitewashed pine fence. "The apartment has an outside entrance," she explained, holding the key between gnarled fingers. "More privacy that way. My husband built the stairs himself years ago when we converted the house into two apartments. After the children left home, you know. The house was just too much to keep up by ourselves."

She handed Helm the key and patted his arm in what seemed a motherly gesture. "Now, Dearie, you take your wife up and show her around and if you like the place, you can tell me when you bring back the key."

Alice Marie started to say, "Oh, I'm not his—" But she caught the twinkle in Helm's eyes and decided to let the old woman think what she pleased.

The woman shuffled a few steps, then turned back, her faded eyes crinkling merrily at the corners. "By the way, you'll see there's an extra bedroom in case you'll be needing a nursery."

Alice Marie's hands went involuntarily to her middle. Had the old woman guessed? No. It was logical that a young married couple might need a nursery. With his hand at her elbow, Helm urged her toward the stairs. He suspected nothing, but still her fingers trembled as she reached for the railing.

Helm unlocked the door, reached inside for a light switch, and stepped aside so she could enter. He followed her inside and turned on a Tiffany lamp that bathed the room in a rosy glow. The quaint wallpapered room was filled with homey furniture and antiques—a flowered, overstuffed couch, maple end tables, a small writing desk, a wicker rocking chair, and a nubby upholstered armchair with doilies pinned on each arm. A colorful hooked rug accented the shiny hardwood floor.

"Yes! This is right for us," Helm said expansively.

When she looked quizzically at him, he said, "I mean, it's right for my father and me."

"It's modest but it looks immaculate," she noted, running her fingertips across the desk.

They walked on to the kitchen. It, too, was neat and clean and even had an icebox. "I like this house. It smells clean," said Helm, examining a cupboard.

"But you haven't even seen the bedrooms and bath."

"Come," he said. "Let's take a look." She followed him into one bedroom, then the other, and finally the bathroom. Each room was spotless and cozy. Eiderdown quilts adorned the beds, hand-painted ceramic water pitchers graced the bureaus, and heavy lace curtains covered the windows.

"I could move in today," said Helm, his excitement growing. "It has everything I need. And my father will be comfortable here. It will remind him of Germany." In his exuberance he turned to Alice Marie and clasped her arms as if to embrace her, then released her just as abruptly. He turned to the window above the writing desk and looked out. "This is where I will write," he told her, his voice still buoyant but with an edge of disquiet.

"A perfect spot," she said, her own heart pounding with a strange excitement.

"So it's settled," he said, crossing the room to the door. "This will be my home. Mine and my father's."

"What about the stairs?" she asked. "Will they be too hard for your father to climb?"

He gave her a grim half-smile. "Climbing stairs will be a small task compared with what my father has endured."

On Friday, October 26, Annie and Alice Marie drove Helm to the Willowbrook depot where he boarded the train for New York. He had promised them he would return a week later with his father and whatever he could transport of their earthly possessions. On the way home from the station Annie was silent, remote. Alice Marie had no desire to converse either;

she never knew what to say to her younger sister. It seemed whatever she said always came out wrong, sounding too arrogant or overbearing.

When they were less than a mile from home, Annie cleared her throat and said coolly, "Alice Marie, I hope you're not getting any ideas about Helm."

Alice Marie purposely matched Annie's coolness. "Ideas? What ideas, Annie?"

"You know what I mean. I've seen the way you look at him and the way he looks at you."

Alice Marie could hear the cattiness steal into her voice. "Really? I hadn't noticed."

"Of course you've noticed. You have your sights on him. It's obvious what you're doing."

Alice Marie rested her hands on her abdomen. "You're going to have to spell it out for me, Annie. Just what is it you think I'm doing?"

Annie gave her a scrutinizing glance. "You're playing your little games again, Alice Marie. I don't know whether you're looking for a mild flirtation to pass the time or a father for your baby. Whichever it is, Helm's not the man."

Alice Marie moved her fingertips lightly over her dress. Perhaps she was touching the very spot where her baby swam in his secret sea. She thought fleetingly of telling Annie how she really felt—her misgivings about facing the future alone and raising a child without a father, her yearning to find someone who would make her feel whole and happy again the way Cary had, the bone-chilling fear that it was already too late to find the kind of happiness other women took for granted. But no matter how she played the words in her mind, they sounded maudlin and false, so she resorted to her usual cheeky bravado. "How do you know Helm's not the man for me, Annie? He's single and available and certainly very handsome. And if I remember right, you're already taken. So why not me?"

Annie jerked the steering wheel too sharply, nearly overshooting the curb as she turned onto Honeysuckle Lane. With a little gasp she steadied the vehicle and drove down the cobbled street to the corner and turned into the winding drive. She parked beside the sprawling, wraparound porch, removed the key from the ignition, and looked solemnly at Alice Marie. "I know you won't listen to me, but I'm going to say this anyway. Helm is a man of vision, a man with a mission. God's hand is on him. Surely even you can see that!"

Alice Marie swung her blonde pageboy with an air of disregard. "I'm well aware of Helm's religious calling, but I don't think God will begrudge me a little of his time."

Annie's face flushed with indignation. "Do you even care about Helm's ministry? Do you have the slightest concern about what God wants for him, or for you, or for any of us?"

"That's your department, Annie."

Annie's gray-green eyes blazed. "You make light of everything, don't you, Alice Marie? Life is one big joke. You go along taking whatever you please, no matter who you hurt. You've spoiled every relationship you've ever had. I won't let you do that to Helm."

"It's not your decision to make, Annie. It's between Helm and me."

"If he knew you the way I do—"

"Say it, Annie. Say what's really on your mind. I tried to steal your husband and break up your marriage. I did it and I can't change it, but that was years ago, and whether you believe it or not, I'm not the same person I was then."

Annie's eyes darkened. "Aren't you? I guess time will tell."

Alice Marie felt a sudden weariness go through her. What she wouldn't give for a few hours of sleep. "I mean it, Annie. I'm not the same. Why won't you believe me?"

"Maybe because I'm not the same either," said Annie, her eyes glazing over. "I'll never be that naive young girl again."

Neither said another word as they got out of the car and went into the house. Mama called from the kitchen, "Alice Marie, that nice young man who works for Knowl phoned you. Dirk Wyman. I think he wants to take you to dinner."

"Thanks, Mama. Let me know if he calls back. I'll be in my room." She climbed the stairs with less energy than she usually felt. Surely it was the pregnancy. With the way she was blossoming she couldn't keep the baby a secret much longer. *Please, dear God, just a little more time!* She caught herself and chuckled. Was she actually praying? Did she really believe Someone was listening—and cared? It was a pleasant notion, but no, prayer was Annie's domain.

Alice Marie stretched out on her bed and closed her eyes. She listened to her own heartbeat, the rhythm of her breathing. She thought of her baby in his secret world, tumbling and swimming and growing—a tiny invisible being alone in the dark of his own private universe.

Alice Marie was also alone in the dark, in a world of her own making—or maybe not of her making; but over the years she had somehow insulated herself from those around her, those who were supposedly closest to her, those tied to her by birth and blood and time and history. They lived in the same house and ate at the same table and breathed the same air, and yet they were strangers—Annie, Knowl, even Mama. Mama loved her blindly, never having read her heart. *If you really knew me, Mama, maybe you'd judge me the same way Annie does.*

Was Annie right? Was she scheming to win Helm over? Was she playing him against Dirk in the hopes of winning one of them, either one, just so she and her baby wouldn't have to face life alone?

The idea repulsed her. She had worked hard over the years to become an independent, take-charge woman. Single-handedly she had carved out a successful career for herself and even earned a modicum of fame. She could do it again if she had to.

But the truth was she had thrown herself into her career to ease the pain of losing Cary when he left her years ago for his girl singer. And for as long as she could remember she had kept everyone at arm's length, so that what people saw was the brassy blonde who could belt out a song and make clever small talk with the best of them.

But that wasn't the person she wanted her baby to know. Then who? What kind of person lay beyond the facade? Someone a baby could love? Someone a man could love? Someone God could love?

She honestly didn't know.

Dirk phoned shortly after Alice Marie arrived home from the train depot. She was weary and dispirited, but she said yes anyway to his dinner invitation. She would show Annie that she wasn't trying to hook her Mr. Schwarz. Besides, Dirk was much more Alice Marie's type; they both loved music, good food, and a good time.

Dirk drove her to a quaint restaurant outside of town called the Old Country Inn that specialized in German cuisine. It possessed the atmosphere of a timeworn German cottage with dark wood beams, old world decor, and shelves of colorful beer steins. A blonde woman in a frilly blouse and long skirt showed them to a long table with a walnut veneer and flickering oil lamps at each end.

"Their weinerschnitzel is delicious," said Dirk as they opened their menus. "The veal is lightly breaded and bathed in the kind of homemade German gravy my mother used to make."

"I'm not very hungry," Alice Marie admitted. Why had she even agreed to come to dinner with Dirk when she was already missing Helm and still smarting over her confrontation with Annie this afternoon?

"The rouladen is good too," Dirk went on in his smoothly lyrical voice. "They stuff and roll thin, succulent slices of beef and drench it in that wonderful gravy."

Alice Marie shook her head. She felt a flutter in her tummy. Was it a stomach upset, or was it the baby? She held her breath for a moment to see if it would come again, but the feeling was gone. *It must have been the baby! He's really there, moving around inside me!*

"Did you hear me, Alice Marie?" Dirk persisted. "If you like pork, you must try the bratwurst."

She smiled distractedly. "I'm not feeling very adventuresome tonight, Dirk. I'll just have something simple—the goulash is fine."

"You seem preoccupied tonight," he told her later as they sampled their entrees. "You look a little pale too. Are you feeling okay?"

"Yes, swell. It's just been a long day."

"We could make it an even longer night, Allie," he ventured with a seductive smile. "You know I find you very attractive."

"I'm sorry, Dirk. It's too soon. Let's just be friends for now."

"For now," he echoed softly. They were silent for a few moments. His voice slightly aloof, he said, "My father told me to give you his regards. He's still planning on you singing at his benefit next spring. You are still planning to sing, aren't you?"

"Yes, of course. I'm looking forward to it. I miss performing."

"And the world misses you too, I'm sure." He ran his finger over a water ring on the table. "Frankly, I'm a little surprised you haven't high-tailed it back to Chicago by now."

She studied him curiously. "Really? Why?"

"When we met you said you would be staying in Willowbrook for only a few weeks. Now, mind you, I'm delighted you're staying longer. I was wracking my brain for ways to keep you here in town."

"You were?"

"Sure. I was serious about us getting better acquainted; I wasn't just making a pass. We're kindred souls—anyone who loves big band jazz the way you do!"

She managed a mirthful chuckle. "You do know me."

He reached across the table for her hand. She didn't pull away. "And I'm hoping to know you a little better every day."

"I'm an old-fashioned girl at heart," she confessed in a softly alluring voice. "My favorite music is a combination of 1936 Benny Goodman and 1942 Stan Kenton."

"I'm with you. One of these days I'm taking you out dancing in the moonlight till dawn. What do you say?"

"I think I'd rather try a concert or a play. Something less exhausting."

"Suit yourself. The play's the thing!" He lifted her hand to his lips. "I got a feeling you're going to be good for me, Allie. You know, I just may come up with some way to keep you here for good. The two of us together."

She smiled. "I'll consider myself forewarned."

Alice Marie saw Dirk three times during the following week. On Tuesday night he took her to a symphony concert at Willowbrook Community College; on Thursday, to a Dixieland revival at a popular club in Fort Wayne; and on Friday he came over for one of Mama's acclaimed roast beef dinners.

After dinner the two of them settled in the parlor to listen to several records she had made years before while traveling with the bands. One of the 78s, "Favorite Hits of Cary Rose and the Starlighters"—a record she had forgotten she had—began to play and brought back sudden, painful memories of Cary. As the sound of his smooth and mellow voice crooning, "I'll Never Smile Again," filled the room, she felt strangely as if he were there beside her. He wasn't, of course, but a tiny flutter deep inside reminded her that Cary's baby was there and growing stronger every day.

Dirk, sitting forward in the wing chair across from her perusing several albums, gave her a searching look and said, "A penny for your thoughts, Allie."

She smiled, her face growing warm, and murmured, "You say that quite often. Aren't you afraid of going broke?"

"It's worth more than a penny if you let me in on your thoughts. Maybe I should up the ante to a nickel."

"Goodness! The last of the big-time spenders."

"But you haven't given me my penny's worth yet. What has you so deep in thought?"

She held up the album jacket. "Cary's band. I hadn't meant to put his record on the turntable."

"My fault," said Dirk. "I put it on. I'm sorry. I didn't make the connection."

She blinked rapidly and kept a smile in place. "It's all right, Dirk. Sometimes I think I'm doing so well at forgetting, and other times it all comes back in a rush and I'm back where I started. Is it just me, or—?"

"They say that's how it goes," said Dirk gently. "I was too young to remember when my mother died, but I know it took my father a long time to recover."

Alice Marie nodded. "Yes, it does take a long time. And it's so easy to slip back into the past."

Dirk came over and sat beside her on the love seat, his arm loosely circling her shoulder. "That's just it, Allie. You don't need to remain in the past. You have your whole life ahead, a wonderful future. Concentrate on that."

"I try, I really do, but—"

"There's nothing to tie you to the past," Dirk continued fervently. "Put it behind you. Let it rest. You're a beautiful, vibrant woman. Get on with living."

Alice Marie looked away, biting her lower lip. Dirk would never understand. She could never be completely free of the past, not with Cary's baby always a reminder of what was.

He turned her face around to his, his thumb and forefinger lifting her chin. "I intend to do all I can to help you forget, if you'll give me a chance."

Before she could reply, her mother opened the parlor door a crack and peeked inside. "Would you children like some hot chocolate to warm you on this cold November night?"

"No thanks, Mrs. Reed," said Dirk, "but I could sure use a cup of coffee if you have any left."

Mama smiled. "I don't mind brewing a fresh pot, if you don't mind waiting a few minutes."

"It'll be worth the wait, Mrs. Reed."

"I'd like a cup too, Mama," said Alice Marie.

Her mother's brow furrowed slightly. "Is that a good idea, Honey? Coffee's not good for the baby."

A dreadful silence settled over the room as the significance of Mama's words became clear. Mama clasped her hand over her mouth, Alice Marie flinched, and Dirk withdrew his arm from Alice Marie's shoulder. The color rising in his face, he stared at her as if she had sprouted two heads.

"I mean—oh, I didn't mean—," Mama stuttered. She looked helplessly at Alice Marie, lifted her hands in a gesture of dismay, and said, "Excuse me. I'll go get the coffee."

Dirk stood up and looked down at Alice Marie, his blue eyes the most intense she'd ever seen them. "What is she talking about, Alice Marie? Did I hear her right?"

Alice Marie stood up and walked around behind the love seat, her polished nails gripping the tufted back, as if for support. "Yes, you heard her right, Dirk," she said defensively. "It's true. I'm expecting a baby."

His anger flared. "No wonder you turned me down for tonight."

"I know I should have told you sooner, but I didn't want anyone to know until—until—"

"Until it became too apparent to hide the truth?"

"All right. Yes! It was nobody else's business but mine."

Dirk raked his fingers through his fine blond hair. "All right, now that I know, you might as well tell me the rest. Whose baby is it?"

She blanched as if he had struck her. "What do you mean, whose baby is it?"

"It's a simple question, Allie. A simple answer will do."

"It's Cary's baby. Is that simple enough?"

Dirk heaved a sigh and sat back down in the wing chair. "How long have you known?"

"A couple of months." She sat back down in the love seat. "I thought you might have guessed."

"No. Never. Oh, I noticed you had filled out a little. In a nice way, of course. I just figured it was your mother's home cooking." He was silent a moment, his jaw taut, before asking, "Did your husband know?"

Alice Marie's eyes filled. "No. Neither did I. Not until I came home and was ill. You remember. I was sick with what we thought was polio. When Doc Elrick ran some tests, he made the diagnosis. I couldn't believe it. A baby. That's probably why I fainted that day at the luncheon."

Dirk picked up Cary Rose's album and studied it absently, then gazed back at Alice Marie. "Have you considered how you'll manage with a baby?"

She shrugged. "Women do it all the time."

"Not single career women. Not women with a talent and a future like you have."

"Well, then, I guess I'll have to prove that it can be done."

"Cary Rose was Jewish, wasn't he?"

"Yes."

"Then your baby is Jewish."

"So what? Do you have something against Jewish babies?"

"Of course not! I just wondered if you've thought about some of the more practical matters you'll be facing."

"You're talking in riddles, Dirk," said Alice Marie. "Say what you mean."

"All right. Will you raise the child as a Jew or a Christian?"

Alice Marie pressed her palms over the slight swell of her abdomen. "For Pete's sake, the baby isn't even born yet and you're worrying about his religious training?"

The redness in Dirk's face deepened. "It's not that—it's just—there are organizations that will place babies in appropriate homes. Jewish babies in Jewish homes, Christian babies in Christian homes. Have you considered—?"

"What? Giving my baby away?" She stood up, clenching her fingers, her voice shrill. "He's mine, Dirk! My flesh and blood. And Cary's! This baby is all I have left of Cary."

Dirk stood up and placed his hands firmly on her shoulders. "I wasn't suggesting that you give up your child. I just wondered if you've considered all the options. A child growing up in a home with only one parent is at a severe disadvantage, socially, economically, emotionally."

She brushed tears from her eyes. "I know the odds are against us, but I've played against the odds before."

Dirk released her and took several steps backward. "All right, Allie, I won't say another word. But if there's anything I can do—"

"There's nothing."

Dirk opened the parlor door and hesitated again. Mama was just coming in the door with the sterling coffee service. The fragrant aroma filled the room. "Coffee's ready," she announced, a bit too politely.

"I don't think Dirk has time for coffee, Mama."

"No time? But I—"

"It smells wonderful, Mrs. Reed," he said, patting her arm, "but it's getting late and your daughter needs her rest." He looked back at Alice Marie. "I'll call you soon, and we'll—we'll plan something—dinner or a concert—okay?"

Alice Marie crossed her arms protectively and rocked slightly on her heels. "Sure, Dirk. Call when—whenever you're free."

"Good night, ladies," he said with an uneven smile, making a little salute with two fingers. "Don't bother. I'll see myself out."

When he had gone, Alice Marie sank back down on the love seat and leaned forward, her arms resting on her knees, her head lowered. Mama came and sat beside her and pulled her into her arms. "I'm sorry, Sweetheart, I didn't mean to tell. It just came out. Forgive me, Honey?"

Alice Marie released her tears in deep sobs. "Oh, Mama, it was awful! He couldn't get out of here fast enough."

"Then he's a fool, Daughter. Forget him!"

"No, Mama! Everybody's going to feel that way. I know it. They'll treat me like a pariah. I can't live that way, Mama! What am I going to do?"

Her mother pressed her cheek against Alice Marie's silken curls. "You'll go on and be strong and hold your head up proud, because you haven't done anything wrong except love your husband and love his child. If people don't like it—if tongues wag—let them. You do what you know is right."

Alice Marie remained in her mother's arms for a long time, both of them silent, only their slow, steady breathing audible. In the stillness Alice Marie felt the flutter once again, and this time there was no mistake. It was her baby doing playful somersaults in his tiny, secret universe, as if to say, *I'm here and I'm well and, no matter what anybody says, I'm going to make my mark in the world!*

14

On Saturday, November 3, Annie and Alice Marie made another trip to the Willowbrook depot, this time to meet Helmut Schwarz and his father coming in on the afternoon train. Tension still bristled between the sisters, although earlier Annie had broken the uneasy silence to inquire why Dirk Wyman had left so abruptly last evening. Alice Marie made no reply, certain that Annie already knew the reason. Mama would have told her, would have lamented her role in revealing Alice Marie's pregnancy to her unsuspecting suitor. So why bring up the subject, except to heap coals on the fire? Or, by chance, was Annie reaching out, seeking a way to offer sympathy and consolation?

Alice Marie would never know, for she had no intention of broaching the subject again. The wound was too tender and the humiliation too great. More painful even than rejection was the risk of appearing vulnerable and needy before the likes of her sainted sister.

Their conversation remained sparse as they stood waiting on the rough-hewn platform with the smell of soot and diesel fumes in their nostrils. The sky was metallic gray and the air chill with the promise of winter's first snow. Alice Marie wore a long wool coat over a loose-fitting corduroy jumper, so surely Helm wouldn't guess that she was pregnant. But still the worry nagged her: If he knew the truth, would he turn against her as quickly as Dirk had?

She watched with a rising sense of panic as the monstrous passenger train roared at last into the station, bellowing like some furious behemoth, its shriek deafening. The platform shook under her feet; she could feel the vibration in her teeth as the rumble and noise encompassed her.

Why did it matter what Helm thought? Or what Dirk thought? Or any man? In the past she had put on a good show of needing no one, of blazing a path to her own success. What was wrong with her now that she couldn't stand alone and face the future in her own strength, free of entanglements? What compelled her to keep looking for someone to fill the empty place inside her? Was it the loneliness without Cary, waking in the mornings with no one beside her in the bed?

The silver-gray coach cars were relinquishing a steady stream of passengers now; there were shouts and laughter as families greeted one another, embraced, and moved into the station in little clusters. Finally Alice Marie spotted a familiar, darkly handsome figure descending the iron steps, his hand steadying the arm of an old man in a tan derby. The two were lost in the crowd for a moment; then father and son emerged and shambled in a swaying gait over the uneven platform.

"There they are!" cried Annie, waving. Even as Annie ran to meet Helm, Alice Marie lagged behind, fighting a flurry of emotions—fear, anticipation, and a surprising swell of affection for Annie's swarthy Jewish evangelist.

Before Alice Marie could collect her thoughts, Helm was at her side and the four were greeting one another, Helm offering each sister a brief embrace, then expansively introducing the quiet, ruddy-faced man beside him.

Helm's father, Gerhart Schwarz—a short, heavy, puckish gentleman— removed his hat and made a little bow. Alice Marie liked him immediately. A stocky, barrel-chested man with a thick neck and round head, he had full jowls and a receding hairline with a healthy mop of gray hair hugging his head like a brush. He reached out and shook Alice Marie's hand with a firm grip, his crinkly brown eyes, so much like Helm's, glinting with a hint of merriment. "How do you do, *Fraulein*?"

"Very well, thank you, Mr. Schwarz," said Alice Marie. "I hope you had a good trip."

He put his hat back on his head, made a so-so gesture with his hand, and said, "Nicht schlecht." Laugh lines, age lines, and fleshy furrows of deep-set pain corrugated his leathery face like an ancient treasure map.

Minutes later, as Helm collected their luggage and urged his father toward the waiting automobile, the old man paused, looking a bit flustered and confused. "Wir gehen nach Hause, nicht wahr?" he asked Helm.

"Yes, Papa. We're going home. Our new home. Our friends are driving us."

"Where are we going?" he asked in English now, with a thick German accent. "This is not New York City."

"No, Papa. It's Willowbrook."

He held his ground. "Who are these ladies? Helmut, do we know these young ladies?"

"Yes, Papa. They are our friends."

Gerhart Schwarz began to move again with a cautious, lumbering gait. Alice Marie fell into step beside him and slipped her gloved hand around his arm. "We're going for a lovely ride, Mr. Schwarz."

A rosy glow touched his lined cheeks. "Danke schon."

"Did you have lunch on the train?" she asked as they strolled toward the car.

"Oy vey!" he said, shaking his head. "I eat, but they serve nothing kosher."

Annie caught up with them. "Then you must be hungry, Mr. Schwarz."

He answered again with a mixture of German, Yiddish, and English. "Ja, I eat at Mittag. Oy! Is no gut, but I do not kvetch. Only a schlep complains, nicht wahr—is it not true?"

Alice Marie and Annie exchanged brief smiles, as if to say, Helm's father is going to be an interesting man to have around!

"Helm, if you're not too tired, Mama would like you and your father to come home with us for dinner," Annie told him as he wedged several battered suitcases into the trunk of the automobile.

Helm straightened his back and smoothed out his trench coat. "Annie, my father is very weary. Another time perhaps?"

She nodded. "That's fine, Helm. Mama thought you might be too tired, so she had a backup plan."

"Yes," said Alice Marie, flashing her warmest smile. "Annie and I will help you settle your father into your apartment while Knowl—"

"Knowl will bring over Mama's special meat loaf and scalloped potatoes and fresh lemon meringue pie," Annie supplied.

Helm laughed. "What do you think, Papa? Shall we let the ladies help us get settled and bring us dinner?"

Gerhart's half-moon eyes crinkled with mirth. "Mein sohn, we would be schlemiels to refuse such offer."

"We're on our way!" said Annie after everyone had settled into the vehicle—Alice Marie and Helm cozily in back and Gerhart Schwarz in front with Annie. It was Alice Marie's doing, of course. It might be her only chance to spend a few moments close to Helm.

"You're looking very well, Alice Marie," he told her, his face mere inches from hers. "The wind puts roses in your cheeks."

"I've looked forward to seeing you again," she murmured demurely. "We've missed you."

"I am here to stay—except for my trip to Chicago."

"When will you be going?"

"Next week, I hope. But there is a problem. I'll need someone to look out for my father."

"I'd be glad to," she said quickly. "I'll take him his meals and check in on him every day."

"That would be asking too much," said Helm softly.

"No, I insist. Your father's a delightful man."

"Then I must find a way to repay you," he said, taking her gloved hand in his.

Alice Marie felt the spark from his touch race all along her spine. "I'll think of something," she murmured, allowing her shoulder to nestle against his.

After a minute Annie said, "Don't worry, we'll make it an early evening, Helm. I know you're speaking in the morning service at church tomorrow."

"Yes. Reverend Marshall asked me to take his place in the pulpit so he and his wife can have a little vacation."

Alice Marie looked at Helm with concern. "I hope you won't be too tired after your long trip."

He chuckled. "I am never too weary to speak my heart to God's people." He was still holding her hand. "You will be there, won't you?"

She hesitated.

"I'm still waiting to hear you sing," he said, his words almost a whisper.

She lowered her gaze. Her face felt warm—a pleasant, excited warmth. "I know. Reverend Marshall has asked me to sing many times, but—"

"Sing tomorrow. Please. For me."

She had no intention of saying yes, but it was the only word that passed her lips. At the moment she couldn't imagine any other word for this man who stirred such volatile and exhilarating emotions in her.

On Sunday morning as Alice Marie stood at the podium waiting for her piano introduction, she wondered why in the world she had agreed to sing today. But, of course, she knew why. Helm's sweet talk had caught her in a moment of weakness. It wasn't that she was afraid to sing; she sang on television without a qualm, knowing that thousands of viewers were watching.

But whenever she sang in church she felt strangely exposed, as if the congregation could somehow read her heart and see that she was an impostor; she didn't even know the God about whom she sang. And now what if Helm realized it too when he heard her sing?

God, help me! she whispered silently as she gazed out at the worshipers in their Sunday finery—women in their pastel dresses and flower-trimmed hats and men in their dark suits and bow ties. The church was nearly full today. Annie, Knowl, and Mama were sitting in the third pew, Mama pleased no doubt to have her in church, whatever the reason. She smoothed the folds of her white flowing choir robe, relieved that at least no one would notice her pending motherhood.

The pianist struck the first chords of "Amazing Grace" and at the right moment Alice Marie began to sing. Her voice felt strong and sure, and with each stanza her emotions rose until the music itself seemed somehow transcendent. God Himself was as near as He had ever been to her, surely within reach. His presence was tangible in the vaulted sanctuary, etched in the upturned faces of the congregation.

When she had finished the last stanza, the room was suffused with an awe-filled silence that Alice Marie knew had nothing to do with her. She had experienced this before—God using her voice to draw others to Himself—a God with whom she had only a nodding acquaintance. How it must have amused the Almighty to minister to His flock through an unsaved jazz singer whose prayers—if she prayed—no doubt hovered several feet below the ceiling.

After Alice Marie sat down, taking her place in the third pew beside Mama, Helmut Schwarz walked to the podium and looked out over the assembly. He gripped both sides of the lectern, drew in a deep breath, and looked directly into Alice Marie's eyes. "My friends, before I speak to you," he said, his umber eyes twinkling, "I must tell you I heard the voice of an angel today. Surely no angel in heaven can sing 'Amazing Grace' better than Miss Reed. I believe she pleases God by giving us a little glimpse of our wonderful Messiah."

Helm's words sent a ripple of pleasure through Alice Marie's heart. Surely God was smiling down on her through this man's benevolent eyes.

If only she could be the person he imagined her to be—if she could somehow measure up to the angelic voice people praised so effusively.

Helm paused for a long moment, cleared his throat, and when he spoke again his voice took on a solemn earnestness that caught Alice Marie's attention. "Dear friends, I am a Jew who has found my Messiah. From childhood I was taught that Jesus belonged to the Gentiles. But when I was still young I heard Billy Sunday preach about Jesus being a man of sorrows, despised and rejected by men. He said Jesus loved me enough to bear my griefs and carry my sorrows. And because Jesus loved me He was wounded for my transgressions and bruised for my iniquities. He poured out His soul unto death to save me.

"I found this Jesus amazingly attractive and compelling. I was gripped by a hunger to know this God-Man who cared so much for me. So I went to my father's rabbi and asked him why we Jews should not accept Jesus as our Messiah. He could give me no reason except to say it is *verboten*; we Jews are forbidden to know this Jesus. I tried to obey the rabbi, but the Spirit of God drew me back to the tent meetings. I knew that God was calling me to accept His Son Jesus—*Y'shua*—God's Anointed One."

Helm went on to speak of his work as an itinerant evangelist, traveling across America, preaching on the street corners of Greenwich Village in New York to Hollywood and Vine in California. He told of traveling throughout Europe and of going home to Germany with his family during the war. Alice Marie had heard some of his stories before, but his accounts of Nazi brutality and his father's bitter sojourn in the death camp chilled her afresh. She could see the raw emotion in his eyes as he spoke of his father's suffering.

Again Helm paused to allow his words to take hold. He removed his handkerchief from his suit pocket and blotted his brow and upper lip. He spoke with a ragged edge to his voice. "Since Adam's fall sin has reigned in human hearts, but in this century some great restraint has been removed, some stopper unplugged, to allow sin to run rampant. If we do not stand up and resist this evil presence, it will burst forth in the decades to come and destroy our children and grandchildren."

As murmuring whispers passed over the congregation, Helm raised his voice, his deeply etched features glistening with a heart-pounding intensity. "Some of you think the evils of Hitler were an aberration in our march toward decency and virtue, and that education and prosperity will usher in a bright, utopian future. But, if we do nothing, I predict we will soon live in a world we hardly recognize, where good will be considered evil and evil, good; and where men will say there is no right or wrong, no truth to build on; where our most treasured values and traditions will be trampled on by godless men."

Helm stopped to catch his breath; it was noon already and several parishioners were glancing at their watches, perhaps thinking of the roasts at home in their ovens. Helm raked his fingers through his thick brown hair and changed his stance, as if preparing to deliver his final blow. "My fellow believers," he declared, leaning forward, one arm outstretched, "we must repent of our lethargy. We must take the Jesus of holy Scripture to the world, the Jesus whose Spirit lives in our hearts. It is not enough that we sit in our comfortable pews; we must take Jesus to all who will listen, until revival spreads through our land."

Helm leaned over the pulpit. "If you have never experienced the reality of the living Christ in your heart, I urge you, accept Him today. Know Him. Serve Him. What we do today will determine what our world will be like fifty years from now when we greet the new millennium. Will God find us faithful?"

After the service, while Helm mingled with the worshipers, Alice Marie waited for him in the vestibule, where several people complimented her on her voice and thanked her for singing. Other parishioners were deep in conversation about Helm's message, and Alice Marie couldn't help listening.

"That fellow's quite a preacher," a portly, gray-haired man told the woman beside him. "He gets right up on his soapbox."

"Yes, he does," she agreed, adjusting her wide-brimmed hat.

"Now I'm not calling him a fanatic," said the man as he buttoned his overcoat, "but after coming through two world wars the way we did, I figure things can only get better."

"You're right," said the woman. "That young evangelist fancies himself an Elijah or Jeremiah prophesying doom."

A younger woman in a fur stole and stylish linen dress agreed. "Such zeal is admirable, mind you, but I say let's take a positive attitude. We've come through the hard years; now let's enjoy life a little."

The man nodded, turning up his coat collar. "There are some things in life that just don't change; they're ingrained in our national consciousness forever."

"Exactly," said the older woman as she worked the fingers of her gloves. "The old verities like love and marriage."

"And don't forget patriotism, motherhood, and apple pie," the man added with a chuckle. "Some things folks just don't tamper with."

"Speaking of apple pie," said the younger woman as the threesome ambled toward the door. "I baked the most delicious . . ."

Alice Marie was so engrossed in the parishioners' conversation, she jumped when she heard a deep male voice behind her. She whirled around and there stood Helm, his trench coat over his shoulder and his Bible under his arm. He grinned and said, "I've greeted everyone here today but you—the lovely songbird who inspired me to new heights."

"I inspired *you*?"

"Yes. I meant what I said to the congregation. God has given you a rare gift. You not only look like an angel, but you sing like one too. I wish my father could have heard you."

"Was he too tired to come?"

"Tired, yes. But he will not enter a Christian church. Out of love and duty he puts up with his *shegetz*—his Jewish boy who fails to observe the proper Jewish religious practices. But perhaps you could come home with me sometime and give an encore performance for an audience of one? Or two, for I would be pleased to hear you sing again myself."

"That could be arranged," she said with a playful smile. "How about today?"

"Today is fine. I will even fix you a real kosher meal."

"You don't have to do that. I could fix something."

"Actually, we still have some of your mama's meat loaf and scalloped potatoes left over."

"That will do."

Knowl and Annie drove Helm and Alice Marie to his apartment. All the way Annie kept saying, "Why don't you and your father come home to our house for dinner? We'd love to have you, and I'm sure Mama's got something delicious planned."

To Alice Marie's delight, Helm declined Annie's offer. "Please understand, Annie. My father is a very private man. He wants to get accustomed to his new home before venturing out to visit others."

With reluctance Annie accepted Helm's explanation, but she was quick to remind him that they must start working together on his book now that he was back in town. Alice Marie stifled a victorious little smile. She couldn't help feeling a bit smug that she would be Helm's first—and only—dinner guest, for today, at least.

"Do you really believe the world will get worse if people don't take drastic measures?" Alice Marie asked Helm as they polished off the last of Mama's lemon meringue pie. They were sitting with his father at the small pine table in Helm's tiny kitchen after a leisurely dinner and an impromptu concert for two by Alice Marie. The radiator was making a clanking sound, as if someone were hitting it with a wrench, and the windows were steamed over with the November chill. When she was a child Alice Marie loved to write her name with her finger on such cloudy windows.

"Not people. *Believers*," said Helm.

"That's what I meant," she said, not sure that was so.

"Oy vey!" uttered Gerhart. "The whole world is Weltschmerz, Sturm und Drang."

"Sorrow, storm, and stress," explained Helm.

"The world has some good things too," said Alice Marie, casting a warm sidelong glance at Helm.

"Ja, so ist es gut." He shrugged philosophically. "Is Weltgeist—what you call 'spirit of the times.'" Slowly, as if his joints ached, Gerhart lifted himself out of the chair, his shirt rumpled, his bow tie uneven. "Helmut, I leave you with your beautiful shiksa who has a voice that is wunderbar! Guten Nacht, Fraulein. Auf Wiedersehen!"

As the gray-haired man trundled off to his bedroom, Alice Marie looked questioningly at Helm. "What did he call me?"

"*Shiksa*. It means a girl or woman who is not Jewish."

But I'm carrying a baby who is Jewish, she thought with a start. Every day her unseen child was growing bigger, making his presence known to her with secret kicks and feather-light somersaults. Soon everyone would know of his existence.

It was time to tell Helm the truth.

But how?

15

Alice Marie glanced toward the walnut-framed, lace-curtained window and wished she could press her flushed cheek against the cold, filmy panes. The radiator was belching too much heat, or perhaps it was her nerves that sent a restless warmth over the surface of her skin. She and Helm had left the dinner table and settled in the quaint living room on the overstuffed sofa. The light was fading, the sun a pale, hard ball slipping behind a distant thicket of bare-limbed trees.

As her thoughts drifted, she found herself comparing Helm with Cary Rose. Cary had excited her physically, but Helm touched her heart, her soul; he stirred a place in her no one else had ever reached. Even Cary.

Helm reached over and turned on the Tiffany lamp, its rosy glow softening the shadows. "Where has this day gone?" he murmured.

"Spent in pleasant company," she replied softly, and thought of her baby, the unseen guest. Her hands moved to the slight curve of her abdomen. She was glad she was tall and slim and that first babies didn't show as early as those that came later. She had seen women who were huge at four and a half months, but with the right clothes she was still able to disguise her condition.

"What are you thinking about so seriously?" asked Helm, turning to face her.

She shook her head distractedly. "Nothing. Daydreaming."

"But you looked so solemn."

"Not all daydreams are happy."

He lifted her chin. "You're here with me in my new apartment and looking so sad?"

She smiled. "Not sad exactly. To be honest, I was thinking of something I need to tell you—"

Her words were cut off by a sudden, guttural, blood-chilling scream from the bedroom. Helm jumped up and bolted down the hall in long, urgent strides.

"What is it?" she cried.

"My father!" he called back before disappearing into the bedroom.

Alice Marie stood up and walked to the window and waited, her arms crossed protectively. The frosty condensation on the glass made it too hazy to see much, except the dusky shapes and colors of neighboring houses and trees. She absently rubbed her elbow and wondered if she had overstayed her welcome. Whatever caused the old man's outburst, it was their business, not hers.

Besides, it was nearly evening and she would have to phone Knowl or Annie to come get her, unless she took a taxi home. Yes, a taxi would be best. If she had known she would be staying so long in Willowbrook, she would have gone out and purchased a car of her own. Maybe she still would.

She turned at the sound of footsteps. Helm crossed the room and joined her at the window.

"Is your father ill?" she asked.

"No. It's—nightmares. They come every night."

"I'm sorry, Helm," she said quietly.

"Nightmares of Auschwitz," he went on, his lips tight against his teeth. She looked at him. His eyes were shadowed, stark with loathing, his jaw set like granite. "He tells me his dreams and there is nothing I can do to make them go away."

"I'm sorry," she said again, helplessly.

"Sometimes the camp's stench comes back to him and makes him violently ill. He dreams he is back in the bunker sandwiched in the barracks with dying men. He sees white bony arms reach out to him and haunted black eyes in gaunt skull faces pleading with him to save them. But he can't, because he is one of them."

He leaned one hand on the chipped brown window sill, his voice ragged now. "My father remembers one guard who beat him over and over, and taunted him, and left him for dead. He sees his face in his dreams. That man is still torturing him."

Alice Marie placed her hand over his. "You must keep reminding him it's over," she whispered. "He's safe now."

Helm turned his palm over and squeezed her hand, almost too tightly. "No, it will never be over, not for my people, not as long as those butchers walk free."

"Butchers? You mean the guard—?" Her words fell away.

He led her back over to the couch and they sat down. The radiator still rattled, but Helm's silence was louder. She waited. Finally, he said, "The Nuremberg trials sentenced only a fraction of the guilty. Countless Nazi murderers escaped to start new lives, many with the help of the United States government."

She stared at him. "How could that be?"

"I have proof."

She sat back and drew in a deep sigh. She hadn't expected the conversation to take this turn. "You must be very bitter."

His mouth twisted slightly, not quite a smile, not quite a grimace. "I suppose I am, but I try not to be. I'm a minister of the Gospel, after all. I preach of God's love for a sinful world."

She shook her head. "How can you serve a God who let so many good people die so brutally? How can you explain it?"

He sat forward, his hands on his knees, his head lowered. "I can't. But we are not puppets pulled by strings. God lets us make our own choices. Our choices have consequences, sometimes deadly. When people choose to do evil, we all suffer."

"It's that simple?"

"That simple, that profound. But I admit, I am not so forgiving as God." He stood up and walked back over to the window. It was dark now; the last vestiges of sunlight formed a sliver of light on the horizon.

"What are you saying, Helm?" she asked, her gaze taking in his solemn profile.

His words erupted in a raw, whispered staccato. "I am saying—if the man who tortured my father—if he were standing in this room—I would kill him with my bare hands." He turned back to her. "There! You know something about me I have told no one. You see? I am two persons in one."

"Is that how you see yourself?" she asked.

His gaze drifted back to the window. "Yes. I am two very different people. And they war against each other." His tone softened. "I am a man who loves God deeply, Alice Marie. When I surrender myself to Christ's Spirit, I am transformed by His love. Transformed. It is the only word to describe it. And I am consumed with preaching His Word to the lost."

"Yes. I saw that person in the pulpit this morning."

"But I am also a man who has been shaken and convulsed by what has happened to my people. In my mind, I know God is still a God of love and that we cannot comprehend His ways. I know we must trust Him even now, especially now. And yet, as a man, I am filled at times with rage that blinds me to God—a hatred so overwhelming I marvel that such fierce and opposing emotions can inhabit one man."

She joined him at the window and touched his face with her fingertips. "Helm, don't be ashamed of what you feel."

He fingered the lace curtain, twisting the hem around his index finger. "Ashamed? No, I'm not ashamed. I am disturbed sometimes by the force of my emotions. But every day I kneel at the cross and claim His love. It is the only thing that keeps me going."

She searched his eyes; his face was a sturdy contrast of lights and shadows. "I've never known anyone who was so honest about his faith, his struggles," she said admiringly.

His hands moved to her shoulders, his touch light and warm. "You make it easy for me to speak. Too often a man of God is expected to be a saint. I am no saint, Alice Marie."

She stifled a smile. "I'm glad. I grew up in a houseful of saints. I could never measure up, especially to Annie. Frankly, I was always the black sheep of the family."

He smiled. "A very beautiful black sheep."

Their gaze held for a long moment. His face drew close to hers until their lips were mere inches apart. She parted her lips, waiting for his kiss, his embrace. It seemed they stood like that forever, so close, yet so far apart. Then, suddenly, he released her and walked back to the couch. "I'm sorry," he said huskily.

"Don't be. I'm not." She followed him back over to the couch. "But it is getting late. I'd better call a taxi."

"I wish I had a car to drive you."

"Don't worry. I took taxis everywhere in Chicago."

"Alice Marie?" His fingers grazed her arm. "Before you make that call, please sit down; let us finish our conversation."

"Our conversation?"

"You asked me a question a few minutes ago, and I'm not sure I gave you the answer you needed."

"What question?"

"You asked how I could serve a God who let my people die."

She nodded. "Not just your people—your own family."

"Yes. My family. Everyone I loved."

"Was there—a girl?"

He looked away, silent for a moment. "Yes. A lovely Jewish girl. We were promised to each other. She died, too, at Auschwitz."

"And you don't blame God? In spite of everything you still serve Him?"

"Perhaps I was too frank about my inner conflicts. I didn't intend to raise doubts in your mind about God's goodness."

"You haven't."

His brow furrowed. "But I sense a guardedness in you, Alice Marie. I see it in your eyes. You, too, struggle with doubts."

She gazed at her hands, absently tracing the cuticle of one long polished nail. "You may as well know, Helm. I'm not a believer like the rest of my family." She flashed him an ironic smile. "I mean, I do believe in God, but I don't think God believes in me."

"You doubt His love for you?"

She shrugged. "I never gave it much thought. Annie, and Mama, and Knowl are the religious ones. They're like you, Helm. They have a heart for praying and Bible reading and that sort of thing."

He studied her closely. "And you have no God-shaped vacuum in your heart, Alice Marie?"

She pressed too hard on her cuticle and it began to bleed. "Drat!" she said under her breath.

He took her hand and blotted the tiny red ribbon with his handkerchief. "Is that better?" he asked, holding her hand gently in his.

"Yes, it's fine," she assured him. "Now I'd better go—"

"Wait, Alice Marie. Let me finish." His expression grew tender and his eyes glistened with an intensity that held her gaze. "I speak to you as a man who still struggles with great, troubling questions," he admitted. "But the love of God is not one of them. God loved us enough to give His own Son to die for us. I don't doubt His love for me, nor His love for you."

She licked the dryness from her lips. "I guess I've never felt that love like you have."

"But it's there," he insisted, clasping her hand between both of his. "You must feel it when you sing. I see it in your face. I hear it in your voice. When you sing you open yourself to Him. The connection is there between you and His Spirit. How else could you sing like that, like an angel?"

"I'm no angel," she said ruefully. "God knows I've done many things I'm not proud of."

"Is that why you resist Him? You're afraid of disappointing Him?"

"No, Helm. I mean, yes, perhaps. I don't know!" She felt the color rise in her cheeks. "I'm just not the type to dash off to church every time the doors open."

"I'm not talking about church," he countered, his grip tightening on her hand. "I am speaking only about you and God. He loves you, Alice Marie. He has always loved you. I believe He has pursued and wooed you all of your life, but He will not force you to love Him."

"It's not that I don't love God in my own way," she said, a sudden swell of emotion constricting her throat. "But I've done things—awful things— I tried to hurt Annie—I tried to break up her marriage. I don't think Annie will ever forgive me."

"I'm not talking about Annie," said Helm. "God will forgive you if you ask Him—if you accept the redemption He offers through His Son. Do you hear me, Alice Marie? God promises to remember your sins no more. That's what you've always longed for, isn't it? I sense that about you— that profound yearning. Tell me I'm right."

She quickly withdrew her hand from his and stood up. She could still feel his touch, the warmth of his hand on her fingers. She could see the questions playing in his eyes, bright and urgent as stars. "I must go, Helm. It's getting late."

He stood up and followed her over to the phone. "It's not too late, Alice Marie."

"Yes, Helm, it is." She picked up the receiver, but who was she going to call? The cab company? She didn't even know the number.

"God loves you," Helm said urgently, his hand on her elbow.

"No," she murmured, her finger unsteady on the dial. She would phone Knowl after all. Knowl would come for her.

Helm refused to be dissuaded. "Dear heart, how can you say no when confronted with such great love?"

For a moment she wasn't sure whether he was speaking of God's love or the love he himself might be offering. Surely she was mistaken; he spoke as an evangelist, not as a man.

His gaze was searing, unflinching. "You are precious in His sight, Alice Marie."

"I can't think about these things now," she told him, fumbling with the dial. How could it be? She'd forgotten her own number! "My head is spinning," she said, her voice low and breathy. "I'm sorry, Helm. I know you mean well, but you don't know me. You see only what you want to see."

"I do know you," he said, clasping her arms, his dark, smoldering eyes searching hers. "I see qualities in you that no one else glimpses, a potential for faith even you do not see."

Tears beaded on her lashes. Why did he persist? Why wouldn't he let her be? She dropped the receiver back into its cradle and looked up at him with sudden fire in her eyes. "You really think you know me? Then you must know I'm carrying a fatherless baby—my dead husband's child! And what will people say when they see me pushing a buggy carriage with no husband at my side? Can you imagine how tongues will wag?"

There! The truth was out! She swayed a little, feeling suddenly weak, wondering if Helm would abandon her as swiftly as Dirk Wyman had. "Did you hear me, Helm? I'm going to have a baby!"

His expression was gentle. "Yes, I heard you. You are expecting your husband's child." He held out his arms to her. "I wondered when you would tell me."

"You knew?"

"I suspected," he said softly.

She allowed herself to sink against him, savoring the warmth of his solid chest against her cheek. His hand cupped the back of her head and his fingers massaged her hair. "Did you think I would condemn you? Why? How could you think that?"

She had no words, no tears, only a deep sensation of exhaustion and relief.

"What a brave woman you are," he said soothingly. "You carry the future, like a great secret, inside you. In spite of death there is life, and with life comes hope."

16

The weeks of November and December passed with surprising swiftness for Alice Marie as life on Honeysuckle Lane settled into a pleasant routine. At Helm's request, she began assisting Annie several days a week in typing and editing his manuscript for Herrick House. And during Helm's increasingly frequent trips to Chicago, she kept his father, Gerhart Schwarz, company and took him nourishing meals.

With a portion of his book advance, Helm purchased a low-priced automobile—Kaiser-Frazer's cozy two-door Henry J; and after church on Sundays, when the frosty winter weather permitted, he would take his father and Alice Marie for drives through the Indiana countryside. She was pleased that the three of them were developing a comfortable relationship. Papa Schwarz, as she called Gerhart, was acquiring a taste for Alice Marie's jazz recordings while she learned Yiddish and practiced fixing sauerbraten, kishke, and schnitzel the way Papa liked.

For Alice Marie it was almost like having back the father she had lost during the war—the father who doted on her and praised her beauty and talent. Papa Schwarz was a very different man from her papa, of course, but when he turned his beaming smile of approval on her, she felt as cherished as a child in her father's arms. And the nice thing about Papa Schwarz was that she saw only affection in his eyes for her and the baby she was carrying.

Helm was as delighted as Alice Marie that his father was so taken with her. "Don't you see it? He adores you. You've given him a reason to live again. He's even looking forward to the baby. He calls it his little Jewish baby," Helm told her one evening after she had served Gerhart's favorite German goulash. She had topped off the meal by coaxing Gerhart to join her in singing several rousing German choruses. Even Helm joined in, and the three of them finally collapsed in breathless laughter around the table.

Before ambling off to his room, Gerhart pinched his fingers to his lips and threw her a kiss. Devotion shone in his dark, misty eyes as he called, "Gute nacht, Liebschen!" She blew him a kiss in return, but couldn't help wondering if Helm felt about her the same way his father did. Was she bringing new meaning to his life too? She sensed that she was; she felt the warmth of his affection whenever he gazed at her and the startling jolt of attraction whenever they happened to touch—during a parting embrace, a welcoming handclasp, or a passing kiss on the cheek; and yet even after all these weeks they remained only friends.

Very good friends, Alice Marie had to admit as the nippy days of December slipped by. Genuine friendship with a man was something she had rarely experienced in her years of meaningless flirtations and passing dalliances. She valued such friendship intensely and wasn't about to complain. And yet, she longed for something more with Helm—the promise of love and romance, a future together; she even found herself dreaming—to her own amazement—of the proverbial cottage with a white picket fence.

But at the same time she realized how unlikely it was for any man to fall in love with a woman who was becoming, as the saying went, heavy with child. She resolved to simply bide her time; after all, she wouldn't be pregnant forever. Or would she? Already she felt as if she was doomed to remain in her "delicate condition" for the rest of her natural life. And she knew her dilemma would get worse before it got better. Presently it appeared that she was carrying around a small cantaloupe under her dress, but before it was over she would look as if she were carrying an overripe watermelon.

As Christmas approached, Alice Marie was determined to endure her pregnancy without complaint so long as she could spend ample time with Helm; and he seemed equally eager to keep company with her in spite of her blossoming shape. In fact, Helm and his father were becoming familiar fixtures around the Herrick household, especially during the holidays. Not only had Knowl and Annie included them for Thanksgiving dinner, but now they would be spending Christmas Eve on Honeysuckle Lane as well.

They arrived in Helm's dashing Henry J automobile shortly before nightfall. Papa Schwarz, for all of his complaining about a Jew celebrating Christmas, allowed little Maggie to take him by the hand and lead him over to the hand-carved manger scene under the towering blue spruce that glittered with bubble lights, angel hair, and tinsel. He sat listening patiently in the oak rocker while Maggie told him in great detail about Mary, Joseph, and the baby Jesus. "Would you like to hold Baby Jesus?" she asked, placing the plaster figure in his hands. His dark eyes widened and his bushy brows arched in surprise, then slowly he eased into a smile. Maggie climbed into the chair beside him and gently he rocked the miniature Christ Child, his eyes glistening with unshed tears.

After Mama's sumptuous dinner of roasted rack of lamb, creamed potatoes, and fresh mint applesauce, the family gathered in the parlor to watch the special television presentation of Gian-Carlo Menotti's opera, *Amahl and the Night Visitors*. Alice Marie made sure she sat on the love seat beside Helm and, as the program progressed, she allowed herself to relax against his arm. When she felt the baby kick with unexpected force, she unthinkingly seized his hand and placed it on her abdomen and cried, "Do you feel it, Helm? The baby's kicking!"

She realized immediately the intimate nature of her overture and released his hand, but he let it remain and flashed her a marveling smile.

"It's truly one of God's greatest miracles," he murmured without embarrassment, and she realized suddenly that she loved him for that.

A week later, on New Year's Eve, Alice Marie accompanied Helm to the nightwatch service at church. As midnight approached, Reverend Marshall called the deacons forward to serve Communion. In the past Alice Marie had always allowed the cup and the bread to pass her by, for she felt little kinship with Christ and His sufferings. But tonight, as Helm handed her the silver tray she promptly took a morsel of bread. She realized she wanted to participate, wanted to honor the Savior Helm worshiped so devotedly. She couldn't pinpoint when she had stopped seeing God through her own cynical eyes and had started seeing Him through Helm's eyes of faith, but the change was evident, undeniable. In her heart of hearts she believed, and yes, hungered for more—the presence of Christ in her life. She bowed her head, the morsel of bread still in her palm, and prayed silently, *God, please listen to me. I'm sorry I've been so selfish and willful and mean. Please let Jesus take away my sins so You'll remember them no more—even what I did to Annie and Knowl. Help me to know You and love You the way Helm does. I don't want to feel empty or alone anymore. I don't want to keep going blindly my own way, always making mistakes and hurting people. I want to serve You and care about people the way Helm does. I don't even know if I can change, but You say You can make me a new person. Please, God, I want to be someone my baby can look up to and love.*

When Helm drove her home that night and walked her through the drifting snow to her door, she told him breathlessly, "I've made my first New Year's resolution for 1952."

He brushed the snow flurries from her upturned face. "You have? Tell me. I hope it's not a resolution to travel the world or go back to your television show in Chicago."

"Neither of those," she assured him. "Actually, it's more than a resolution." She reached out for his gloved hand and held it against her cold cheek. "Helm, I prayed during Communion. I told God I want to know Him the way you do. I don't know what it all means yet; I don't even know if I'll change and be a better person. But the empty place inside me is filled now. I know Jesus loves me. I—I just wanted you to know."

He drew her into his arms against his nubby overcoat, so tightly she felt the baby flinch inside her. "I've prayed for you since the day we met," he whispered against her hair. "Thank God, He heard my prayers."

New Year's Day, 1952, started out on a buoyant note for Alice Marie in more ways than one. Not only had she discovered the peace she had always yearned for, but when she shared the news with Knowl, Annie, and Mama, they reacted as if she had scaled the highest mountain or won the Nobel Prize. She hadn't expected such a fuss—tears from Mama, a warm but brotherly hug from Knowl, and both a hug and tears from Annie.

Their excitement and enthusiasm embarrassed her. What if next week she realized she was the same person she had always been? What if she only thought God had changed her? What if she turned out to be just as spiteful and mean and stubborn as ever? Would God say, *Whoops, I made a mistake with Alice Marie. She's not saint material after all!*

But her doubts were quickly dispelled by Annie's joy. "All these years I've dreamed of the two of us being not just sisters, but sisters in the Lord!" Annie cried as she clasped Alice Marie's hands.

Sisters in the Lord. It had a nice ring to it, especially since they had never felt like sisters in any sense of the word. But something was still nagging at Alice Marie, as piercing and deeply entrenched as a burr under the skin. So when Mama went to the kitchen to work on dinner, Alice Marie detained Knowl and Annie in the parlor. "Wait, please. We still need to talk." She felt a sour taste at the back of her throat, but she forced the words out anyway. "I need to tell you," she began, looking from Annie to Knowl and back again. "I don't know how to say this—I'm sorry—I was wrong—and I knew what I was doing—it's not like I didn't know—

and it's been there between us all these years, like a shadow, like a festering wound."

She was weeping now, actually weeping. "All those years ago, I was so hurt by Cary running off, leaving me, that I wanted to hurt someone else. I wanted to hurt you, Annie. You had everything I didn't have—a loving husband, a beautiful home, a good life; and suddenly I had nothing. But that's no excuse. I know that now. I was wrong."

Annie drew close and ran her hand over Alice Marie's hair, gently fingering her golden curls. "You don't have to get into this now."

Alice Marie clasped Annie's hand. "But I do! I deliberately tried to break up your marriage, Annie. I tried to win Knowl back, and when I couldn't, I lied to you. When you phoned from California, I made you believe Knowl and I were back together. I robbed you of two years of your marriage, and I can never give that back." The two sisters were in each other's arms now. "Will you forgive me, Annie? Can you possibly forgive me?"

"God help me, I've wanted to resolve this with you for so long," said Annie. "I've struggled, praying it was in the past but knowing it wasn't, knowing there was so much to be said before we could ever put it behind us." She held Alice Marie at arm's length, their hands still entwined. "Yes. Of course, I'll forgive you—if you'll forgive me."

"Forgive you? For what?" Alice Marie asked blankly. "You've always been a—a saint!"

"No, I haven't." Annie's dark lashes were laden with tears. "You're not the only one who was wrong. I've been hateful in my own way. I've been unloving and . . . and self-righteous. I liked being the good sister and thinking of you as the bad one. I liked feeling that I was better than you and that you got the troubles you deserved. I've tried not to let my resentment show; I've tried to be kind."

"You've been more generous than I had a right to expect."

"But not in my heart," said Annie as the tears rolled down her cheeks. "When you came home last summer, I didn't want to let you back into my life. I didn't want to share anything with you, not my home, or Mama, or Maggie. And I surely didn't want you to become friends again with Knowl."

"I don't blame you," said Alice Marie. "Why should you trust me? I wasn't worthy of your trust."

"But I didn't even want to share Helm with you," said Annie. "I was possessive and jealous. I had no right to feel that way."

Knowl came over and drew Annie to him, while Alice Marie stepped back, brushing away her own tears. She managed an ironic little smile. "At least now I know you're human, Annie. Frankly, I feel much better, knowing I'm not the only sister with shortcomings."

Alice Marie looked up earnestly at Knowl. "Will you forgive me too, Knowl? I won't blame you if you don't. I won't blame you if you feel you still can't trust me. I know it was wrong of me to leave you at the altar all those years ago, and it was unforgivable of me to try to make you violate your marriage vows. I'm sorry. Will you forgive me?"

A tendon tightened along his temple. She could see his eyes misting behind his glasses. "I have forgiven you, Alice Marie. It was the only way I could live in peace—to put what you did, and the way I felt about you, behind me. But, as long as we're being honest, there's more. I think it has to be said."

"More?"

He paused and cleared his throat. "This isn't easy to say, and, Annie, I hope you'll understand."

She looked at him with concern. "Understand what, Knowl?"

He gazed solemnly at her, a mixture of emotions playing in his face. "What happened between Alice Marie and me, it wasn't entirely her fault. It was mine too. Annie, we talked about it when you first came home from California. I don't know if you even remember."

"Of course I remember, Knowl."

He reached over and touched her long burnished hair. "Then you know I'm not saying your sister and I did anything wrong—overtly." He looked back at Alice Marie, a patina of moisture glistening on his forehead. "But, if I'm honest, Alice Marie, I have to admit I was flattered by your attentions. I think I gave you the impression that if you pursued me enough, I might respond to you. Call it the remnant of a school-boy crush or a bruised ego after you left me at the altar. Whatever the case, I'm afraid I left the door open just enough to encourage you."

Alice Marie wasn't sure what to say. She was new to this whole business of laying the truth on the table. And what if the truth just made things worse? "So you encouraged me, Knowl? Is that so bad?" she questioned, casting a sidelong glance at Annie for her reaction. "Since we're being so candid, I'm kind of glad you saved a little place in your heart for me."

"But I gave you mixed signals, and for that I'm sorry."

"It's okay, Knowl. You always were too hard on yourself." She crossed her arms over her expanding middle and rocked back slightly on the balls of her heels. She looked at Knowl and Annie and for the first time didn't feel a twinge of guilt. "I'm glad we've got this whole thing out in the open after all these years. Maybe now we can concentrate on just being a family."

"A wonderful family," said Annie with a smile. She and Knowl were standing together, his arm draped over her shoulder and her arm circling his waist. They looked happy and content—an expression Alice Marie realized mirrored what she herself was feeling at this very moment.

But with everything settled and life so at peace, why did she still feel a small sense of foreboding, as if something were about to shatter this newfound tranquillity?

17

The storm of controversy started even before Helm's book went to press. On Saturday, February 16, 1952, the *Willowbrook News* ran a feature story on *From Darkness to Dawn: Lessons of the Holocaust*. That morning, as Alice Marie sat at the breakfast table with her family, Knowl read the advance review aloud. "Schwarz's book is not for the squeamish or faint of heart, nor for those who like their reading sugar-coated," wrote the reviewer.

"Writing in a style that is forthright, assertive, and pulls no punches, Schwarz jabs the human conscience by presenting an unsettling portrait of mankind at mid-century. He demands answers to many troubling questions: Have we gotten so caught up in our comfortable lives that we've forgotten the evil cataclysm of the past decade? Have we forgotten how the earth shuddered and convulsed with the slaughter of twelve million people? Do we look at the past and say God has forsaken us, when in truth we have forsaken Him? Do we shrug and say it's none of our business what others do as long as our own lives remain undisturbed? If we remain in our complacency, what catastrophes will shake our world in the decades to come? And Schwarz's most pressing question—Where are the Christians whose hearts are so tender to God and one another that they are wholly committed to changing the world for Christ's sake?"

The article went on to highlight the lives of Helm and his father in both America and Germany, and concluded with the observation, "While some may resent the suggestion that Americans, and Christians in particular, could have done more to deliver their world from evil, let us hope that most of us are willing to take to heart the admonitions this Jewish evangelist presents so vividly and poignantly."

When he had finished reading, Knowl set the newspaper down and looked around the table. "Well, it looks like that pre-publication copy of Helm's manuscript we sent the press did its job. What do you think? Will the readers be as favorable to Helm's book as this reviewer? Do we have a winner on our hands?"

"I think so," said Annie. "At first people are just going to be curious. They're going to want to know what Helm has to say. But after they've read the book, they'll never forget it."

"I think so too," said Alice Marie. "Sure, the book's going to be controversial, but sometimes that's what sells books."

"We're not publishing it to be controversial," said Knowl.

"Of course not," said Annie, "but sometimes the truth is controversial, and I'm proud we're the house giving Helm a chance to be heard."

"The editor at the paper says this article on Helm's book may be picked up for syndication. It could appear in every major newspaper in the country."

"Because it's controversial?" asked Alice Marie.

"Because it's news, I suppose—a Christian Jew speaking out so frankly about issues that should concern us all."

"I'm excited about what's in store for Helm and his book," said Annie. "I think we should be proud of a job well done."

"Me too," said Knowl. "But before we get too pleased with ourselves, we'd better be prepared for a backlash as well."

Annie's mouth puckered slightly. "A backlash?"

"Helm's book may make some people extremely angry, and angry people have a way of striking back in unexpected ways."

"Let them get angry," said Alice Marie. "They're the very people Helm is trying to reach."

"But I just want us all to be prepared for the criticism that may come along with the praise."

"Well, I'm going to think only positive thoughts," said Alice Marie, resting her hands on her ample middle. Even through her denim bib-front jumper she could feel her tiny baby thrusting about, an elbow here, a foot there, as if he were already aware that his accommodations were getting a bit too cramped.

"Yes, only positive thoughts," Annie agreed. "That's important for expectant mommies. Positive thoughts, gentle lullabies, and whispered prayers keep Baby content. I found that true when I was carrying Maggie."

Alice Marie smiled wanly. "It works except at night when I lie down. Then Baby thinks it's time to do jumping jacks and somersaults. He gets so restless and rambunctious, he leaves me exhausted."

Knowl leaned over to Annie and squeezed her shoulder, his brown eyes twinkling. "Darling, all this talk about babies makes me think maybe it's time for Maggie to have that little brother or sister we promised her."

Annie slapped his hand away. "Bite your tongue, Knowl!"

He shrugged. "It was just a thought, Darling."

"And that's all it'll be, unless—"

"Yes? Unless—?"

Annie's expression softened and her voice took on a playful tone. "Unless you really do think Maggie needs a playmate."

Alice Marie pushed her chair back from the table and stood up—a feat that was becoming increasingly difficult with her expanding girth. "I think I'll leave you lovebirds alone and go help Mama with the chores," she said lightly. But her thoughts were less sunny. Observing the easy banter between Annie and Knowl only reminded her that she had no husband to share the joys and, yes, the trials, of impending motherhood. There was Helm, of course, but they were only friends, so there was only so much she could share. And since he had no personal stake in this baby the way Cary Rose had, she couldn't expect him to share her excitement and anticipation—and yes, her worries and fears.

But then again, she did have Someone to share the deepest yearnings and secrets of her heart, but even her new relationship with God was still uncharted territory. It was like getting acquainted with a new friend; every day she discovered something new, something she hadn't known before; and every day she learned to trust this Friend a little more; but there was still so much she didn't know and so many bridges to build.

Helm was helping her, of course. Whenever they spent time together at the publishing house, at his apartment, or at her home, he would read a few verses from the Bible and pray with her, as if she were a Sunday school of one. He would always encourage her to ask questions and she enjoyed challenging him with every outrageous question she could think of. *What does God look like? Will there be jazz in heaven? When we die, will we remember the people on earth we left behind? How does God communicate with Christians all over the world at the same time?*

"Sometimes I think you come up with questions just to try to stump me," Helm told her that night as they sat in the parlor eating fresh-baked pumpkin pie—Mama's contribution to their celebration over the favorable newspaper review of Helm's book.

Before she could answer she felt a swift jab under her ribs that momentarily stole her breath. She gasped and pressed her palm against her sore rib.

"The baby?" asked Helm, eyeing her with concern.

She nodded. "I think he's going to be a little bandleader like his dad; he's already got the swing down pat." She placed Helm's hand on the spot where the baby's elbow moved back and forth and up and down. "Feel it?" she asked. "I think he's practicing for the Big Bands."

"He's doing a good job of it too," said Helm with a note of awe in his voice. "He's a frisky little tyke, isn't he? I never felt anything like it in my life."

At moments like this Alice Marie almost felt as if Helm were truly connected with her and her baby, but then the moment would pass and Helm would go home, and she would be alone upstairs in the rosebud room with her invisible God and her unseen child.

"I'll be going to Chicago again this next weekend," Helm told her as he prepared to leave. "Some pressing business."

"Again?" she lamented. "I was hoping you and your father could come to dinner."

"We will. Soon. I promise."

"I don't know how many weekends I'll have left before the baby comes. After that, I hear my freedom will be severely curtailed." She paused, an idea brewing in her mind. "I know, Helm. I'll go with you to Chicago. I've been wanting to get back there to see Rudy, the producer of my television show, and to pick up a few things in storage at my old apartment."

"It's out of the question."

"But, Helm, I really need to go. Rudy called me just the other day. He's been talking with the network and he thinks he can convince them to bring me back to my television show after the baby comes. It's the break I need."

Helm's gaze moved over her with obvious solicitude. "How can you go to Chicago now? You—you're so—"

"Heavy with child?"

"That's one way of putting it."

"So?"

"So you shouldn't be traveling."

"Nonsense, Helm! I feel wonderful. All right, my ankles are swollen and I'm a little slow on my feet, but otherwise—"

"It's not a good idea, Alice Marie," he insisted. "It's not just your health. Who will look after my father while I'm gone?"

She gestured reassuringly with her hands. "Annie would love to check in on him, I'm sure. Or maybe even Mama."

He paused and his face reddened. "What if . . . I mean, the baby. You'd be so far from home. What if the baby started coming?"

She broke into laughter. "Oh, Helm, I'm sure with your *savoir faire*, you'd have no trouble delivering a baby."

He stifled a chuckle and gave her belly a paternal pat. "Please, I entreat you! Don't be in a hurry, little one."

She brightened. "Are you saying you'll take me with you to Chicago?"

"We'll see." And that was his final word on the subject.

On Sunday, after the evening service at Willowbrook Church, as Helm drove Alice Marie home he suggested they stop downtown at Walgreen's Drug Store for a bite to eat. A waitress showed them to a back corner booth that provided an aura of privacy, and when she asked what they wanted, Helm gave Alice Marie a wink and said, "Let's throw caution to the wind and order juicy hamburgers with the works and thick chocolate shakes."

"You'll get no argument from me," she answered with a conspiratorial smile. But minutes later, when the waitress brought their order, Alice Marie shook her head and said, "Oh, my goodness! The baby will get the hiccups for sure!"

"Don't despair," said Helm, generously dousing his burger with catsup. "If he's a typical lad, he won't be able to resist a good hamburger. But please don't tell anyone I've led you down this path of temptation when you should be home eating—uh, whatever expectant mothers are supposed to eat."

"Lots of fruits and vegetables," she said between bites, "but tonight I'm living it up and eating anything I please."

"Then you don't blame me for being a bad influence on you?"

"Not at all." She tossed her head jauntily, a smile playing on her lips. "Actually, you've been a wonderful influence, Helm. Don't ever doubt it.

Without you I never would have come to know God or been reconciled with Knowl and Annie."

He reached across the table and patted her hand. "Then I won't feel guilty for leading you astray in a few small things."

"Such as thick, juicy hamburgers?"

"And marvelous chocolate shakes."

She searched his eyes. "But why do I feel you have something else on your mind, something you're reluctant to talk about?"

"Is that what you think?"

"It's true, isn't it? Beneath your little jokes about the food, you're upset about something."

"No, I'm not upset."

"But I see it in your face—a dark, brooding look."

He grimaced. "You read me too well."

"What is it, Helm? Please tell me. What's wrong?"

He glanced around, as if to see who might be within earshot. There was no one around except a young couple sitting at a table across the room and several teenage boys in wool caps and jackets at the lunch counter. "This is probably the wrong place to talk, but I didn't want to go to your place or mine, and it's too cold to sit in the car somewhere."

"Talk about what, Helm? You sound serious."

"It is serious." He traced a water ring on the shiny laminated table-top. "It's something I should have told you before, but I didn't want you involved."

"Not involved? Why? What is it?"

He pushed his plate aside and leaned forward, his arms resting on the table. "About Chicago—the reason I don't want you to go with me."

She leaned forward too. "What about Chicago?"

"I'm going there to meet a man named Simon Golding. We met just after the war. He, too, had relatives who died at Auschwitz. In fact, he was the only one in his family to survive the *shoah*." When she looked blankly at him, he explained, "*Shoah* is Hebrew for holocaust."

"Why are you meeting him?" she asked.

"It's a long story, too long to tell you all the details tonight. Simon is one of many Jewish survivors searching for the men who persecuted them and murdered their families."

Alice Marie felt a chill of comprehension. "Are you talking about Nazi war criminals? Is that what you're doing, Helm? Tracking down Nazis?"

The muscles in his face tightened and his eyes narrowed. "You say that as if you think I am doing something wrong."

"No, it's not that," she assured him. "It just sounds so—so dangerous and improbable. Isn't that something better left to the authorities?"

His lips curled. "Do you really believe the authorities will do anything to capture and punish Nazis?"

She slipped her hand over his. "Yes, I do, Helm. Why wouldn't they?"

"Perhaps they do not believe the Nazis are guilty of such heinous crimes. Or they do not care. Do you know, Alice Marie, as early as 1925 Hitler laid out all his vicious plans for the world to read? It's all there in his autobiography, *Mein Kampf*. He said he would form a dictatorship in Germany, annihilate the Jews, enslave the Slavs, and dominate Europe."

His hand tightened under her palm. "For years he carried out his insane plan while people looked the other way. Even Americans said, 'Oh, the Germans are too smart; Hitler won't last six months.' In the 1930s, when newspapers began reporting Hitler's atrocities, people said, 'Oh, he won't be able to get away with that.' But he did. And everything he said he would do, he did."

"But the war is over, Helm. Hitler is gone. We won!"

"Did we?" He ground his jaw, his lips taut, skeptical. "What have we won, Alice Marie? Have people changed?"

"If they haven't, then what was it all for? Where's the justice?"

"That is my question," said Helm. "People are too busy to worry about justice—too busy trying to find jobs, or trying to keep jobs. They have their own lives to think about, so war criminals go free. But Simon and

I and others like us will not let the matter go away. We will find these evil men and see that they are brought to justice, whatever it takes."

Alice Marie stirred the straw around in her shake. "It sounds very dangerous, Helm."

"I suppose it is, but it is what I must do."

"But you can't track them down by yourself, Helm. Even a handful of men isn't enough."

"You'd be surprised at what we've accomplished."

"I'm listening."

"Simon and I have traced the very guard who persecuted my father. He is living somewhere near Chicago."

"You know where he lives?"

"Not exactly. But Simon Golding has been working on this for some time. He has promised to have the necessary papers ready when I go to see him next Saturday."

"Surely you're not planning to—to take justice into your own hands. Please, Helm, tell me. What will you do when you find the man who tortured your father?"

Helm stared down at his fingers as they drummed the tabletop. "I don't know, Alice Marie. God help me, I don't know."

She reached for his hand. "You're afraid of what you might do, aren't you?"

A tremor of rage filled his voice. "That one man represents all the evil and brutality that was done to my people. As much as I love God, I hate that man. Before I die, I want to look deep into his eyes and try to comprehend how one human being could torment another so cold-bloodedly. I want to know how his mind works, because it was that kind of mind that poisoned the German nation, that made butchers of ordinary people, and turned cultured citizens into a heartless society that saw a great malignancy infecting their country and looked the other way."

"But, Helm, if you locate these criminals, you must turn the information over to the authorities and let them see that justice is done. It's not your place to—"

"To avenge the wrong done my father and millions like him? He was once a strong man, Alice Marie. I wanted to be just like him. But they humiliated him, crushed him, made him a helpless victim who relives the Nazi horrors every night in his dreams."

Alice Marie clasped his hand firmly. "Your father is not a weak man, Helm. He is strong in spirit; no one can take that from him. And he is a survivor. The Nazis wanted to destroy him, but they didn't; he lives, and that means he has won."

Helm lifted her hand to his lips and kissed her fingers. "You are very good for me, Alice Marie. In your own way you are a survivor too. I love that about you."

His eyes searched hers. "Your husband who died—he was Jewish?"

"You know he was."

Helm smiled. "Well, then, perhaps your little Jewish baby—as my father calls him—will face a better world than we have known. I pray that no one will taunt him, or persecute him, or shun him because he has Jewish blood in his veins."

Alice Marie felt a chill. "You almost frighten me, Helm."

"I don't mean to."

"It's just—I—I've worried about my baby being a fatherless child, but I never thought of him being treated badly because of his Jewish heritage."

Helm's lips relaxed in a smile. "If I have anything to say about it, your child will never experience such prejudice. I would give my dying breath to make this world a better place for him."

Alice Marie returned his smile. "Oh, Helm, don't you see? You've already made it a better world for him."

18

Early Monday morning Alice Marie answered the phone and was startled to hear Dirk Wyman's voice. Her immediate impulse was to hang up on him. Since learning of her pregnancy he hadn't asked her out socially and he hadn't phoned, except to discuss some business matters with Knowl. It was probably business now, too, so she asked coolly, "Do you wish to speak to Knowl?"

"Yes, I do," he replied, sounding uncharacteristically agitated. "It's important, Allie. He hasn't left for the office yet, has he?"

"No, he hasn't. Is there a problem?"

"Yes, I'm afraid so. Will you get him please?"

She called Knowl from the kitchen and slipped out of the room while he took Dirk's call. Minutes later she heard Knowl call her name and Annie's. They quickly joined him, Annie still in her robe.

Knowl urged them to sit down while he took the wing chair opposite them. "That was Dirk. There's been some trouble at Herrick House."

"What kind of trouble?" asked Alice Marie.

"It looks like—some vandalism."

"Vandalism?" echoed Annie. "Oh, Knowl! What happened?"

He pushed his tousled hair back from his forehead. "Nothing that can't be fixed, I'm sure, but Dirk says it's not a pretty sight."

"Tell us, Knowl," prompted Alice Marie.

"Dirk says it's mainly broken windows and graffiti painted on the walls. Red paint everywhere. Inside. Outside."

Annie shook her head, bewildered. "Graffiti?"

"Yes, Annie. I'm sorry. It's ethnic slurs and expletives. Swastikas, things like that."

Alice Marie sat forward. "Knowl, are you saying this attack is aimed at Helm?"

He nodded, his jaw rigid, his hazel eyes darkening behind his wire-rimmed glasses. "It looks that way. Apparently someone who read the article in the paper isn't happy about our publishing Helm's book."

"I knew some people wouldn't like it," said Annie. "I assumed we'd get some nasty letters, but I never expected this."

"Me neither," said Knowl, standing up. "I've got to get over to the office."

"What can we do?" asked Annie.

"Not much. Sit tight. Pray. Dirk has phoned the police. I want to be there when they arrive."

The next few days were painful and harried for the entire household, as well as for the employees of Herrick House Publishers. The *Willowbrook News* ran an article with large photographs of the damage on the front page of Tuesday's paper; the headlines read, "Vandal Attack Tied to Controversial Book." Several wire services picked up the article and by Thursday the story appeared in a televised thirty-second spot on NBC's fifteen-minute *Camel News Caravan* with John Cameron Swayze.

That week a flood of letters arrived at Herrick House, not just from Willowbrook and other Indiana cities, but from cities across the country. Half the letters supported the publication of Helm's book and half criticized or condemned Herrick House for needlessly stirring up trouble.

One letter was typical of many: "Dear Herrick House Editors: I read about the trouble you had with somebody defacing your property, and if you want my opinion, most folks I know just want to forget the war, the depression, and every other negative thing we had to go through in the past twenty years. People are finally getting jobs, getting married, having kids, and settling down in their own little house somewhere. Don't begrudge them finding a little happiness in life. And don't make them feel guilty for wanting to forget the bad things, like Nazis and Commies and poverty. I say dump your depressing book in the trash and let us live in peace." It was signed, "A concerned reader in Terre Haute."

On Friday, February 22nd, Knowl called an emergency meeting of the publishing company's board of directors. He told Annie, Helm, and Alice Marie the results of the meeting at dinner that evening. "It was one of the most rousing, vocal gatherings we've ever had," he said solemnly, ignoring the food on his plate. "A regular tug of war, I'm afraid. Dirk Wyman was the first one to say, 'I told you so,' and he went so far as to suggest that we cancel your book, Helm."

"Oh, Knowl, you wouldn't!" cried Annie.

"Surely you wouldn't change your mind now, would you, Knowl?" asked Alice Marie.

"Don't worry, ladies. I've made a commitment. I'll keep it, especially when it's one I believe in with all my heart. The book will be released as scheduled, about the middle of April. Meanwhile, let's hope the furor has died down and that we can enjoy some peace and quiet in our lives again."

"What did the board say about your decision, Knowl?" asked Annie.

"The majority went along with me. There's still the question of whether the bank will withdraw their financial backing."

"I'm sure Robert stood with you," said Annie.

"Naturally." Knowl glanced over at Helm. "You met Robert Wayne. My sister Catherine's husband. And co-owner of Herrick House."

"Yes, of course. A nice fellow."

Knowl nodded. "The rest of our directors are just hoping all the attention will result in high sales of your book, Helm."

"But what if the negative publicity results in poor sales?"

"Then Herrick House had better tighten its belt in some other area."

Helm's brows furrowed; he clenched his fists. "It's all my doing, Knowl. I don't want your publishing house to suffer because of me."

"God will take care of us, just as He always has." Knowl paused, adjusted his glasses on his nose, and added, "There is one thing I should mention."

Annie looked at him. "What, Knowl?"

He reached over and took her hand. "Among the letters we've received—a few disgruntled writers have made actual threats. I don't think any of us are in real danger, but you should be aware there may be a few lunatics out there. Just keep your eyes open, all right? And, Annie, keep an eye on Maggie when she's out playing."

Annie's hand flew to her throat. "You've received threats against our daughter?"

"Not directly. But yes, a few veiled threats against our family. No sense in taking any chances."

Helm turned to Alice Marie. "I don't think I should risk taking you to Chicago tomorrow."

"Please, Helm, I'm going. Besides, with all that's happening here, I need to get away."

"We may need to stay overnight at my friend's home."

"I don't mind, if he has room for me."

Helm nodded. "We can make suitable arrangements. But are you sure the drive won't be too tiring?"

She managed a wry chuckle. "I know I'm getting as big as a barn, Helm, but I can still get around okay—if you don't mind being seen with a lady in my condition."

His cheeks reddened. "I'm honored to be seen with you in any condition."

"Now that's an interesting proposition," she mused slyly.

He met her gaze with a whimsical smile of his own. "You may not be so eager to accompany me when I tell you I will be here to pick you up at six sharp in the morning."

She heaved an exaggerated sigh. "Ah, night person that I am—somehow I'll survive!"

But when Helm knocked on the door at 5:30 the next morning, Alice Marie was tempted to send him on his way alone.

"Bring a pillow and a blanket," he suggested, "and you can sleep while I drive."

"Sleep sitting up?" she inquired. "In your little Henry J?"

"You may curl up in the backseat if you wish."

She sighed. "I think I'll take my chances in the front."

Fortunately Mama insisted they eat a hearty breakfast before hitting the road, giving Alice Marie a few minutes to savor a cup of hot cocoa along with Mama's date muffins and a cheese omelet.

But by seven they were bundled in their heaviest coats and traveling on the two-lane highway out of Willowbrook, treading a light snowfall that had transformed the pavement into a glistening sheet of ice.

Alice Marie felt too disquieted to sleep; instead, she propped her head on the pillow and kept her gaze squarely on the road ahead. There were swirls of frost etched on the windshield and white flurries whirling at them, as if God were shaking out His feather pillows on the earth.

When she shivered, Helm asked, "Are you cold?"

"A little," she replied between chattering teeth.

"Dear girl, why didn't you say so?" Helm turned up the heat and within minutes the air inside the automobile turned from frigid to stifling. The close warmth of the car, the rhythmic whir of the tires, and the early hour wafted her into a drowsy slumber. For what seemed forever she teetered between nodding wakefulness and a dreamlike sleep.

She awoke with a start when Helm pulled into a gas station and told the uniformed attendant to fill up the gas tank and check the oil; the attendant cleaned the icy slush from the windshield as well. The sun was shining high in the sky now, making Alice Marie feel as if she had just come out of hibernation.

"You must be hungry," Helm told her as he pulled back onto the highway. "I saw a little cafe nearby. We'll stop and have an early lunch."

"How far are we from Chicago?" she asked, running a brush through her long, tangled curls.

"Less than an hour. Look. Here we are. Pearl's Country Cafe." He pulled up beside a modest white-frame building with cafe curtains and Coca-Cola signs decorating the plate glass windows. Helm got out and came around to her door. "What do you say, Alice Marie? Will a good hot meal lift your spirits?"

She took his hand and eased herself slowly out of the cramped automobile. "I'm awake, but my legs are asleep." She leaned her full weight on him until she was sure her legs could support her.

They entered the cozy, unadorned restaurant, sat down at a small table covered with a red-checkered oilcloth, and ordered vegetable soup and chicken salad sandwiches. As they ate, Alice Marie asked Helm to tell her more about the Holocaust survivors tracking down Nazi war criminals. "I have a feeling you've told me only part of the story, Helm. Please tell me how involved you are with this group and what information you've uncovered."

He was reluctant to speak at first, but slowly, bit by bit, he revealed the scope and breadth of their operation. For some time he had been making contact with other Jews in Europe and America; they had traced hundreds of war criminals who had assumed new identities and resettled in North or South America. He told her about his contact, Simon Golding, who had infiltrated a German group in Chicago responsible for bringing Nazis and their families secretly into the United States.

"Now Simon has his hands on a list of names of Nazis who were resettled here in the Midwest," said Helm. "If we can get their names, their American aliases, and current addresses, we will turn the information over to the proper American authorities. I pray they will rout out the Nazis and deport them back to Germany to stand trial for war crimes against humanity."

"I thought you didn't trust the authorities."

"I don't entirely. But when we have enough evidence the press can sway public opinion and force the government to deal with these criminals."

"And you believe Simon Golding has located your father's guard from Auschwitz?"

Helm's hand shook slightly as he spooned up a mouthful of soup. "Yes, the guard who tortured my father is living somewhere in the Midwest under another identity."

"Helm, when you find him, promise me you won't take justice into your own hands. You'll let the authorities handle matters, won't you?"

He stirred his soup, his gaze downcast. "I'll know what to do when the time comes."

After lunch, they drove on to downtown Chicago and by mid-afternoon they pulled up in front of a two-story brownstone in an old neighborhood off North Michigan Avenue.

"Simon lives in an upstairs apartment," Helm told her as they climbed the steps of the trellised front porch. He opened the heavy door and a shaft of light revealed a long, gloomy hallway. The stairs were steep and narrow and the air had an old, musty smell. Alice Marie was out of breath when they reached the second floor, and the baby squirmed inside her, so she held back and leaned against the railing while Helm went to the door on the right and knocked.

He looked back at her and asked, "Are you feeling okay?"

"Yes," she assured him. "Just a little discomfort." It was more than discomfort, but she didn't want to admit it to Helm. Lately her abdomen tensed and sometimes grew hard as a fist when she exerted herself. Annie called it false labor and told her, "Your body's practicing for the big day." She didn't want Helm thinking this was the day.

He knocked again, but there was still no answer. "It's okay," he told her. "Simon gave me a key. If he's out, we'll make ourselves at home and wait for him." He tried the key and the door opened. "Simon!" he called.

"Simon, old man, are you here? I've brought a guest. I hope you're decent."

When there was no response he beckoned Alice Marie over and they went inside. Even with the scant winter light barely dispelling the shadows, she could see what he saw. His grip tightened on her arm and he groaned, "Oy vey!"

The room was as empty as a tomb.

"Simon!" Helm called again, urgency turning his voice shrill. "Simon Golding, are you here?"

The silence was chilling. They walked from room to room, only to find what they already knew. Simon Golding no longer lived here. Nothing remained to suggest that anyone had inhabited the place.

"Not a single stick of furniture," marveled Alice Marie. "When he moved he took everything."

"He didn't move," said Helm, his tone hushed and confidential. "He would not have left without notifying me."

"Then where is he?"

Helm went to the closet and threw open the door. Nothing. Empty hangers, empty shelves. He strode to the tiny kitchenette and opened the cupboards one by one, and slammed each door, venting his frustration. "Where could he be? He would not leave of his own free will. I know that about him!"

"When did you see him last?"

Helm opened the dilapidated oven and felt inside along the black wire racks. "I saw him two, maybe three weeks ago. He told me he was getting very close to finding the evidence we needed. He told me to come back this weekend and he would have it for me."

Alice Marie crossed her arms and shivered. "Maybe we should call the police."

"And tell them what? My friend was here and now he's gone?" Helm walked back to the living room and inspected the radiator; he scrutinized the dingy overhead globe and looked under a loose corner of the threadbare carpet. He strode down the narrow hall to the tiny bathroom and examined the medicine cabinet and the small drawers under the chipped enamel sink. Nothing. "I was so sure Simon would leave some clue, something!"

Alice Marie placed a consoling hand on his arm. "Maybe we should talk to someone else in the building. They might know something."

Helm brightened. "You're right. Simon's landlady lives in the apartment downstairs. Come!"

They rushed downstairs—Helm nearly flying, Alice Marie treading behind; Helm crossed the dingy hallway and pounded forcefully on the scarred pine door at the end of the corridor. After a moment the door creaked open and a squat woman in a frowsy housedress peered out. Alice Marie caught a glimpse of frizzy, blue-gray hair and a weathered face with a dot of rouge on each cheek. The woman's gray eyes narrowed and her thin lips curled in a sneer as she demanded, "What do you want, Mister, banging my door down like that?"

Helm was breathing hard. "My friend, Simon Golding—he lives upstairs. At least, he was there three weeks ago. Tell me, where did he go?"

"Oh, my goodness! You be lookin' for Simon Golding?" Her pinched brows arched in surprise. "You be too late, Mister. He ain't here no more."

"I can see that," said Helm. "Please, Mrs.——"

"Mrs. Morrissey, it is."

"Please, Mrs. Morrissey, do you know where he is?"

She shook her head forlornly. "They come and took him away."

"Who?" demanded Helm. "Who took him away?"

"Why, the ambulance." She craned her neck and looked more closely at Helm. "You come visit this man and you don't know what happened?"

"No. I told you, it's been several weeks. Is he ill?"

She shook her head again. "It's a sad thing, it is."

"Mrs. Morrissey, please!"

"I'm sorry, Mister." She shrugged and held up her hands in a gesture of helplessness. "Simon Golding is dead."

Alice Marie felt a painful lurch deep in her stomach. She stretched her hand out to Helm and saw that his face had paled to an eggshell white.

"There must be some mistake," he said in a strangled voice.

"Oh, no. No mistake," said Mrs. Morrissey. "I saw it myself. The accident. Plain as day. It happened right in front of this house. Mr. Golding was coming home from his usual walk, minding his own business. He always buys the paper from that little newsstand on Michigan Avenue, you know. So he was coming home—I seen him walking down the block, almost home. I was sweeping my porch, you see, and I waved to him and he waved back, friendly as can be. Then he steps off the curb and out of nowhere comes a big black car and hits him. Poor Mr. Golding. The car didn't even try to miss him. It hit him and knocked him into the air and just kept going. Saddest thing I ever seen."

For several moments Helm didn't speak, but Alice Marie could see the shock and emotion moving in the muscles of his face. At last he moistened his lips and said, "Did the police find the driver?"

"Not that I know of. Such a shame. He was a nice man, Mr. Golding was. Always paid his rent on time, and never noisy or unruly. Always treated me kindly, he did. A real gentleman."

Helm removed his handkerchief and blew his nose. "Was there a funeral?"

"Just a quiet burial. Last week it was. Monday morning. He didn't have no family. Just a handful of friends who came and went. Real private fellows, they were. Never met them. Never knew their names. Couldn't even call 'em with the news." She squinted up at Helm. "Saw you here once or twice, I think."

"What about his apartment?" asked Helm. "Everything is gone—the furniture, his belongings—"

Mrs. Morrissey nodded. "Oh, yes! Merciful heavens, it's all gone, and I don't mind saying, the whole ordeal was mighty upsetting."

"What was upsetting?" Helm's tone was edged with impatience.

Mrs. Morrissey stepped into the hallway and said confidentially, "A man came. Said he was Mr. Golding's brother. Had an accent. German, I think, like Mr. Golding's. Anyway, he come to collect his things. I gave him the key but he never brought it back. When I went upstairs to see if I could help, the man was gone, and Mr. Golding's apartment—it looked like a cyclone had come through."

Helm gripped the woman's shoulder. "What happened?"

She drew back from his touch, her eyes growing steely with suspicion. "I'm saying somebody went in and smashed Mr. Golding's furniture. They threw everything around like they was looking for something and couldn't find it. I had to have the junk man come and take everything away. Couldn't save nothing!"

Helm rubbed his chin, his eyes shadowed with consternation. "What junk man, Mrs. Morrissey?"

"Don't remember, but the fellow carted the whole kit and caboodle away just last Wednesday."

Helm turned imploringly to Alice Marie. "We were so close—so close!"

"Only one thing left of that poor man," Mrs. Morrissey was saying. "But I'm saving it for a certain party."

Helm looked at her. "What, Mrs. Morrissey? You're saving something of Simon's?"

She nodded. "He asked me to—a week before the accident. He says, 'Mrs. Morrissey, I need you to do me a favor,' and, of course, I says I will. And he gives me this envelope, all sealed and looking so mysterious. And he says, 'You save this for my friend, and if anything happens to me, you give it to him when he comes calling.'"

"Was it for his friend Helmut Schwarz?" demanded Helm.

"Why, let me think—yes, it was a German name. Schwarz. Helmut Schwarz. Yes, come to think of it, that was the name." She peered at Helm. "Do you know him?"

"I am the man," said Helm. "Please, Mrs. Morrissey, give me the envelope Mr. Golding gave you."

She cocked her head at an angle. "Do you have something with your name on it, Mr. Schwarz—some sort of proof, you know? I promised Mr. Golding I'd take good care of his parcel."

Helm showed her his driver's license. She seemed satisfied and went back inside, then appeared moments later with a thick manila envelope in her hand. "Just so you know, I didn't look inside, Mr. Schwarz. I was curious as a cat, but I let it be. I respect other folk's property. Especially him being dead and all. I didn't even tell the police."

Helm thanked her and handed her a twenty dollar bill for her trouble. With the brown envelope securely under his arm, he ushered Alice Marie outside, down the steps, and back to his waiting automobile. Before Alice Marie had even settled comfortably into her seat, Helm was revving the engine and swerving away from the curb.

"Why the sudden hurry?" she asked.

He didn't reply. Instead, he accelerated, his foot pressing the gas pedal until his Henry J was traveling ten miles over the speed limit.

"Where are we going?" Alice Marie persisted.

"Back to Willowbrook," he said, his words clipped.

"But I thought we were going to see my producer. And I have to go to my apartment. Don't you remember? I have some things to pick up."

"We can't," he said sharply. "Don't you see what has happened?"

"Yes, Helm, and I'm sorry—truly sorry—your friend was killed. It was a terrible accident!"

Helm spoke through clenched teeth. "It was no accident. Simon was murdered."

Alice Marie felt the baby twist inside her, as if he were taking the brunt of this shocking news. She gasped and crossed her arms over her middle, as if to quiet the infant and herself as well. At last she found her voice. "Are you sure, Helm?"

"I have no doubts. Everything I have waited for is in that envelope. And someone wanted it more than I."

Alice Marie turned the envelope over in her hands. "But now you have it," she said with a note of awe. "Now you'll have your answers you've searched for for so long."

"But at such a high price. Poor Simon. And for what?"

"Wouldn't you have been willing to die to bring these evil men to justice?"

"Of course I would."

"Then I'm sure Simon felt that way too. And look how he managed to get this information into your hands, Helm. He died, but he will have won too."

"If I'm able to get the information to the proper authorities."

"There's nothing to stop you now."

He looked over at her, his expression solemn. "I pray to God you're right."

They were silent for several minutes, listening to the steady roar of the engine and the whir of the tires on the ice-slick pavement. It was snowing again and the temperature had dropped sharply in the past hour as a pale rose-blue sun hovered forlornly on the horizon.

"Have you thought about what you'll do when this is over?" she asked.

"Do you mean when my book is published, or when I've brought my father's guard and the rest of those Nazi hoodlums to justice?"

"Both," she replied. "Will you stay in Willowbrook?"

He kept his gaze on the road. "What does it matter? You plan to go back to Chicago."

"But what about you?"

"I haven't thought that far. Except, someday, before my father dies, I want to take him to Israel."

"Israel? To visit?"

"No, not just to visit. Since '48, when Israel became a state again, I have wanted to go there and help my people rebuild their land. And my father longs to set foot on Jewish soil. But with all my unfinished business, I couldn't allow myself to think about going, nor to dream of it."

Through her wool coat Alice Marie lightly massaged the place just below her ribs where the baby arched his back, as if protesting Helm's surprising news. Alice Marie hadn't thought about Helm leaving Willowbrook, hadn't stopped to imagine what her life would be like without him. Didn't he feel it too—the growing connection between them? How could he talk so blithely about going away, going halfway around the world away from her? How could he leave her when she loved him so much?

The realization struck her with such force that she pressed too hard against the baby and he kicked back at her hand, stealing her breath. Or perhaps she felt breathless at the thought of losing Helm—a man who was never hers to begin with. Never had he spoken to her of love, never had he made any promises. He saw her only as a friend, and that was why he could tell her he would go to Israel to live without even wondering if she would care.

So engrossed was she in her thoughts that she almost didn't hear Helm's sudden exclamation of dismay. She looked at him; he was staring into the rearview mirror.

"What's wrong?" she cried.

In the hasty glance he gave her, she saw alarm vivid in his eyes. "Don't look back, Alice Marie," he warned, "but that black car behind us—I think it's following us!"

19

The sky at the horizon was a metallic gray with a thin ribbon of glinting silver; overhead the dusky, snow-heavy clouds were melting into streamers of inky blackness. It would be dark soon. Helm turned on his headlights, the yellow beams cutting a swath through the mud-crusted snow bordering the two-lane highway. He pressed his foot on the gas, his knuckles white on the steering wheel. Even in the coldness of the automobile, a sheen appeared on his forehead and a stray strand of hair drifted toward his furrowed brows.

Alice Marie watched the speedometer climb to fifty-five, sixty, sixty-five. She looked around and saw that the black car had accelerated too.

"He's been behind us since we left Chicago," said Helm. "It looks like a new Packard sedan."

"Who could it be?" she asked. She couldn't see the driver, but she noticed the hood ornament—a fancy swooping eagle with wings spread skyward.

"Maybe it's someone who was watching Simon's apartment."

"Watching his apartment? Why?"

"Possibly waiting for someone to show up looking for Simon."

"But how could he know we were looking for him?"

"He might have planted someone in the apartment; maybe even the old woman told him; or perhaps he saw us through the window searching Simon's place."

"Or maybe it's just our imagination, Helm."

He glanced again in the rearview mirror. A tendon tightened along the stubble of beard that shadowed his solid jaw. "Let's find out. I'll take the next turnoff."

"Why? It's just a one-horse town. Logansburg. There's nothing there."

"Good. I'll drive through town and get back on the highway. If he's still behind us, we'll know we're in trouble."

Helm turned off the highway and drove down the narrow, cobbled Main Street where tire tracks made hachures in the muddy slush. He passed a Texaco station, Clackton's General Store, a Dairy Queen, and Sandusky's Bar and Grill, then followed the snowy street through an old residential neighborhood of large frame houses with steep roofs and screened porches. Smoke curled from red brick chimneys in smudgy charcoal spirals. After half a mile the cobbled street gave way to uneven pavement, and the rows of vintage houses dwindled to an occasional farmhouse nestled among sprawling cornfields or wheat fields.

Helm drove another mile and turned back onto the highway. "I think we lost him," he said with a note of relief, but as his gaze turned to the rearview mirror, he sighed heavily and said, "I spoke too soon. There he is. Still behind us."

"Maybe you should slow down and let him pass us," suggested Alice Marie.

He looked over at her. "I'm not sure that's a good idea."

"Try it, Helm. We have a long stretch of road ahead and no cars coming this way. He'll probably go right on by us."

Helm slowed his vehicle, allowing the black car to advance several car lengths. Alice Marie looked back. "Oh, Helm, he's almost riding our back bumper."

"No, he's coming around, passing us."

The shiny black automobile swerved into the oncoming lane and rode parallel with Helm's car, keeping pace, slowing when he slowed, accelerating when he sped up. "What is this bloke trying to prove?" said Helm through clenched teeth.

Alice Marie craned her neck to get a view of the driver, but she could only catch a glimpse of a shadowy figure in a dark overcoat and narrow-brimmed derby.

Helm gunned the engine and his Henry J shot ahead of the black vehicle, leaving it several car lengths behind. "What'd you do that for?" Alice Marie asked, bracing her gloved hand against the dashboard.

"I need you to do something," Helm told her in a confidential voice, as if afraid someone might hear.

"What?" she asked, puzzled.

"Open the glove compartment and take out the copy of my manuscript."

She did as he asked. "What do you want me to do with—?"

"Remove the contents of Simon's envelope and put the papers under your coat."

"Under my coat? Why?"

"Just do as I ask."

"With the baby there's hardly room."

"Do the best you can. Hurry."

Alice Marie unfastened the top buttons of her heavy wool coat, slipped the thick packet of papers inside, and buttoned the coat up to her collar.

"Now fill the manila envelope with my manuscript pages," said Helm. "Quickly. The man is gaining on us."

Alice Marie stuffed a handful of Helm's manuscript pages into the envelope until it resembled the original parcel. "Now what?"

"Seal it and leave it on the seat here between us."

"You think that man is going to try to get this envelope, don't you?"

"He won't if I can help it."

But already the black automobile was crossing into the oncoming lane and advancing on Helm's car. The two rode side by side for a minute along the empty highway; then the black vehicle veered suddenly into Helm's Henry J. Helm swerved before their fenders touched, but his tires skidded off the pavement into the slush along the soft shoulder.

"He's trying to kill us!" cried Alice Marie.

"Hold on!" shouted Helm.

She braced her legs and pressed her palms against the dashboard. The car slid several feet and the chassis shuddered as Helm wrenched the wheel. Within seconds they were back on solid pavement.

But already the black car was crossing the center divider, its bumper kissing their fender. The vehicles touched lightly, metal grazing metal, and rebounded. Helm accelerated, hitting seventy, seventy-five. His Henry J groaned with the effort.

The Packard was beside them again, edging them off the road. Helm clutched the wheel and came back, hugging the middle line. The Packard swerved, its heavy chrome bumper ramming Helm's fender with a dizzying, ear-splitting jolt. Helm cranked his steering wheel left against the impact, and for a moment the two cars raced fender to fender along the highway like conjoined twins.

"Dear God!" Alice Marie whispered. "My baby, take care of my baby!" It was the only prayer she could utter.

The Packard eased off momentarily, but was swiftly back for another attack. Engine roaring. Whitewalls screaming over slick pavement. Bumper glancing against bumper. The two vehicles caromed and ricocheted over the desolate highway like cast-iron model cars.

Helm was losing ground, his right wheels skidding off the shoulder, plowing through snowdrifts, the Packard crowding him toward the abutment. Alice Marie clutched Helm's arm and buried her face against his sturdy shoulder.

She felt another crashing impact, steel colliding against steel. A jarring, scraping noise ringing in her ears as Helm's Henry J careened off the road. For an instant the automobile seemed airborne; she had the sensation of slow-motion flight. She stared out the windshield and saw a flurry of snow and brambles and night sky assailing them, felt herself flying forward, the soft flesh of her body slamming against the rock-hard dashboard. Then: Raw cold. Shooting pain. A twisting sensation in her abdomen.

She was lying crumpled against the door, Helm's solid frame against her shoulder. The car was at an odd angle, on an incline, headed downward, tilted crazily to the right. The coldness was creeping through her veins, turning her hands and feet numb; or was she paralyzed? She was vaguely aware of a noise outside—a crunching sound in the snow. Footsteps. Someone coming. She groaned as someone forced open the car door. She was aware of a bulky figure leaning in on the driver's side; a gloved hand reached for something. She caught the familiar fragrance of Old Spice, the same aftershave Cary had worn. Then the figure drew back and she heard the sound of heavy boots retreating back to the highway.

"Helm," she rasped.

His hand touched her back. "Don't move until he's gone."

When they heard the Packard drive away, Helm stirred, drawing her close to him. "Are you hurt?"

She tried to shift her torso, but pain radiated through her body. "I can't move," she told him. "Oh, Helm, the baby—something's wrong!"

He moved his hand over her abdomen. "Is the baby coming?"

She moaned. "It can't be. It's not time yet. I still have two months!"

"Tell me what you're feeling."

"It hurts!"

"You'll be okay. I promise." He moved over to the door, stepped outside, and eased her down gently on the seat.

She gasped. Every move was excruciating.

Helm peeled off his overcoat and spread it over her. "Don't move. I'm going for help."

She clutched his hand. "Don't leave me."

He tucked his coat gently around her shoulders. "I'm just going to the highway to flag down a motorist. We need to get you to the hospital."

She hugged herself, the biting cold mixing with the waves of pain convulsing her belly. Her sense of time and place dimmed. She was vaguely aware of being alone, the night wind whistling through the cogs and joints of the automobile.

She was aware then of someone coming and gathering her into his arms and carrying her to another vehicle—not a car; some sort of truck, huge. She was riding in its cab, rumbling over the uneven highway, the smell of cigar smoke thick in the overly heated air. She sat curled like a wounded child in someone's comforting embrace. Yes, it was Helm's strong arms around her. It was Helm whispering words of endearment. *Be strong, my darling. Don't give up. I don't want to lose you.*

Was it truly Helm she heard? Speaking like a man in love? The question faded as another sensation overwhelmed her—constant viselike contractions hardening her belly with explosive force. "The baby," she whispered to Helm. "I can't lose my baby!"

"You're not going to lose this baby," he assured her. "Enough Jewish babies have died. This one is going to live!"

It seemed as if hours had passed before they arrived at Willowbrook General—the closest hospital available, according to the truck driver; yet perhaps it was only minutes; Alice Marie had lost all sense of time. Her entire concentration focused on the upheaval within her own body.

Again, Helm lifted her in his strong arms and laid her on a gurney. Hastily he removed the papers from under her coat and slipped them into his overcoat pocket. Hospital attendants covered her with blankets, then whisked her into the sprawling two-story concrete building, down one long corridor after another. At last they passed through wide double doors into a large room sparsely furnished with utilitarian tables and beds, its high, narrow windows covered with pull-down shades and walls painted dreary gray.

"Call Dr. Elrick," she told the attending physician, who introduced himself as Dr. Blarcom—a pale young man with deep-set gray eyes, sunken cheekbones, and a receding hairline.

"We have, Mrs. Rose," he said as he palpated her abdomen. "He'll be here momentarily."

Mrs. Rose. No one had called her that in months. She looked up at Helm standing at her bedside, his hand massaging her arm. The accident had left him with a cut above his brow and a bruise along his temple, but thank God, he was here with her!

She gasped as a sudden wrenching pain stabbed her low in her pelvis; it was as if the baby were ramming his head against the floor of her womb and splitting something apart. She seized the doctor's sleeve, her heart racing with fear. "I feel a—a terrible pressure. Is my baby okay?"

"That's what we're going to find out."

She forced herself to remain motionless as Dr. Blarcom listened with the stethoscope. "The baby's heart is good, Mrs. Rose, but it looks like you're in labor."

She blanched with alarm. "I can't be. The baby's not due for two months."

"The accident likely brought on premature contractions. We'll do all we can to make sure you deliver a strong, healthy infant." He looked up at Helm. "You can stay with your wife for now, Mr. Rose, but when she goes to delivery, you'll have to go to the father's waiting room down the hall."

"I'm not Mr. Rose," Helm explained evenly.

"You're not? Then who—?"

"And I'm not the father of this baby."

Dr. Blarcom looked bewildered. "Oh, well, I assumed—"

"And I'm not leaving Alice Marie," Helm went on with conviction, "until I know she and her baby are safe and sound."

"Well, obviously you can't accompany her to the delivery room."

"Please," begged Alice Marie, "let him stay with me."

"I assisted in many deliveries in Germany during the war," said Helm. "I helped deliver babies while bombs were dropping and buildings exploding."

Dr. Blarcom's pale eyes widened. "I'll let Dr. Elrick decide whether you remain with Mrs. Rose during her delivery, Mr.—"

"Schwarz. Helmut Schwarz."

"Well, Mr. Schwarz, it's highly irregular, but if Dr. Elrick gives permission for you to stay, you'll need to wash and put on a surgical gown." He patted Alice Marie's hand. "I'll go now and send in the nurse to prep you. I trust Mr. Schwarz is willing to be separated from you for a few minutes at least?"

When Dr. Blarcom had gone, Helm came around the bed and looked searchingly at Alice Marie. "I never should have taken you to Chicago!"

"You had no choice. I insisted."

"Are you sure you want me to stay?" he asked, smoothing her tangled hair back from her forehead.

"Yes. Don't leave me alone, please. I need you."

"Then I'll be here as long as you wish."

"I'm so afraid for my baby," she whispered, tears stinging her eyes.

He leaned over and kissed her forehead. "God will protect you and your little one."

"How can you be so sure?"

"It's my fervent prayer." He clasped her hand and his voice grew tender. "I'm not your baby's father, Alice Marie, but I carry him in my heart as if he were my own."

"Oh, Helm," she murmured. She wanted to say more, but the words wouldn't come.

The nurse—a tall, big-boned woman with prominent features and prudent brown eyes—appeared then and shooed Helm out of the room. Dr. Elrick arrived minutes later as the nurse was checking Alice Marie's contractions. "About three minutes apart, Doctor."

Doc Elrick sidled over, looking a bit like a wise and kindly walrus in green pajamas, his black eyes merry under his tent-like brows and his doughy double chins burrowing into his bountiful neck. He patted Alice

Marie's hand and said in a wry, fatherly voice, "Looks like this little tyke is in an awfully big hurry."

She could taste the anxiety at the back of her throat. "Will my baby be okay, Doc? He's got so much against him. First the polio, and now this accident."

"You just stay calm, Dear. We'll take good care of him."

"I want Helm with me."

"Well, if we give you ether, you won't know who's here."

"No ether! I want to be awake when my baby's born."

Doc Elrick nodded. "Holding back on the anesthesia is best with a premature birth. But I must warn you, it won't be easy."

"As long as Helm is—"

"He's already scrubbing."

She raised her head slightly. "How, how long before the baby comes?"

"Not long," he said after he had checked her. "You're completely effaced. The cervix is dilated at eight centimeters. We'll probably be taking you to delivery sometime in the next hour."

The next hour was a blur for Alice Marie as she rode the waves of one contraction after another. Just when one was behind her, the next surged in on its heels, even more powerful and consuming. Helm sat beside her, smoothing her hair, wiping perspiration from her face, moistening her lips with chips of ice, and through it all whispering words of comfort and encouragement.

At last even Helm's presence meant little; no one could go with her where she had to go. It was just Alice Marie and this cataclysm rocking her body; she had to go with it, catch its violent rhythm, keep from being submerged under its colossal deluge. She shrieked, "Help me! I've got to push!"

"Not yet," said Doc Elrick. "We're going to delivery now, Alice Marie."

As if on cue, attendants appeared and pushed her bed into another room more spartan and gloomy than the one before. They lifted her off her bed and placed her on a hard table with the thinnest of mattresses.

They placed her cold feet in stirrups and covered her trembling body with a sheet. "Helm?" she cried.

"I'm here, Alice Marie." He stood by her head, his hands caressing her clammy forehead, her tangled damp hair. "You're doing fine. It won't be long now."

Doc Elrick sat at the foot of the delivery table. "All right, Alice Marie, it's time to push."

She pushed and pushed again, exhausted, her breathing ragged, her mind drifting, near delirium.

Doc Elrick seemed to be speaking from a great distance. "You're crowning now, Alice Marie. One more push!"

One more push? What did he want? She was turning herself inside out and it wasn't working. She had nothing left to give.

"You can do it," Helm told her, his mouth beside her ear.

Yes, God help her, she was strong, a survivor like Helm. She gulped for air. Clenched her fists. Bore down fiercely. Every sinew of her body bombarded that intractable wall. She felt something give.

Doc Elrick uttered an exclamation of approval. "We've got his head, Alice Marie. One more good push and he's out."

The last push came easier. She could feel the solid angles of her baby as he emerged from the birth canal.

"It's a boy!" said Doc Elrick. "Born at 12:53 A.M. Sunday's child."

Alice Marie caught a glimpse of a tiny, glistening, bluish-white body. She heard a soft mewing sound and then a plaintive cry.

"Is he okay?" she cried.

"He's a small one. Under five pounds, I'd say." Doc handed the baby to a nurse, who whisked him away, then brought him back moments later wrapped in a small flannel blanket. She placed the bundle in Alice Marie's arms.

She drew back the blanket and gazed at the purplish, pinched face of her son. "Oh, he's so little!"

"He's beautiful," said Helm, bending close. "Just like his mother."

She managed a smile. "Are you kidding? He looks like a little old man!"

"All right, a very handsome little old man."

Alice Marie gazed up at Helm. "I couldn't have gone through this without you."

"I wouldn't have been anywhere but here with you."

"Do you want to hold him?"

He scooped the bundled infant up in his arms and rocked him gently. "He's as light as a mother's kiss."

"We'd better get the lad into his heated bassinet," said the nurse, taking him from Helm. She eyed the baby closely and said, "Doctor, his respirations are shallow. He's turning blue."

The doctor's voice was edged with alarm. "Let's check his nose and throat for mucus and get him into the incubator. Now!"

Alice Marie raised herself up on one elbow. "Doc, is my baby okay? Tell me, Doctor! Please! Dear God in heaven, don't let him die!"

The final frosty days of February were filled with a bittersweet ache that consumed Alice Marie. The days were bitter as she waited to see whether her baby would survive; but they were also unexpectedly sweet as Helm accompanied her to the premature nursery to sit by the incubator, hold her hand, and pray for her child's healing.

During the ten days she remained a patient at Willowbrook General, Helm came every afternoon and walked with her down the hall to that sterile, white room with its rows of incubators, heated cribs, and bassinets. She was thankful to have him beside her; how else could she face seeing her child in his lonely Isolette in that bleak, cheerless room? It was nothing like a healthy baby's nursery, nothing like the nursery she had at home with teddy bears and dolls everywhere, a rocking chair by the window, and painted animals on the wall.

Perhaps the staff was afraid to make this nursery sunny and bright because these babies hovered so tenuously between life and death. The room's blank, anonymous walls offered no promises so that no promises would have to be broken. One wall held utility shelves filled with cotton shirts and diapers, flannelette nightgowns, receiving blankets, towels, and rubber crib pads. Against the opposite wall, a long laminated table held bottle warmers, sterilizers, baby scales, gauze bands, cotton balls, and assorted bottles and jars of creams, powders, and oils. Everything neat and in order. Nothing frivolous or playful for these babies who might never have a chance to play.

And that was the question that weighed on Alice Marie's mind every hour while she sat watching her son's frail chest rise and fall as he gasped for air. Would he ever run and play like other children? Would she experience the ordinary concerns of other mothers—whether her son wore his galoshes to school, or skinned his knee, or came home late for dinner? Such concerns would be precious gifts compared with this constant, gnawing fear that this child who had not yet tasted life might succumb so easily to death.

And yet her son was a fighter. Everyone said so—the doctors, the nurses, even other parents who came to stand watch over their own ailing infants. Her son was a fighter just like his namesake. Chilton Reed Rose—named after Alice Marie's brother who had died at Pearl Harbor—was five pounds of plucky, feisty boy. And what a fight he had on his hands—to develop strong lungs so he could breathe on his own, healthy lungs that would withstand the constant threat of infection and pneumonia.

It grieved Alice Marie's heart to watch her tiny son struggle so valiantly. She was his mother, and yet there was so little she could do to help him. At least she was able to supply the breast milk the nurses fed him every two hours through a feeding tube or medicine dropper. She who had never considered herself motherly was sustaining her son with nourishment from her own body.

And every day she watched as a nurse slipped her hands into the round openings of the incubator and rubbed warm oil on her baby's translucent skin. Sometimes his little puckered face would turn in Alice Marie's direction and his rosebud mouth would open as if to speak, but only a faint mewling sound would emerge; yet she was sure his dark gray eyes were trying to focus on her.

"Mommy's here," she would croon, pressing her palm against the glass of his Isolette. "Mommy's here, my sweet little Chip. Mommy's right here."

"And your Uncle Helmut is here too," Helm would declare, tapping the incubator with his forefinger. "You hurry up and grow strong so we can play baseball together."

Helm would sit with her and chat amiably, exchanging simple pleasantries; he would carry on long, one-sided conversations with tiny Chilton; and he would hold Alice Marie's hand and pray aloud for her baby. Every day she realized she was depending more and more on Helm's quiet strength and warm compassion.

One afternoon she found herself reminiscing with him about her brother, Chip. "Did you know, Helm, the December my brother died he was supposed to marry Knowl's sister, Catherine? She was already carrying his child. Little Jenny. He never even knew he was going to be a father. I promised myself, if I ever had a son, I'd name him after Chip, so there would be someone to carry on his name." She paused and brushed a tear from her cheek. "Ironic, isn't it? I don't even know if my baby will live long enough to carry on Chip's name."

"He will," said Helm, squeezing her hand. "I am convinced God wants your baby to live a long, productive life."

She smiled through her tears. "You always give me hope." She leaned toward the incubator, watching her son's mouth make feeble sucking motions as he lay in a dreamless slumber. She glanced back at Helm. "Do you know how my brother got the name Chip?"

He smiled. "No, but I'm sure you will tell me."

"Well, you see, my mother named him Chilton. She thought it was such a regal name. Stalwart and noble as a king. But my dad called him Chip. He said it was because his son was a chip off the old block. And that's how I always thought of Chip—strong and handsome and honorable just like my father. And that's how I want my son to be."

"I am curious about something," said Helm gently. "Why didn't you name your baby after your husband?"

"After Cary?" She thought a moment. "I don't know. I suppose it would have been the right thing to do, wouldn't it? I'll tell Chip about his father, of course. I want him to know what Cary was like." She lapsed into another silence, then said quietly, "It's strange, Helm. I don't know if I can explain it. I loved Cary *in spite* of what he was, not *because* of what he was. I suppose that sounds horrible, but I don't know how else to say it."

"I think you've expressed yourself quite well."

"But there's more," she said, the insights coming now as quickly as she could say them. "I'm no longer the same person who fell in love with Cary Rose. I don't look at life the same way. I'm not the same woman; I hardly remember her." She stared at Helm as if the truth were dawning for the first time. "It's true. I don't want to be the woman I was with Cary."

Other thoughts came with a clarity that startled her, but she held back, silent, embarrassed, wondering what Helm would think if he knew. *I want to be the woman I am when I'm with you, Helmut Schwarz. You bring out the best in me. You tap into qualities I never knew I could possess. You make me feel alive, and valued, and cherished in a way no man has ever made me feel.*

"You look as if you're about to say something else," Helm said, his dark eyes twinkling with curiosity.

She felt the color rise in her face. "Yes, I was thinking something. I'll tell you someday, but not now."

"I'll hold you to that promise."

She studied his solid, deeply etched features, the way lights and shadows played on his face, revealing wonderful subtleties of expression. "We've talked about my marriage to Cary," she said engagingly, "but why haven't you ever talked about the women you've loved?"

He sat back and made a bemused sound low in his throat. "The women I've loved? Now if that isn't a leading question!"

"I know there was someone special. I can see it in your eyes. The girl you were promised to during the war. But you don't want to talk about her, do you?"

He sat forward on the spindle-backed chair and cracked the knuckles of one hand, then the other. "There's not much to say."

"Really?" She pushed a long, flaxen curl behind one ear and flashed an inviting smile. "Tell me about her, Helm, please."

He grimaced, still massaging his knuckles. "You're a persistent lass, aren't you?"

"Isn't that what you like about me? I don't give up."

He met her gaze. "Neither do I. And, yes, there was a girl. A long time ago. I met her in Munich during the war. She was with the German resistance movement. We didn't have much time together, but we promised each other we would be together after the war. If it had been another time, another place, I would have married her."

"What was her name?"

"Eva Schiller."

"What happened to her?"

He lowered his gaze and the muscles in his face tensed, his furrowed brows shadowing his eyes. "She died at Bergen-Belsen six weeks before the war ended."

Alice Marie reached over and clasped Helm's hand. "I'm sorry. You lost so much. I don't know how you can be so strong."

He shook his head. "I am not strong. God is strong. I lean on Him."

She smiled wistfully. "That's what I'm trying to do too. But it's hard giving up your expectations and trusting Him. Don't you see, Helm? I'm afraid to open my hands and give everything to Him."

He caressed her slim hand between his rough, warm palms. "My dear girl, when I stood at the gates of Auschwitz after the war, I learned a lesson that God teaches me over and over again. When you come to the place where He is all you have, you realize that He is all you need."

She blinked back sudden tears. "For most of my life I was convinced I had to keep taking and taking or I would lose everything I had. But the more I took, the emptier I felt. Now I'm beginning to understand why."

"And now you are discovering another mystery," he said quietly, his warm eyes searching hers. "The more you give up, the more you gain."

She averted her gaze. "Are you saying I should be willing to let God take my baby?"

"No, dear heart. No! I am only saying there is an excitement, a delicious sense of risk, an electrifying joy, in trusting God so fully that you open your hands wide to Him, knowing He will do nothing that is not for your good."

"I wish I could be like you that way," she said, her hand still warm between his palms.

"I am not that man yet," he confessed. "But at times I have stumbled upon His grace and caught a glimpse of what He is capable of doing when I give up all to Him."

"I want to live like that, with that kind of faith," she said. "Perhaps someday . . ." Her words drifted off and they were silent for several minutes.

After a while he released her hand and glanced at his watch. "I should get home to Papa. He's cooking tonight. He'll be up to his elbows in schnitzel."

"How has he been?" she asked. "I've been so caught up in my life here at the hospital and in this nursery, I forget life continues on beyond these walls."

"Papa's fine," he replied. "Annie has been staying with him while I've been here visiting you. I don't like to leave him alone, you know."

"Of course not. I'll be sure to thank Annie the next time she comes to visit me. I couldn't have gotten through these days without all of you, especially you, Helm."

"Yes, you could; you are stronger than you think. But I hope my presence has made these days more tolerable."

"It has." She fingered the lace sleeve of her long, blue silk dressing gown. "Helm, there is something else we haven't talked about. I'm sure you've avoided the subject for my sake, but I'm feeling stronger now, and we need to talk about it."

He gazed at her. "You sound so serious."

"You know what I mean. The accident."

"If you're wondering about my automobile, I'm happy to tell you the damage wasn't serious. I've already had it repaired. My Henry J is as good as new."

"Did you report the accident to the police?"

"No, I don't want them involved. Besides, what could they do? It was a hit-and-run. There must be a hundred black Packards on the streets just like the one that hit us."

"It's not just the accident, Helm. What about the packet your friend Simon left you—the papers the man in the black car thought he retrieved that night?"

Helm's expression sobered, the tendons along his jaw tightening. "Don't worry. I'm taking care of things."

"What things?"

He drew close, his voice a whisper. "I don't want you involved in this any further, Alice Marie. I was foolish to take you with me to Chicago. That trip almost cost you your baby's life. It could have cost your life as well."

She stared hard at him. "You don't want me involved because you think our lives are still in danger. That's it, isn't it?"

He glanced around, as if scouting for eavesdroppers. He looked back at her, his gaze riveting. "I don't know that we're in danger, but I do know that someone wanted those papers, and he may try again."

"Where are the papers?"

"They're safe. I sewed them into the lining of my overcoat."

"How clever. And surely you've looked at them. Studied them. Will they help you locate your father's guard?"

He shifted restlessly in the spindle-backed chair. "The papers are incomplete, Alice Marie," he said under his breath. "They are lists of German names—war criminals, I'm sure—with biographical information about each one, plus additional notes in some sort of code. There must be a matching set of papers that reveals their American aliases and current addresses. I think the man who ran us off the road has that matching information and wants these papers back before someone deciphers the code. I think if I could get my hands on his papers I would have the evidence I need to send these men back to Germany to stand trial."

She moistened her lips, feeling a chill of uneasiness. "You think this is a significant find, don't you, Helm?"

"These papers were important enough for Simon Golding to die for—and we almost died as well."

"I think you should go to the authorities now," she urged.

"What good would it do? Without the matching papers we have no real proof of anything."

"You have the names of Nazis who have escaped to America to start new lives. You can begin with that."

He nodded. "I am already doing some investigating. I have contacted several colleagues in Chicago, Detroit, and New York. They may turn up something. Beyond that, my dear girl, the subject is closed. I want you to forget all of this mysterious intrigue and concentrate only on your baby."

She smiled. "Yes, Sir, Mr. Schwarz."

He returned the smile. "Besides, I think your son wants some attention from his mother."

"My darling Chip?" She leaned over beside the incubator and smiled at her son. Chilton Reed Rose was kicking his spindly legs and making a soft whining sound. He looked beautiful to her. His little round face was ruddy with the effort of crying and his plum-colored eyes seemed to be seeking her out. She longed to reach into the Isolette and touch his fine, downy black hair and hold his tiny, grasping fingers.

"I think my baby's getting stronger," she told Helm. "Look how he's kicking. He's eager to get out of his little glass cage and go home with Mommy."

Helm gave her a long, searching look that prompted a tickle under her ribs. Surely she was reading him wrong—it was her own secret desire she perceived, not his—but those sable-brown eyes seemed to be saying, *Wouldn't it be perfect if the three of us were going home together?*

21

On Tuesday, March 4, 1952, ten days after her baby's premature birth, Alice Marie was released from the hospital—without her son. Little Chip—tiny and delicate and precious as a porcelain doll—had to remain in his incubator until he could breathe on his own. But the doctors wouldn't tell Alice Marie when that might be—and privately she wondered if her son would ever come home.

Helm came to pick her up at the hospital that cold, blustery morning. Outside her window skeletal trees swayed and bent in the wind and dead leaves rustled in skittish whirligigs over the frozen ground. Inside, she felt as frozen as that frigid landscape, her hands clammy, her emotions on ice. She was sitting on the side of her bed wearing a fleecy lambswool sweater and a pleated mid-calf skirt Annie had brought her. She wanted to go home, but she didn't want to go. How could she leave without her son?

Just when she was about to tell the nurse she couldn't possibly leave yet, Helm walked in with a beaming smile and winter's kiss in his ruddy cheeks. He was wearing his overcoat, a wool scarf, and his black derby, and in his arms he carried a dozen long-stem red roses, which he placed gallantly in her arms.

"Oh, Helm, where on earth did you find these?" she cried, touching one soft, velvet-red petal.

"It wasn't easy," he admitted, tossing his hat on the bedside table and leaning over to kiss her forehead. "But it was worth every penny just to see your eyes light up."

"They're beautiful! Thank you." As she turned her face up to his, his lips moved from her forehead to her mouth, but only for a moment. His kiss was as light and soft as the velvet rose petal and left her yearning for more.

He sat down in the armchair by the bed. "Are you okay? The doctor hasn't changed his mind about letting you go home, has he?"

She shook her head. "No. It's just—" Her voice wavered.

He nodded. "You're going home without your baby."

She reached for a tissue and dabbed her eyes. "I feel so empty inside, as if everything that mattered has been torn from me. My arms ache to hold my son. It's a physical ache, Helm. I feel as if I'm leaving my soul behind. How can I leave him? What kind of mother forsakes her child?"

He took her hand. "You're not forsaking him, Alice Marie. I'll drive you over here to see him twice a day if you wish."

"I can't ask you to do that."

"You're not asking. I'm volunteering."

"But with your book coming out soon, Knowl must have your schedule filled with interviews and publicity campaigns."

"I don't care if he has me booked in Alaska. Chip comes first."

"You mean that, don't you?"

"I always say what I mean." He stood up. "Now, do you have a suitcase for me to carry?"

"Over by the dresser. And there's a basket of diapers and baby supplies, compliments of the hospital."

Helm was halfway across the room when Doc Elrick trundled in, the buttons of his tweed suit straining against his ample girth, his capacious grin rippling over the folds of his thick jowls. "Well, looks like my number one patient is ready to go home," he said in a jolly, resounding voice.

Alice Marie shook her head. "No, Doc. I'm not ready."

He raised one bristly eyebrow and said in jest, "You mean the hospital food is that good?"

"You know what I mean. How can I leave my baby? Even though I couldn't hold him, it was comforting knowing he was just down the hall."

Doc massaged one of his chin rolls. "I had a feeling you might be thinking that way. That's why I stopped by the nursery just now."

Alice Marie's fingers tightened around the prickly, tissue-wrapped stems of her bouquet. "Is Chip okay?"

"Oh, my yes. A fine lad. Gaining quite nicely. An ounce or two a day. In fact, I talked with the pediatrician and he's pleased with the boy's progress. He tells me your son is breathing on his own for short periods of time and should be weaned from the incubator soon. I would guess, barring any unforeseen complications, your son should be able to go home in a few weeks."

"You're sure, Doc?" Tears rolled down Alice Marie's cheeks. She stood, dropping the roses on the bed, and went into Helm's arms. "Thank God! Oh, thank God!"

Doc Elrick gave her shoulder a paternal squeeze. "I'll go tell the nurse to bring the wheelchair. Our patients always ride out to their automobiles in grand style."

Alice Marie hardly heard the doctor leave the room. She could think only of her baby getting well and the delicious warmth she felt sharing her joy with Helm. She looked at him and saw tears in his eyes too. "My son's going to be okay," she whispered, laughing and crying at once. "Think of it! I'll get to take my baby home!"

Helm swung her around in his arms. "I told you so!"

"I'll never doubt you again." She pressed her cheek against his chest. His embrace tightened. She felt safe and protected in the solid warmth of his arms. Without thinking, she looked at him and said, "I love you so much."

"I love you too," he said.

His mouth sought hers and it was as if a barrier had broken, unleashing long pent-up emotions; love, joy, grief, and desire commingled in one long, impassioned kiss.

Afterward he held her for a long while, neither of them speaking. As she felt his tears spilling onto her hair, she thought, *This is the man I was born to love. At last I've found him!*

Finally he released her and held her at arm's length, his mahogany eyes still brimming with emotion. "I won't say I'm sorry for what just happened," he told her quietly, "because I'm not. I have wanted to kiss you like that for so long. But our paths have crossed for only a short time, Alice Marie, and our destinies will take us to very different places. Me to Israel, you to Chicago. We must not let our feelings make it even more difficult for that unhappy day when we must part."

She stared at him as if not quite comprehending his words. They had just confessed their love for each other, and now in a handful of hurtful phrases he was taking it all back, dashing her hopes with his callous, shortsighted reasoning.

She drew away from him, her mind reeling. She had been about to promise him her heart, her love, her life, but he wasn't asking for promises; he was telling her they would never be more than friends. She brushed impatiently at her tears and forced a smile in place before turning to face him. "Don't sound so gloomy, Helm," she said, summoning a lighthearted tone. "And don't mistake gratitude and friendship for passion. I know we're just friends. Surely you don't think I expect anything more."

A shadow of disappointment passed over his darkly lashed eyes, but he said only, "I'm glad we have an understanding." Minutes later, when they were both settled in Helm's Henry J and heading home to Honeysuckle Lane, his mood turned merry again. "My father and I have a surprise for you," he said with a hint of mystery. "A gift for you and your baby."

"Where is it?" she asked, too brightly.

"At my house. We can stop by and pick it up, if you're not too tired."

"All right. And I can say hello to your father."

"Yes, he'll like that." Helm turned right at the next intersection and headed north toward his brownstone apartment. "Papa's eager to see you again. You and your baby are all he speaks of lately."

"Is Annie staying with him today?"

"No, she was busy with little Maggie, so I left Papa alone. I don't like doing that, but I knew I wouldn't be gone long. And he seems stronger lately, less confused."

Light flurries were falling when Helm pulled into the driveway beside the venerable, old two-story brownstone. He held Alice Marie's arm as they walked gingerly through the fresh snow to the back entrance and ascended the slippery narrow pine stairs. Helm was about to put his key in the lock when he noticed the door was ajar. He cast her a puzzled sidelong glance and stepped inside. Alice Marie followed.

"Why would your father leave the door open?" she asked, but even as she spoke her eyes swept over a living room in shambles—tables and chairs overturned, the Tiffany lamp broken on the floor, papers spilling out of the small writing desk and covering the room like confetti. "Oh, no!" she cried, the sour, galling taste of horror rising in her throat.

Helm ran across the room and down the hall. "Papa! Papa, where are you?"

She hurried after him, sidestepping the debris. Helm shoved open his father's door and they burst inside. The furnishings in this room, too, were mangled and dismantled—dresser drawers hanging out, blankets ripped from the bed, clothing in disarray, curios, vases, books, shoes, and personal effects scattered everywhere.

"Papa!" Helm shouted.

Then they saw him—a crumpled, trembling, disheveled figure sitting in the corner on the floor behind the bureau. Sweat glistened on his high, round forehead, his thick brush of gray hair was mussed, and his deep-set eyes stared unseeing into the distance, glittering with an unspeakable vision.

Helm bent down and embraced his father, cradling him in his arms like a child until his trembling subsided. Then gently he lifted him up and helped him onto the bed. "Papa, are you hurt? Can you hear me, Papa? It's me. Your son Helmut." When the old man didn't reply, Helm spoke to him in German. Gerhart made a low, moaning sound that seemed to erupt from some secret place in his soul, but he remained slumped over, arms useless at his sides, his expression dazed.

"I'll call someone," said Alice Marie. "Who? Doc Elrick? The police?"

"No, wait," said Helm. He sat down on the bed, gripped his father's shoulders, and looked him full in the face. "Papa, who was here? Who did this?"

The old man shook his head and the moaning became louder, more tormented. Alice Marie brought Gerhart a glass of water, which he sipped, then pushed away. She found a washcloth in the bathroom, ran warm water over it, and gently bathed his face. He seemed to rally a bit and his frightened eyes focused on her. "Liebschen," he murmured, his shaky fingers reaching out to her. He said something in German and Helm responded, their voices urgent and strained.

"What is he saying?" she asked.

"He says someone was here looking for something. Papa was not harmed, only shoved a little, knocked to the floor."

"Who was here?" cried Alice Marie. "Was it—it couldn't have been— the man in the black car?"

Helm shook his head. "No. He says—Deiter Weyandt. The Nazi guard from the death camp at Auschwitz."

"But that's impossible, isn't it?"

"That Nazi thug may be living somewhere in this country," Helm agreed, "perhaps even here in the Midwest. But for him to come to this very house where my father lives? Unlikely. But for my father, any intruder might resurrect images of that vicious butcher-guard, Weyandt."

She searched his eyes. "Then you do think it was the man in the black car who broke in?"

"Who else? He was obviously looking for these papers." Helm patted the right pocket of his overcoat. "Did he think I would be foolish enough to leave them lying around?"

"How could he have known where to find you?"

Helm heaved a sigh. "My manuscript pages. My name and address were on them."

"Of course."

"The man must have been watching my house since the accident, but someone was always here, Annie or Anna or me. Maybe he didn't even know about my father being here. I'll have to find another place to hide these documents. He'll figure if they weren't here that I have them."

"You've got to go to the police, Helm. Your life is in danger."

"And what can they do, except to perform a cursory investigation and then dismiss the case as a minor break-in and vandalism? I doubt anything was taken."

"You must tell them about Simon Golding and this whole operation to turn Nazis into ordinary American citizens."

"I have no proof without the other half of these lists."

"Then we're back where we started." She shook her head in dismay and sat down on the bed beside Gerhart Schwarz. She slipped her arm around him and placed her head on his shoulder. "Are you feeling better, Papa?" she asked.

He made a sniffling sound and reached out, fumbling for her hand. "The baby," he murmured. "How is the baby?"

"Growing stronger, Papa. He will come home soon, and I will bring him to see you."

The old man looked at her, his crinkly eyes misting. "Ja, es gut. Danke schon, Liebe."

"You're welcome, Papa." She looked at Helm. "Let's take him to my house to rest. I'll call Doc Elrick to come check him over. Then you and I can come back here and clean up."

"We'll take him to your house, but no work for you, dear girl. You just got out of the hospital."

She nodded. She did feel suddenly weary and a bit weak in the knees.

"I've got to check on something before we go," said Helm. "I hope it survived the attack." He left the room and was back moments later carrying a polished, hand-carved oak cradle in his arms. He set it on the floor beside Alice Marie. "This is for your son. Papa made it. He's been working on it for months. I helped a little, but he's the one who carved all the intricate figures and designs."

Alice Marie gazed dumbfounded at the handsome crib, its deep, rich grain embellished with tiny angels and frolicking lambs, its craftsmanship superb. "It's the most beautiful thing I've ever seen! Thank you, Papa. Thank you, Helm. I'll treasure this always." She gave Helm a quick kiss on the cheek, then gave Papa a warm embrace. "I'll always love you," she whispered. "You're the father I haven't had in so many years."

He patted her cheek, his glistening eyes tender, his heavy jowls quivering. "Ja, es gut." Then his expression turned solemn, shaggy brows knitting together over flashing, umber-brown eyes. "Now you tell Helmut—you tell my son—I see Deiter here. In this room. Only Deiter. No mistake. I know him better than I know my own face. Deiter Weyandt was here!"

22

It was like a homecoming on Honeysuckle Lane when Alice Marie arrived at the old homestead with Helm and Papa Schwarz. For a few moments she was so caught up in the sweet, warm confusion of greeting everybody and exchanging hugs and kisses with Mama, Annie, Knowl, and little Maggie that she forgot the pain of coming home without her baby. But only for a moment, and then the bitter reality struck afresh. She was home now, but her son was still in the hospital struggling to get well. Even as the tears sprang to her eyes, she vowed to keep smiling for the sake of her family.

"How's our darling little Chilton?" Mama asked, a catch in her voice, her pale blue eyes glistening with unshed tears.

"He's doing better, Mama. Doc says if he keeps improving he'll come home in a few weeks. Are you glad I named him after Chip, Mama?"

Her mother cupped Alice Marie's face in her palms. "Glory be, he's your brother's namesake! Nothing could make me happier."

"Chip would have loved him, Mama. He's so tiny, but he's a regular little trooper, fighting so hard to get strong."

"I'm proud of him, and proud of you too," said Mama, choking up. She released Alice Marie and looked around, the tears escaping now. "Come, everyone, let's go to the parlor. I've got tea and warm biscuits waiting." Mother and daughter linked arms as they walked down the hall. "You look wonderful," Mama told her as they entered the parlor. "Look at you, Daughter. You've already got back your figure!"

"It was the ten days of hospital food that did it, Mama. If I'd had your home cooking I'd still be, uh, pleasantly plump."

"You do look grand," said Knowl, taking the wing chair by the fireplace. "Being a mother agrees with you."

She sat down on the love seat with Helm. "I just wish my son was here so I could start acting like a mother." A wellspring of tears caught her by surprise. Helm handed her his handkerchief. "I promised myself I wouldn't cry," she said between sobs. "I should be happy. Like I said, Doc says Chip is doing better. But he's so tiny and helpless. And there could still be complications—infection, pneumonia, who knows what all!"

Annie came over and put her arms around Alice Marie and hugged her again. "I know it's hard not having your baby with you. But he'll be home before you know it. And until then I'll go with you every day to visit him."

Mama turned to Helm's father who had settled into the overstuffed armchair by the window. "It was so nice of you and your son to bring Alice Marie home, Mr. Schwarz. Is there anything I can get you? You look a little peaked."

Alice Marie and Helm exchanged solemn glances and Helm said, "There's something you all should know. Someone broke into my apartment today and messed things up a bit. Papa's still quite shaken over it."

"Goodness gracious!" Mama went over to Gerhart and put her hand on his arm. "Are you all right, Mr. Schwarz? Would you like to go lie down?"

"Nein, nein, Frau Reed. I am gut. Danke."

"Did you call the police, Helm?" asked Knowl.

"No, not yet. I wanted to get Alice Marie and Papa out of there as soon as possible."

"Yes, that was wise." Knowl turned and paced the floor, his gaze lowered, his expression troubled. "I never imagined we'd see this kind of violent reaction to your book, Helm. Sure, we've had crackpots writing nasty letters and even vandalizing the publishing house, but for someone to break into your house like this!"

Helm ran his fingers through his thick, chestnut hair. "I'm as stunned as you are, Knowl. But who knows? It could have been a random act, unrelated to my book. We may never have the answer." He looked from Knowl to Anna. "But for now I'm wondering if my father could stay here for a day or two, until I get the place cleaned up?"

"Of course," said Knowl.

"Of course," echoed Mama. "Your papa can stay as long as he wishes. I'll enjoy his company." She looked at Gerhart, the color rising in her cheeks. "Do you like to play Chinese checkers, Mr. Schwarz? And, if you enjoy music, we could play Wagner and Strauss on my old Victrola."

Gerhart grinned, his onyx-black eyes brightening in his leathery face. "Ja, gut! Do you play Benny Goodman also?"

Knowl turned to Helm and said, "I'll be glad to go over and help you get things back in order at your apartment. And you can tell me the whole story of what happened."

"I will, Knowl. In time," said Helm. "But first I have something to bring in for the baby." He looked at Alice Marie. "Do you want me to take the cradle up to the nursery?"

"No, take it to my room. The rosebud room. That's where Chip will sleep until he's big enough for the crib."

She went upstairs with Helm to show him just where to place the cradle. "Here by the dormer window so he'll have the warm sunlight streaming in on him. They say sunlight is good for babies."

Helm set the cradle down and she brought a small eiderdown quilt from the dresser, knelt down, and laid it in the tiny bed.

Helm gave her a wistful smile. "You look beautiful kneeling there, like an angel."

She ran her hand fondly over the quilt, reminiscing. "My Grandmother Alma made this quilt. It was my father's, and then mine when I was a baby. I didn't think I'd ever get to use it. I never considered myself the motherly type. But now—oh, Helm, I just pray—!"

"I know." He took her hands and lifted her to her feet. "Your son will enjoy his quilt and his new cradle. I promise."

She searched his eyes. "I wish I had your faith."

"You do," he whispered, "and you have a house full of love. I feel it in this very room. Generations of love are stored here in these charming, timeworn walls. Am I right?"

She gazed around her familiar childhood room, seeing it through Helm's eyes—its homey Victorian furnishings and canopy bed, her wicker rocking chair beside the cedar hope chest, Papa Reed's antique writing desk, and above it the curio shelf with Annie's storybook dolls. And, of course, the delicate rosebud wallpaper graced with Catherine's exquisite watercolors in their hand-carved frames.

"I do feel it," she admitted, "the love and memories of generations of Reeds—and Herricks—who lived in this room. Anyone who has ever had this room has loved it and found healing here."

"Then it's the perfect place for your son," said Helm. "The healing comes from the God who watches over you here."

She smiled up at him. "You're right, of course. That's the real secret. God is here."

Helm turned and examined one of the watercolors—a bouquet of lush purple lilacs in a milk glass vase. "Knowl's sister is a very talented artist."

"Yes, she is. The older I get, the more I appreciate Catherine's work." Alice Marie ran her fingertips over the edge of the frame. "This painting has hung here for years. It's a permanent fixture." She paused and looked suddenly at Helm. "I have an idea. You said you need a place to hide Simon Golding's papers. Why not here?"

He looked at her. "Here? Where?"

"In this room. Behind Catherine's painting."

He shook his head. "No. That wouldn't work. I wouldn't consider risking your safety and Chip's."

"You wouldn't be. No one would suspect this room." Alice Marie lifted the painting off the wall and turned it around. "Look, Helm. There's a cardboard backing. You can remove it and slip the pages between the painting and the mat. No one would think to look for them there."

Helm was silent a moment. When he spoke, an undercurrent of excitement animated his voice. "You're right. It could work."

"Of course it could," she agreed, her own excitement rising. "This house—the rosebud room—would be the last place anyone would expect to find those documents."

He took the painting and examined the back. "Are you sure about this, Alice Marie? You know I wouldn't do anything to put you or your family in danger."

"We won't be in danger, Helm, because, like I said, no one will suspect Simon's notes are here. Not even my family will know." She drew close to him. "I realize how important these documents are to you. Where else can you put them?"

He nodded. "I'll do it, but only until I find a better hiding place—or until I find the matching pages to provide the evidence I need for the authorities." He set the painting face down on the bed. "I'll need some tools—a hammer, screwdriver."

"I'll get them."

After Helm had loosened the frame's backing, he ripped open the lining of his overcoat and removed the packet of papers. He held them up to Alice Marie. "One day—God willing—these documents may help bring many war criminals to justice."

"Wait, Helm," she said, touching the small bundle. "Before you put them in the painting, may I see what we're hiding?"

He frowned. "It would be better—safer—for you to remain uninformed. That's why I haven't told Knowl or Annie or anyone else what I've uncovered."

"I agree that the fewer who know, the better. But I've already shared so much of this with you, Helm. I feel as if your battle is my battle, your cause, my cause. But I need to know what we're dealing with—and who we're looking for."

"All right." He spread the papers out on the desk. "Here we have copies of surveillance photographs, false citizenship papers, passports, and identity cards of S.S. officers. They were Hitler's right hand, the elite guard of the Nazi party who did all the dirty work. You see beside each name some sort of code. I believe that code reveals their new American identities and where they are living now."

She shivered. "It's frightening to think of those vile men assuming the lives of ordinary American citizens."

"It's a blasphemy against God and all that is good," said Helm. He handed her several sheets written in a small, uneven script. "These pages give accounts of Nazi criminals who escaped after the war. They turned for help to their families and friends, to former comrades, or secret networks of ex-Nazis, and even to the church. Many escaped over the Austrian Alps and hid in the vast woodlands or in remote villages, in farmhouses and barns. Most deplorable, they financed their escape by confiscating gold, money, and jewels from Jews sentenced to the death camps."

Alice Marie placed a consoling hand on Helm's arm. "How can you bear to read these papers when they open such painful wounds?"

"I do it because it is only by remembering the past that we can safeguard the future. If people forget, then hatred will grow again in the hearts of tomorrow's children."

She nodded, her hand still caressing his arm. "You are so wise." After a moment she turned her attention back to the finely scripted pages. "Does it say where the Nazis settled?"

"Everywhere. Europe, South America, Australia, Canada, the United States. According to these documents, many have found safe havens in German communities in Argentina, Bolivia, Paraguay, and Brazil. Argentina's President Juan Peron actually welcomes Nazis to his country."

He handed her another document. "This is perhaps the most troubling. It tells of fugitive Nazi officers being recruited by the U.S. Army Intelligence Corps for espionage purposes. Even as we speak, Nazis are helping the American government uncover Soviet secrets."

She shook her head. "Surely our government wouldn't stoop to such devious tactics."

"It's all here in these secret police files. Apparently our country is more concerned these days with the threats of Communism, the Cold War, and the atom bomb than with bringing Nazis to justice."

She sat down on the bed. "This whole ghastly thing—it's more far-reaching than I ever imagined. What can we do?"

He sat down beside her. "When I track down the code-breakers to these documents I'll turn them over to the United States Department of Justice and pray that they'll take action. I'll also make a lot of noise to the press to make sure the State Department doesn't just look the other way."

"You think the State Department would ignore such evidence?"

A tendon in Helm's jaw tightened. "They did in the past. During the war they knew about the genocide of the Jews and chose to ignore it. They made the immigration of Jews to America a bureaucratic nightmare with all their red tape. Jews needed financial sponsors, and they were extremely hard to find. Immigration quotas were strict, the rules inflexible. It didn't have to be that way. I know this much—if I could have brought my relatives to this country, they would be alive today."

"That's such heavy burden to carry, Helm. I wish I knew what to say."

A faint smile softened the smoldering rage in his eyes. "I don't wish to burden you with these things, dear girl, especially when you've just gotten home from the hospital. Anti-Semitism has been around for a long time, and I suppose it will exist as long as we Jews survive. But God is with us, even if we are not always with Him. For now I am determined to bring about a small measure of justice for my people."

She looked earnestly at him. "About these papers—do you really believe you'll uncover the rest of the evidence you need?"

He patted her hand. "I won't stop until I do." He stood, gathered up the documents, and slipped them into a plain manila folder, then tucked the folder between the painting and the cardboard backing. Then he carefully hammered the fasteners back into the frame and returned the painting to its proper place on the wall.

"There, it's done!" he said, turning to face her. "I can't tell you how grateful I am for your help, Alice Marie."

She gazed for a long moment at the painting. It looked the same as it always had. No one would guess the secret it held. She smiled grimly at him. "I guess we're in this together now."

He drew her to him and gave her a brief embrace. "No, dear heart, this is my battle, not yours. You go on with your life. Bring your baby home and go back to Chicago and have a wonderful career. And someday, sooner or later, I will drop by Honeysuckle Lane and insist on buying Catherine's painting of the lilacs hanging here in the rosebud room, and no one will need to know why until those Nazi fugitives are on their way back to Germany to stand trial."

"Goodness, I'd better tell Catherine the painting is reserved for you so no one else takes it."

"Yes, yes, please do!" He paused and his expression sobered. "Now, I don't want to frighten you, but if you should hear that I've met with a little accident—"

Her heart lurched with alarm. "No, Helm, don't even say it!"

"I must, Alice Marie. You've got to hear me out." He put his finger to her lips to silence her. "In the event of my death, I want you to turn the painting over to the proper authorities and tell them all that I've told you."

"Please, Helm. You're scaring me."

"I'm simply erring on the side of caution."

She touched his cheek with her palm, her fingertips caressing his hair. "You really do believe your life is in danger, don't you? Is that why you want me to go back to Chicago?"

He placed his hand over hers, warm and reassuring. "I only want you to be safe and happy, you and your son, wherever that might be. Now don't look so worried. A frown only mars your beauty."

"But I am worried. I can't help it."

"Now listen, dear girl. Not a word to anyone about these documents or where they're hidden. It's our secret, okay?"

She smiled, masking a torrent of anxieties. "Yes, Helm. Of course. It's our secret."

23

On Saturday, March 8, Dirk Wyman phoned and asked Alice Marie if he could drop by to talk with her about the upcoming benefit concert to raise money for Europe's displaced persons. She tried to put him off; she had no wish to see him after the way he had distanced himself from her after learning she was pregnant. But with his usual sardonic wit and charm, he convinced her to see him—just to talk business.

He arrived at five sharp and suggested they go to the Brandwynne for dinner for old time's sake, but she refused and suggested they discuss their business in the parlor and then he could be on his way in time to invite someone else to dinner.

"There's no one else I'd rather take to dinner than you," he told her as he took the love seat and she sat in the wing chair by the fireplace. He looked impeccable in a light blue suit that brought out the brightness in his azure eyes and accented the golden highlights in his professionally styled blond hair.

"Thank you for the invitation, but Annie and I will be going up to the hospital this evening," she said coolly.

Dirk sat forward, massaging the knuckles of his right hand. She caught the mingled scents of spicy lime, Dentyne gum, and expensive wool. "I was sorry to hear about your baby, Allie. Truly sorry. I hope he's doing better."

"Yes, he is. He should be able to come home soon."

Dirk cracked his knuckles. His face was ruddier than usual, his forehead shiny. "That's good. Swell. Listen, Allie, I want to apologize for the way I acted when you told me about the baby. It's been weighing on me for months—my stupidity, my lack of sensitivity. It's just—I thought we had something good going between us, and suddenly there was this baby, and it was like your husband had stepped back into the picture. I didn't feel I could pursue you under those circumstances."

"Pursue me?"

"Yes. Date you. Take you out. I suppose it was foolish of me to feel that way, but I felt I needed to give you space and time. You had enough to deal with without an eager suitor hanging around, complicating things."

She gave him a reproachful glance. "Actually, I had the impression you couldn't wait to escape. Admit it, Dirk. You dropped me like a hot potato."

He met her gaze, his low-slung brows shadowing his crinkly eyes. "You're right, Allie. I was a jerk. I didn't know how to handle you carrying another man's child. Will you forgive me? Give me another chance?"

She turned her gaze to the fireplace with its toasty, crackling fire. "The old Alice Marie would have held a grudge," she conceded, "but too much has happened for me to hold on to negative feelings. You're forgiven, Dirk, but that doesn't mean I want us to pick up where we left off."

"That's okay. I'm a patient man." His gaze moved over her slowly, appreciatively. "You look gorgeous, Allie. A real knock-out. No one would guess you just had a baby."

She shifted, ill at ease, instinctively smoothing her slim jacquard skirt. "You said you wanted to talk to me about the benefit concert. So, what about it?"

"Well, as you know, it's coming up on Saturday, April 5. The publicity has gone out around the state—in fact, to several states. It's going to be quite the gala affair, Allie. Invitations have been sent to the governors of every state in the Midwest. I hear even the mayors of Chicago and Detroit may attend."

She felt her mouth go dry. "I had no idea it was going to be such a big deal. You know, I haven't performed in months."

"Allie, with a few rehearsals under your belt, you'll be back in top form. Besides, you haven't heard the half of it. We sent an invite to the producer of your television show—Rudy whatshisname—and he's excited about the publicity this benefit is generating. He thinks it'll be just the promotional vehicle to get people excited about you coming back to your show."

"But I haven't even decided whether I'm going back to Chicago or not."

"Of course you'll go back. Any girl singer I know would give her wardrobe and hairdresser for a chance like that. You're lucky that opportunity is knocking a second time."

"Maybe so, but I don't have to decide my future today."

"No, and it never hurts to keep them guessing either, does it? Meanwhile, I've got your rehearsal schedule here." He handed her a sheet of paper with dates and times. "And now, Allie, here's the big surprise—and I think when you hear what I've done you'll forgive me for everything."

She stared curiously at him. "What are you talking about?"

"I hope you'll be as pleased as I think you will." He sat on the edge of the love seat and reached for her hand. "You've been so involved lately with your baby and all, I went ahead and made arrangements for an orchestra to accompany you at the benefit."

"Good. I hadn't even thought about an orchestra."

"And here's the best part. I've booked the band you traveled with several years ago—the American Stardust Dreams Orchestra. They just happened to have that date available."

She broke into a gratified smile. "That's wonderful! They're the best in the business."

"Then you're happy with my selection?"

She squeezed his hand. "I couldn't be happier, Dirk. Thank you for thinking of them. They're a great bunch of guys. It'll be swell seeing them again."

He stood up and straightened his jacket. "I'll run along, if you're sure I can't persuade you to dine with me."

"No, thanks anyway, Dirk. Another time. I promise."

She walked him to the door, her hand on his arm.

In the foyer he turned to face her, with a boyish, earnest expression she found unexpectedly endearing. "I want you to know, Allie, how much your performance means to my father. You know he's your greatest fan, and your willingness to help him raise money for his pet project—I mean, this displaced persons program, it's his whole life; he's thrown his heart and soul into it—and I'm just trying to say how grateful he is that you're going to be a part of it."

"I'm glad I can help."

"Oh, one more thing," he said, as he reached for the door knob. "After the benefit my father is throwing a huge party at our home. To celebrate the success of the benefit, you know. He's pulling out all the stops. Everybody who's anybody will be there—Willowbrook's richest and finest; the mayor, of course, and maybe even the governor. And your whole family is invited, naturally." His tone softened as his blue eyes searched hers. "Allie, I'm hoping you'll let me be your escort for the evening."

She hesitated, thinking of Helm. But he would probably be traveling, doing advance publicity for his book. And he would have little interest in going to some black tie affair anyway.

At last she matched his smile. "All right, I'd like that, Dirk. It sounds like it's going to be an exciting evening."

For Alice Marie, the last days of March flew by like bright leaves in a brisk wind. She split her days between rehearsals for the benefit concert and visits to the hospital to see her son. Chilton was out of the incubator now and growing stronger every day, but he still hadn't gained enough weight to go home. She worried that maybe she wasn't providing enough breast milk; she was so exhausted these days, and there was hardly enough time to pump the life-giving nourishment Chip needed. How she yearned for the day when he could suckle at her breast the way nature intended.

On the evening of April first, Alice Marie found it difficult to drift off to sleep. Her mind was jumping from one thing to another—her son, the concert, Helm. Helm had been out of town for over a week now promoting his book; it was scheduled to be in bookstores by the middle of April. She knew authors' tours were a necessary part of the publishing process, but she dreaded being separated from Helm for days at a time.

She was constantly thinking of things she wanted to tell him or share with him—the way Chip looked up at her when she held him in the nursery, a romantic new song she had learned for the concert, something funny his father had said at dinner.

She wanted to tell Helm how close Gerhart and Mama were growing since he moved in with them after the break-in—how they played Chinese checkers in the parlor every evening and listened to symphonies and jazz and even hymns on Mama's Victrola. *You should be here, Helm, sharing all that's happening to the people you care about and the people who care about you. You should be here to hold Chip and feel his tiny hand clasp your finger. You should be here to tell me I'll be a smash at the concert, and to laugh at Mama teaching your papa how to make cherry cobbler and him teaching her how to make schnitzel.*

A troubling question stirred inside her as she lay tossing and turning that night. When had she started depending on Helm so much that her life seemed incomplete without him? She loved him and knew in her heart of hearts that he loved her too; but love wasn't enough when two lives were going in opposite directions. Helm had his calling, his ministry, his commitment to his father and to Israel; she had her commitment to her son and her career; there was no way two such contrasting lives could merge. And there was Helm's obsession with bringing Nazi fugitives to justice, a lifestyle fraught with danger and uncertainties, obviously not a life she could subject her son to.

So it was best that she and Helm were drifting apart, that any hope for a future with him was slowly unraveling. Now she must somehow remove Helmut Schwarz from her affections and purge him from her thoughts. But how?—when he had become part of the very texture of her being? That was the question on her mind as she finally ebbed into a restless, dreamless slumber.

Sometime in the night Alice Marie emerged from the murkiness of sleep, startled, her senses alerted by something not quite right. Slowly she became aware of the unthinkable. Someone was in her room with her. She heard a rustling sound, sensed a presence, then steps moving stealthily, a drawer creaking open, the flutter of papers. She lay still, rigid, heart pounding, listening. Maybe it was little Maggie sleepwalking; she had wandered around the house from room to room once or twice before. But no, Maggie wouldn't be rifling quietly through her desk drawers!

Alice Marie caught the pungent scent of Old Spice and her stomach turned; she had smelled it the night of the accident. She turned her head slightly and saw a large shadow hovering in the darkness over her desk; the pale moonlight carved a luminous profile of a malevolent figure in a black hooded sweatshirt and black pants.

Her heart raced. *The man in the black car!*

Should she scream? Tell him to get out? Her throat was already constricting with terror. *Don't move,* she told herself. *Pretend to be asleep and pray that he leaves. Pray that he doesn't find Helm's papers in Catherine's painting!*

After several excruciating moments she heard his footfall in the doorway, then his covert steps going down the hall. Thank God, she was alone again. She lay still for several seconds, listening, gasping, trying to calm herself, her heart pounding so hard she thought her eardrums would explode.

Surely the intruder had gone downstairs now, had perhaps even left the house. She rose gingerly from her bed, knees weak, wrists trembling, and hurried to Annie and Knowl's room. She knocked lightly on their door, then slipped inside, stole over to the bed and shook Knowl. "Don't make a sound," she whispered as he raised up groggily. "There's a prowler in the house."

Annie stirred from sleep as Knowl scrambled out of bed and grabbed his robe. The three of them were padding down the hallway when they heard a commotion downstairs—glass breaking, something crashing, and Mama shouting, "Get out, you hooligan, you no-good scalawag! Get out and don't come back or I'll have the police after you!"

Knowl bounded downstairs with Annie and Alice Marie rushing headlong behind him, only to find Mama standing at an open window with a broom in her hand. She was wearing a long flannel nightgown and her silver-blonde hair was tied in rags.

Knowl darted to the window and looked out as the two daughters hurried to their mother's side and embraced her.

"Are you okay, Mama?" cried Alice Marie.

"Did he hurt you, Mama?" cried Annie.

She waved them both off. "You girls stop fussing. I'm perfectly fine." She turned to Knowl. "He's gone now, that yellow-belly swine. I gave him a good thrashing."

"What happened?" asked Annie as she led her mother over to the sofa and the two sat down.

"It all happened so fast." Mama's voice was sounding a trifle strained now. The reality of what she had just done was setting in.

"That's okay, Mother Reed. Relax. Take your time." Knowl closed the window and locked it, while Alice Marie picked up the overturned brass lamp and straightened the shade. Then they sat down in the wing chairs and waited for Mama to speak.

She pulled a rag from one of her curls and wound it nervously around her finger. "I came downstairs for some warm milk," she said, steadying her voice, "and what do I find? Some strange man rummaging through our things." She gestured with a swoop of her hand. "Snooping through the desk and buffet drawers and cupboards, almost as if he knew just what he was looking for. I got the broom and took after him. Surprised him so much he stumbled over the end table and knocked over the lamp. I chased him with the broom and he scrambled out the window, the same way he got in."

"I noticed the lock was jimmied," said Knowl.

"He didn't get away with anything," said Mama. "At least not that I could see."

"Why did he break in here?" asked Annie. "We've never had a burglar before. Why now?"

Knowl shook his head. "It can happen to anyone any time. There's no rhyme or reason to it."

"I know why," said Alice Marie solemnly, under her breath. "He was here because of Helm."

Knowl looked at her. "You mean because Herrick House is publishing Helm's book? That makes no sense. Sure, some disgruntled reader might conceivably vandalize our house, but why break in?"

Alice Marie lowered her gaze, silent, remembering Helm's warning; it was safer for Knowl and Annie not to know the truth.

"Well, I'm calling the police," said Knowl, standing up and tightening the sash on his robe. "Let's pray they can catch the thief before he commits another robbery in our neighborhood." He walked to the phone and picked up the receiver. "We might as well all have some hot milk. It looks like it's going to be a long night."

Alice Marie felt a shiver travel the length of her spine and goose bumps rose on her skin under her nightgown. *When will this nightmare end?* she wondered. *And who else will be hurt before it's all over?*

As Saturday, April 5 approached, Alice Marie was already dreading performing at Max Wyman's gala benefit concert.

The much ballyhooed event—to be held at Willowbrook's spacious Majestic Theater—came on the heels of the break-in, a cursory police investigation, Helm's return from his publicity tour, her hospital visits with Chip, and two days of exhausting rehearsals with the American Stardust Dreams Orchestra. She juggled all these concerns under the looming threat of the sinister man in the shiny black Packard.

When he learned of the break-in, Helm was even more distressed about it than Alice Marie. On Saturday morning, as he drove her to the Majestic Theater for her final rehearsal, he said, "I never should have hidden Simon Golding's papers in your room. I must have been out of my mind to put you and your family at risk like that."

"But it was my idea," she told him. "Besides, we don't know for sure that the intruder was the same man who forced us off the highway that night."

Helm turned his gaze from the road momentarily. "You don't have any doubt, I know you don't. I can read it in your eyes."

"All right, I do believe it was the same man, but he didn't find the papers, Helm. That's what's important."

"But he'll be back. He won't stop until he's found what he's looking for."

She shook her head distractedly. "I can't think about that today, Helm. I've got to concentrate on the benefit tonight. If I don't stay focused on my singing, I'll never pull this off." She held her hands up. "Look, my palms are clammy. I'm actually suffering stage fright."

He reached over and clasped her hand warmly. "You'll be wonderful tonight. I've heard you at rehearsals, and you're tops in my book. Believe me, this town is in for a treat."

She pressed his hand against her cheek. "Thank you, Helm. You're good for me. I'm glad you'll be in the audience tonight."

"You couldn't keep me away. Papa and I will be sitting right there on the front row, cheering you on. Your show is all Papa can talk about these days."

They were silent for several moments before she released his hand and said cautiously, "There's something I should tell you, Helm. I hope you don't mind. I told Dirk Wyman I would go with him to the party tonight after the show."

"Dirk Wyman?" He looked annoyed."But I thought we—"

"I'm sorry, Helm. I wasn't even sure you'd get back from your tour in time."

"You know I wouldn't miss your performance tonight."

"But you never mentioned going to the party. I didn't think you'd even want to go to one of those stuffy black tie affairs."

"You're right. I wouldn't want to go."

"Then you don't mind that I accepted Dirk's invitation?"

Helm gave the steering wheel a white-knuckled grip. "No, why should I mind?" His tone was detached, almost morose. "We both agreed it's time for us to get on with our lives."

"It's true, Helm. We can't remain in limbo forever."

"Not when we both know we have no future together," he agreed coolly. "We're two driven, headstrong individuals. We live by our passions and have too little in common."

"I'm afraid that sums it up quite well."

"You'll be moving back to Chicago to do your television show, and I'll do some promotional tours for my book before taking Papa to Israel. It's all settled then, isn't it?"

She felt her heart wrench, but she said evenly, "Yes, I guess it is. I suppose there's nothing more to say."

"Nothing more at all." His knuckles grew whiter. "Maybe Dirk Wyman is the man for you after all," he said recklessly, in a voice she'd never heard before. "Is that what you're thinking, Alice Marie? He's a nice enough chap, and he could do a lot for your career."

"Yes, I suppose he could," she said. "But I'm not looking for a suitor or romantic attachments right now."

Helm's tone softened. "Nor am I."

It was 10 A.M. when Helm dropped Alice Marie off at the theater for her final rehearsal. He picked her up again at two and drove her to the hospital to see Chip. For nearly an hour she held her son, rocked him, nursed him, and crooned lullabies.

Helm held the boy too, cradling him against his broad chest and chatting with him as if the lad could understand every word. He smiled proudly as Chip's tiny hand wrapped around his index finger and wouldn't let go. "What a grip!" he exclaimed. "He's as plucky and tenacious as his mother!"

Alice Marie took the infant in her arms and nuzzled his tiny pink ear. "Chip will need all the backbone and grit he can muster in this tough world," she murmured, breathing in the talcum fragrance of his skin and downy-fine hair.

When it was time to go, it was all she could do to tear herself away from her son. She kissed him on both dimpled cheeks, placed him back in his crib, and ran out of the nursery, blinking back tears as his pitiable cry pierced her heart.

Helm's earlier irritation was gone as he slipped his arm around her and walked her out to his Henry J. "You know, I love that little guy as if he were my own," he said softly.

"I'm glad you do." But Alice Marie couldn't help thinking, *If only you loved his mother with that same kind of devotion!*

They both lapsed into silence as he drove her home. He urged her to get a few hours of rest before her performance. She tried, but she was too keyed up to sleep. At six he drove her back to the theater and dropped her off at the back entrance with her garment bag and makeup case. "I'll go pick up Papa and be back in an hour," he told her.

"Come see me backstage before the show," she said offhandedly as she stepped out of the automobile. She still felt uneasy about their little rift over Dirk.

"All right. I should be back in plenty of time."

"Good. See you soon." As she walked along the narrow corridor to her dressing room she wondered if Helm had any idea how much she needed to see him before she performed. Surely not. She had tried to sound nonchalant, just as he had when he spoke of their relationship. How, she wondered, had they slipped into this painful charade of pretending they meant nothing to each other?

With less than an hour before show time, Alice Marie put the finishing touches on her makeup and slipped into her dress—a shimmering pearl velour evening gown with a draped neckline, fitted bodice and waist, and a long, sweeping skirt. She had styled her lustrous blonde hair in a graceful chignon with delicate ringlets at her temples and at the nape of her neck.

Annie arrived in time to zip her up, fasten the ankle straps on her satin pumps, and make sure every detail of her appearance was perfect. "You've never looked more beautiful," Annie told her as they gazed into the floor-length mirror on the back of the dressing room door.

Alice Marie flashed an appreciative smile. She had never felt closer to Annie. "What a gal won't do for charity, huh?" she quipped, squeezing her sister's hand.

They were startled by a knock, and Dirk Wyman promptly poked his head in the door. "How's our girl?" he asked, stepping inside, looking urbane in his black tuxedo and silver-blue cummerbund.

"It feels like a wedding," she said with an ironic smile.

"Now that's not a bad idea," he said, his clear blue eyes sweeping over her. "You can be the bride on my wedding cake any time you like."

With a polite little wave Annie excused herself. "I'd better go. Knowl's saving seats on the front row for the family."

As she slipped out, Max Wyman burst inside, looking a bit like a short, round penguin in his shiny black tuxedo and white cummerbund. His rosy jowls shook as he grinned expansively and clasped both of Alice Marie's hands in his. "Land sakes, you look breathtaking, Miss Reed."

"Thank you. You look quite dapper yourself, Mr. Wyman."

"Max, please. I'm always Max to you, dear girl. You don't know how much I've looked forward to this evening. I know everyone will be as enchanted by your music as I am, and, of course, I expect tonight to be our biggest fund-raiser ever."

"I hope you're right, Max."

"Oh, I am, I know I am. Do you know who's out in the audience? The governor himself! Not to mention the mayors of Detroit and Indianapolis, plus a stellar group of Midwestern politicians, businessmen, and educators. The press is here too, thank heavens, giving us plenty of invaluable coverage. By tomorrow evening I expect this benefit to be written up on the society page of at least a dozen leading Midwestern newspapers, or my name's not Maxwell Wyman."

Dirk placed a steadying hand on his father's shoulder. "Watch it, Dad. The show hasn't even started and you're excited as a cat on a high wire. Don't forget your blood pressure."

"I'm fine, Son, and my blood pressure's fine. Leave me be." He leaned in close to Alice Marie, his blue eyes twinkling, and said, "I'll be on stage to introduce you, Miss Reed. And I'll come back at intermission and then wrap things up at the end." He patted his jacket pocket. "I've got my little speech right here, urging folks to be generous."

"Dad," warned Dirk, "if you do your usual spiel you'll have the audience sleeping in their seats."

"I don't intend to bore anybody, Dirk." Maxwell's voice grew conspiratorial. "Miss Reed, I've got a little surprise for the audience. I've invited several of the displaced persons we helped in years past to appear on the show. I'll have them right up there on the stage saying a word or two to inspire folks to open their wallets wide. It'll be a real showstopper. What do you think?"

"Yes. It should be quite moving."

"Exactly." He squeezed her elbow. "And you'll be joining us for our party after the benefit, of course. I have a lot of important people I want you to meet."

"Yes, I'll be there."

"Come on, Dad," urged Dirk. "The show starts in a few minutes and we still have some last-minute details to tend to."

Moments after Dirk and his father left the dressing room, Helm appeared, slipping in the door without even a knock. She knew by his unsettled expression that something was wrong.

"What is it?" she asked.

He drew her close and spoke in a whisper. "I don't want to alarm you. Maybe I shouldn't even tell you this."

"Tell me what? What's wrong, Helm?"

He glanced around to be sure they were alone. "When I arrived with my father a few minutes ago, I noticed a car in the parking lot. A black Packard."

Her hand flew to her mouth. "No, not the car!"

"I'm afraid so." Helm's breathing was labored. "I brought my father in and got him seated. Then I went back outside and examined the vehicle. Its right front bumper is damaged. I'm sure it's the car that ran us off the road."

She clutched his arm, her blood running cold. "That means the man who murdered Simon Golding—the man who tried to kill us—is here in this theater."

The veins in Helm's temples throbbed. "I don't know why he would come here. We could call the police, but what would we tell them?" He pulled her against him and held her close, a protective, consoling embrace. "You don't have to do the benefit, Alice Marie. If you're afraid—"

"Of course I'm afraid, but I've got to go on with the show. What else can I do, Helm? I can't step out on the stage and say, 'Ladies and gentlemen, don't be alarmed, but a dangerous man—a murderer—is in the theater. We don't know where. We don't know who he is. We don't even know his name or what he looks like!'"

"You're right. Such an announcement would cause utter pandemonium."

"It might even force the man's hand and turn him violent among all these innocent people."

"We can't risk that," said Helm.

"So I have no choice but to do the show."

"Can you handle it?"

"I think so. Surely he won't do anything foolish with over a thousand people watching."

"May God be with you and protect you," Helm murmured, pressing her head against his chest.

Helm's words rang in Alice Marie's thoughts a half hour later as she stepped out on the sprawling stage and gazed out at the sea of faces. The house lights were on, making it easy to spot Knowl and Annie, Robert and Catherine, Helm, Papa Schwarz, and Mama in the first row. But beyond them the faces were anonymous, one blending into another as the audience—a capacity crowd—welcomed her with high-spirited applause.

One of you is a murderer, she thought. *Why are you here? What do you plan to do?*

Her dark thoughts broke and scattered as the orchestra began playing and the theater lights dimmed. Where the colorful mosaic of faces had been there was now only a vast black expanse. The glaring brightness of the overhead spotlight illuminated her in its moon-white circle. She closed her eyes, breathing deeply, shutting out the world, and plumbed the secret, nameless reserves of her creative being to become, as always, the consummate performer.

The transformation complete, she launched effortlessly into her first song, *Someone to Watch Over Me*, in the rousing, heart-tugging tradition of Ella Fitzgerald. One thing she had learned in all her years of traveling with the Big Bands—when you step into the spotlight you forget every trouble and care you ever had and you play to the audience, woo them, love them, as if nothing else existed except you and them.

Alice Marie continued her first set with several more Gershwin hits. Piano, guitar, drums, and bass accented her fluid, lilting soprano as she explored a wide range of melodic variations. Joined by the string section for her second set, she sang *The Lord's Prayer* and *Motherless Child*, in a style reminiscent of Sarah Vaughan.

She followed with a selection of Les Brown favorites, *Taking a Chance on Love, We'll Be Together Again, Sentimental Journey,* and *Twilight Time*. The program was moving along superbly, the audience avidly responsive. The warm, easy interplay between Alice Marie and the audience buoyed her, sent her spirits soaring; this was why she loved to perform—for this heady, dazzling sensation that anything and everything was possible.

In her final set she sang a medley of Cole Porter numbers in her own upbeat styling, including several of his songs from the musical comedy hit *Kiss Me, Kate*. She closed her program with a poignant rendition of *Tenderly*, the six-bar intro opening with unison saxophones and soft, open harmonic support from the brass section. The audience was spell-bound.

She received a standing ovation. The applause went on for two full minutes.

After she had sung three encores to more wild applause, Max Wyman strode out onto the stage, handed her a dozen long-stem red roses, and gave her a congratulatory embrace. As the houselights came up she realized she hadn't thought once about the ominous stranger during her entire two-hour performance. Now, thank God, the show was almost over and there had been no mishap or interruption.

"Isn't she fantastic, ladies and gentlemen," said Max, clapping, giving her his own personal round of applause. "She has the voice of an angel—and she even looks like an angel, doesn't she, folks? Well, we certainly know she's Willowbrook's angel. And tonight she's been an angel to help us raise the funds we need to help the beleaguered children of Eastern Europe."

Max Wyman stepped onto center stage, his arms outstretched in a gesture of beneficence. "Your gifts tonight will help us sponsor hundreds of needy children and families—innocent people whose lives were uprooted and torn asunder by the war. These are good people who have found themselves homeless and destitute, living for years in displaced persons camps across Europe. With your help, ladies and gentlemen, these people will be brought to America where they will be settled in jobs and homes in communities like ours, so they can become productive citizens of our great country."

Max paused to catch his breath, his grin spreading from jowl to jowl. "And now I have a marvelous surprise. On this very stage you will have an opportunity to meet several of these deserving persons we've already had the pleasure of helping." Max held out his hand to a man and woman with two small children, who shuffled out on the stage looking ill at ease and blinking against the bright lights. The couple looked like ordinary folks one might see on the streets of Willowbrook, plain of face, the man's dark hair slicked back and the woman's pulled back in a tight bun, their clothing neat and unadorned, and the children beside them clean-scrubbed and polite.

Max Wyman pushed the microphone into the man's face and he spoke a few halting words with a thick Slavic accent while the woman smiled, her rosy, round cheeks dimpling. When the man had finished speaking, he made a little bow and the audience applauded.

Max took the microphone back and declared in a booming voice, "Now, ladies and gentlemen, I'd like you to meet the man who first inspired me to begin this charitable, humanitarian project to aid displaced persons." His voice took on a husky, sentimental tone. "My very own brother, Douglas Wyman, found himself a displaced person after the war. His home in Munich had been seized and his family had nowhere to go. I used my own funds to bring him and his family to America. And that's when I realized that there were hundreds more like my brother waiting for someone to help them. I knew I couldn't do it alone, and that's why I have turned again and again to you generous people. Please welcome my brother, who has come from Chicago to be with us tonight."

The audience applauded as a tall, broad-shouldered man in a tweed suit strode across the stage and clasped Max Wyman's hand. He had straight brown hair, heavy arched brows, and a full mustache over pale, thin lips. Alice Marie could see both Dirk and Max Wyman in the man's sturdy features and ruddy complexion, but there was a coldness, a mesmerizing shrewdness in his flesh-pocked, narrow, ice-blue eyes. And something more; she caught a whiff of a spicy, masculine fragrance. Old Spice!

As the applause died down, the strapping man stepped to the microphone and said in a heavy German accent, "Thank you, ladies and gentlemen, for allowing me to speak to—"

His words were interrupted by a sudden, piercing, blood-chilling shriek from the front row. Papa Schwarz had jumped up out of his seat and was waving his fists in the air. "Nein, nein, nein! Is not man named Wyman! Is Deiter Weyandt. Is Nazi guard who beat me! Monster of Auschwitz! Murderer of Jews! Stop him! Somebody stop him!"

Papa Schwarz was shouting now in German, shaking his fist at the stage as Helm and Alice Marie's mother tried to quiet him. Alice Marie, on the right side of the stage, saw Max Wyman's face turn pasty as oatmeal and his pale blue eyes bulge with disbelief. His brother, Deiter Weyandt or Douglas Wyman—Alice Marie wasn't sure now who he was—tightened his grip on the microphone and glared down red-faced at Papa Schwarz. She heard him growl something in German under his breath.

For several moments the audience sat in stunned silence, watching the improbable scenario in the front row, but as Papa continued his tirade, waves of baffled whispers rolled through the theater. Amid the commotion, Max Wyman, his color returning, waved his hands and shouted, "Please remain in your seats, ladies and gentlemen. We've had a little interruption, but the program will resume in a moment. The ushers will pick up your commitment envelopes and then we'll be dismissed." He turned his attention to the front row. "Will someone please take this poor, distraught old man outside? He's obviously ill. He needs a doctor."

Alice Marie watched, immobilized, as Knowl and Helm led the combative, bellicose Gerhart Schwarz out of the auditorium. *He's not ill!* she wanted to shout. *He's outraged, frightened, in shock.* Her astonishment over Papa's outburst was already spiraling into grim questions and horrifying suspicions. Had something triggered his memory causing a flashback to the war, the death camps? Was Papa in his delirium seeing a Nazi in every face or was he speaking a ghastly, unthinkable truth?

Somehow she got through the remaining minutes of the show, but as soon as the curtain closed she ran backstage, hoping to find Helm. He wasn't there, but a tidal wave of fans and well-wishers was already advancing toward her, programs raised for an autograph. She waved them away with the brightest smile she could muster and fled to her dressing room.

There was Helm, waiting, a look of alarm and revulsion jarring his usually stoic expression. She went into his arms and he held her, but she felt a disquieting chill in his embrace. "How is Papa?" she asked.

He looked at her, his eyes grim, shadowed. "He's okay. He's in Knowl's car with your mother. She's the only one who can comfort him. Knowl will drive them home, and Annie will phone Dr. Elrick, just as a precaution."

"What happened, Helm? His outburst—what does it mean?"

His arms remained loosely around her waist. "I think it means we've found the man in the black car. The man who killed Simon Golding and forced us off the road. The man who ransacked my apartment and your home. It's the man who stood on that stage tonight."

"Max Wyman's brother?"

"And if Papa is right, he's the Nazi guard who beat my father at Auschwitz."

"He can't be, Helm."

"Why not?"

"Because he's Max Wyman's brother, for heaven's sake! He looks like an ordinary guy, not a Nazi killer. Surely Max would know if his own brother was a—a Nazi!"

"I think he does know. I think the whole family knows. I think they're all part of this whole grisly operation."

Alice Marie shook her head. "They can't be. I'd know if they were evil like that. Wouldn't people know? Wouldn't we sense such evil in our midst?"

Helm clutched her hand. "You've got to trust me, Alice Marie. I believe we're on the verge of uncovering a terrible thing here—an unspeakable injustice, a conspiracy going on right under our noses. Your Max Wyman and his brother are so arrogant they think no one will find out. They think no one will believe a confused old man. But I believe him. And tonight I'm going to find the proof I need."

"How?"

"I'm going to Max Wyman's home—to the party."

"And what do you expect to find there?"

"Documents that reveal the code in Simon Golding's papers."

"You're going to search Max Wyman's house? With dozens of people milling about, partying? You can't be serious."

"I'm deadly serious."

"But how? Max will catch you. Or worse, his brother."

"I'll take my chances."

"I can't let you do this, Helm."

"You can't stop me." He lifted her chin. "I'll be careful, don't worry. But I need a favor. Tell Dirk and Max you've invited me to the party, that I decided at the last minute I wanted to go."

"Won't he be suspicious?"

"Not if we act like nothing's wrong. And even if he is suspicious, he doesn't dare tip his hand and give himself away. Don't worry, Darling, everything will be fine."

She nuzzled her head against his chest. "I'm scared, Helm."

"I know, but if I find the evidence I need, this will all be over, and we can get on with our lives."

"You mean . . . go our separate ways."

He looked at her. "You know I wish it could be different."

Her voice was small, pained. "So do I."

Minutes later, when Dirk came by her dressing room, Alice Marie did as Helm had requested, telling Dirk she had invited Helm to the party, and surely he had no problem with that, did he?

Dirk shrugged. "He's welcome as long as he knows you're my date, not his."

Alice Marie rode to the party with Dirk in his British Nash-Healey sports convertible. The weariness from performing was just setting in, but even more exhausting was the dread of what she and Helm might encounter this evening. What would Helm find? What perils lay ahead? This was to have been such a wonderful evening. How could it have turned so ominous? Or was she allowing herself to be swept up by Helm's paranoia? How could he believe a respected, upstanding family like the Wymans could be involved in something so loathsome?

"You're awfully quiet," noted Dirk as he turned onto the highway out of town.

"I'm always fatigued after a concert."

"You did a magnificent job." He reached over and squeezed her hand. "I'll tell you a little secret, Allie. I watched you tonight, and all I could think about was how much you mean to me. It hit me like a ton of bricks. I'm falling in love with you and I want the whole world to know."

She pulled her hand away. "Dirk, please, I'm flattered, but I can't even think of such things tonight. Let's just keep things casual for now, all right?"

"Whatever you say, Babe, but I had to speak my mind. So now you know the truth. What you choose to do with it is up to you."

They followed the main highway for nearly fifteen minutes, finally turning off on a private road that wound through a wooded area; after half a mile they arrived at a sprawling gated estate flanked by a forest of firs and blue spruce.

"You've never been to my father's house, have you?" asked Dirk as he drove through the open wrought iron gate.

"No, I haven't. It's beautiful."

"You can't see much in the dark, but it is magnificent. An authentic English Tudor mansion. A wonderful blend of Gothic and Italian Renaissance styles. And charmingly cozy, considering its grand size. I suppose that's why, even at my age, I still live at home. Where else could I enjoy such comfort and luxury?" He pulled into a circular driveway and parked beside the massive residence—a handsome ivy-draped fortress of stone and oak, with large bay windows, pointed arches, and towering chimneys.

"We have over ten acres," he told her as he walked her up to the carved double doors. "It makes a nice getaway from the hassles of life."

"Yes, I can imagine," she agreed. They entered an enormous marble foyer lined with exquisite copper engravings by Albrecht Durer. At the end of the hall a wide, circular staircase led up to the second floor. Overhead, a crystal chandelier cast a warm, burnished glow on several pieces of classic Greek and Roman sculptures, including a bust of Plato or Socrates. Or maybe it was Homer. Alice Marie hadn't excelled in history, so she couldn't be sure which man it was.

Dirk showed her around the house. The elaborately decorated rooms—from the high-ceilinged living room to the graceful sitting room and dining room—revealed a rich, eclectic style, an American amalgam of French, English, and German tastes.

Dirk escorted her finally to the great room where most of the guests had already gathered. Dominating the room was a massive stone fireplace flanked by huge colorful murals depicting German history; bronze urns and ceramic vases graced the sturdy oak mantle. A Steinway grand piano occupied the opposite wall by the bay window. The heavy dark mahogany and rosewood furniture had a rich timeworn patina in stunning contrast to the ivory-white, damask-covered sofas and armchairs.

Gray-haired men in tuxedos and finely coifed women in sequined gowns milled about, chatting pleasantly, sampling silver trays of hors d'oeuvres, and sipping goblets of white wine.

"May I get you something to drink?" asked Dirk.

"Thank you. A ginger ale would be fine."

"Don't move. I'll be right back."

While Dirk was gone, Helm stole over and drew her aside. "I'm going upstairs as soon as I can slip away," he whispered. "If you don't hear anything from me in an hour, I want you to get out of here. Call Knowl to come get you and when you get home, call the police."

"You're scaring me, Helm. Please be careful."

But before Helm could break away, a tall, burly man approached, stepping between Helm and Alice Marie, a knowing gleam in his frigid blue eyes as he offered Alice Marie his hand. A chill rippled over her as she recognized Maxwell's brother Douglas Wyman. Or more accurately, Deiter Weyandt.

"You were splendid tonight, Miss Reed," he said in his thick brogue. His cunning gaze shifted to Helm. "Don't you think so, Herr—?"

"Schwarz," Helm replied stonily.

"You are a friend of Miss Reed?" he inquired.

"A good friend," said Helm, tight-lipped.

"I hear in your accent that we are countrymen, Herr Schwarz."

"Countrymen? That is your word for it, Herr Wyman."

"How long is it since you left Germany?"

"Just after the war."

"Oh? You are one of my brother's—how do they say—protégés?"

Helm's jaw stiffened. "No, I am most definitely not."

Alice Marie broke in. "So you drove over from Chicago, Mr. Wyman? Have you lived there long?"

"Long enough to call it home."

"Yes, it was my home too for several years." Alice Marie felt the tension between Helm and Deiter growing. The greater her unease, the faster she talked. "But I enjoyed Chicago's hustle and bustle. There's no place like Chicago, is there, Mr. Wyman? It's so different from Willowbrook."

"Very different."

"You must have an amazing story to tell," she went on animatedly. "I'm surprised Max didn't tell us about you ages ago."

"The feeling is mutual, Miss Reed."

She lavished him with her most brilliant smile. "I hope we have a chance to get better acquainted before you head back to Chicago."

Deiter clasped her hand firmly, graciously. "I think that is quite possible, Miss Reed. It is very good to make your acquaintance." He turned to Helm and offered his hand. "And yours too, Herr Schwarz. I think we have more in common than we know."

"You speak the truth," said Helm, hesitating a moment before accepting the handshake.

The strapping man gave them both a small, adroit smile, then turned and slipped smoothly back into the crowd. Alice Marie clasped Helm's arm and whispered, "You're a marvelous actor. I know you wanted to wring his neck."

He inhaled sharply. "You have no idea how close I came to confronting him with my suspicions."

"You can't, Helm. Not here, not yet. He's got your hands tied until you find the evidence against him."

"Now is the time," Helm whispered. "I will find it. Remember what I said. Wait an hour. Then go home and phone the police."

Her hand tightened on his arm. "Helm, please! Don't take any unnecessary chances."

"I won't. Say a prayer for me." He kissed her cheek, then gave her a lingering smile before disappearing into the crowd.

"Helm?" she whispered. She had a sudden, desperate impulse to go after him, but several people had already stepped in the way and were approaching her with eager smiles.

"Miss Reed," said a matronly woman in a black, embroidered evening dress, "your performance was absolutely marvelous! I can't tell you how long I've wanted to meet you. Why, I used to watch your television show every day. Didn't I, Felix?"

"Every day," said the wiry bald man beside her.

"And, Dear, I hear via the grapevine that you're going back to Chicago to do the show again. I can't tell you how pleased I am to hear that. In times like these the world needs to hear a lovely voice like yours."

"Thank you, Mrs.—?"

"Oh, I'm Josephine Crawley. My husband, Felix, is on the board of directors at the bank." The woman turned and beckoned another couple over. "Darlings, come meet Miss Reed. She's just the most precious thing." She wheeled back to Alice Marie. "Dear, have you met Eleanor and Vernon Frasier? They own Frasier's Department store downtown. It's a delightful place to shop, but then I'm sure you know that already."

Alice Marie offered her hand, but her thoughts were on Helm. She glanced around the room, seeking the slightest glimpse of him. "I'm glad to meet you both," she said, forcing her gaze back to the smiling couple. "Yes, of course, I shop at Frasier's. Where else? In fact, I got this gown there."

"And it looks divine on you, Darling," cooed Josephine.

"Perfectly divine," agreed Mrs. Frasier.

"Thank you. You're both too kind." Alice Marie looked around again— a hurried, stealthy glance. *Helm, where are you? Why did I let you run off alone on such a dangerous mission? If anything happens to you—!*

"Darling, did you hear me?" Josephine Crawley wrapped her silk-gloved fingers around Alice Marie's wrist.

Alice Marie blinked. "I'm sorry, Mrs. Crawley. What did you say?"

"I was saying you really must tell us about some of the glamorous stars you've met. You're one yourself, of course, but you know what I mean. I remember the show where you sang with Dinah Shore. It was superb!" Her voice grew smugly confidential. "Tell me. What's Dinah like—really like? In person, I mean."

Alice Marie groped for words. "She—she's wonderful—exactly the way she seemed on television." *Now please let me get out of here and find Helm!*

Josephine looked faintly disappointed. "Oh, really? The very same?"

Alice Marie sighed with relief when she spotted Dirk wending his way through the crowd with her ginger ale. She accepted the crystal goblet gratefully and stepped back, letting Dirk pick up the conversational thread with Josephine Crawley. *She'll keep him talking all evening!*

As Alice Marie contemplated slipping away and looking for Helm, Max Wyman strolled over and gave her a welcoming hug. "Come, my dear, I have scads of important people waiting to meet you." He took her arm peremptorily and guided her over to a cluster of starched, stout aristocrats looking rather like pompous penguins. "Very influential people, these are, Miss Reed," he confided. "Starting with the mayor and the governor himself!"

Max made the introductions with a grandiloquence that would have amused her if she hadn't been so worried about Helm. She responded with what she hoped was her usual flare and aplomb, although her laughter was a bit forced and her smile felt pasted on. "Really? . . . You don't say! . . . Is that so?" she heard herself saying over and over. For what seemed an interminable length of time Max's colleagues exchanged banal pleasantries with her, pausing only to let the waiter refill their drinks or to sample a stuffed mushroom, a morsel of smoked salmon, or shrimp cocktail.

Even as she smiled and nodded politely, Alice Marie found it impossible to concentrate on the conversations buzzing around her head like insistent bees. Her mind kept drifting back to Helm. *If I could just go find him and help him. Dear God, please keep him safe. Let him find the evidence he needs!*

Finally, as Max and the mayor became absorbed in an impassioned discourse on some recent legislation, Alice Marie saw her chance to escape. She excused herself and headed for the stairs, only to encounter another couple eager to compliment her on her concert. She paused for just a moment and was promptly surrounded by jovial, ardent partygoers who insisted on regaling her with their latest story or joke. Some wanted to know how to get their second cousin's uncle into show business, while others wondered if she could sing for their next PTA or auxiliary meeting.

Their voices grew distant as Alice Marie gazed distractedly around the room. *Helm, where are you? Be careful. Come back to me!*

"Looking for someone, Darling?" Dirk's voice.

"Oh, there you are," she said, wishing it were Helm.

Dirk breathed a sigh of exasperation. "I finally managed to extricate myself from that stultifying conversation with Josephine Crawley. I hope you weren't getting lonely."

She forced a smile. "Not a chance. Your father introduced me to all his friends."

Dirk draped his arm fondly around her shoulder. "Well, now it's my turn. I want to show you off to my friends."

For the next half hour they greeted more guests, one after another, endlessly. Again, Alice Marie smiled cordially, making small talk, listening and making the proper responses, until her face ached and she feared her smile might freeze in place.

When she finally glanced at her watch, she realized time had run out. She had to escape these fawning, reveling merrymakers, had to find Helm. She whispered to Dirk, "Please excuse me. I need to go to the powder room."

"Use the one upstairs," he suggested. "It won't be so busy. Second door on the left."

"Thanks, Dirk. You're a doll." She hastened down the hallway, holding her gown several inches off the floor, and climbed the stairs to the second floor. The powder room was empty, thank goodness, so she wouldn't have to make small talk with anyone. She sank down on a small Chippendale love seat in the lounge and caught her breath. She looked again at her watch and shivered. Well over an hour since she had seen Helm. Nor had she seen Max Wyman's brother lately. Had he discovered Helm snooping through Max Wyman's papers? Had he already silenced him?

Dear God, please, no!

Helm had told her, *If I don't return in an hour, go home and call the police.* But she wasn't about to go home and leave Helm alone facing who knew what. She had to stay, had to find him. She had bought herself some time with Dirk—ten minutes or so perhaps—but where should she begin looking for Helm?

She slipped out of the powder room and stole down the hall, quietly trying each door, only to find a linen closet and several bedrooms, dark and empty. At the end of the hall she encountered heavy carved double doors, rosewood or mahogany, with a cornucopia motif. She turned the brass handle and peered inside. It was a library and the lights were on— a brass lamp on the writing desk and a floor lamp between two leather armchairs. Ceiling-high bookcases covered two walls; striped gold wallpaper adorned the other two, broken only by several ornate Postimpressionist paintings. Lush Oriental rugs graced the gleaming hardwood floors.

Gingerly Alice Marie stepped inside, her breathing shallow, her pulse racing. The room looked empty.

"Alice Marie?"

She whirled around at the sound of the familiar voice just behind her. "Helm, you scared me out of my wits! What are you doing behind the door?"

He shut the door noiselessly and whispered, "I jumped back when I heard the door open. I thought you were Deiter Weyandt."

She put her hand to her heart. "That's who I thought you were."

They chuckled mirthlessly. "I thought I told you to go home and call the police," he said, his smile fading.

"I couldn't leave you, Helm. I had to know you were all right."

"I'm fine. Now go."

"Have you found anything?"

"Nothing of importance. I checked every room. Max Wyman is either innocent or very good at covering his tracks."

"You didn't find anything?"

"Not in the bedrooms. I was just about to search the library."

"I'll help you."

"We have to move quickly and quietly."

"Where shall I start?"

"You take the writing desk; I'll go through the cupboards in the book-case."

She sat down at the gleaming rosewood desk and opened the center drawer. It looked like any normal drawer, brimming with stationery, ink pens, postage stamps, paper clips. Nothing out of the ordinary. She gently shifted the contents around, satisfying herself that the drawer held nothing of consequence. She explored the side drawers, first the three on the left, then the three on the right. It felt strange rummaging through someone else's belongings. She felt a wave of guilt, then reminded herself that lives were at stake.

"There's nothing here," she told Helm. "Just a few letters, newspaper clippings, old photographs."

"Are you sure you haven't missed something?" asked Helm, sounding disappointed.

"Go ahead. Look at the letters, if you wish. They sound like letters anybody would write." She opened the upper right-hand drawer and reached for the letters.

"No, that's okay," said Helm. "I'll take your word for it."

She started to shut the drawer, but it caught momentarily. She gave it a shove and it closed.

Helm looked over. "A problem?"

"No, just a sticky drawer."

Helm came over. "Try it again."

"Why? It's just one of those temperamental drawers every desk has."

"Try it anyway," he hissed.

She opened the drawer and closed it. "See? It works fine now."

"Try it again."

"Really, Helm, this is silly." She opened the drawer and started to close it, but it stuck again, making a squeaking sound. "If I keep this up, someone will hear us."

"That's enough." Helm pulled the drawer out and held it up. Gingerly he felt underneath, along the runners. "Well, what have we here?"

"What is it?"

He smiled triumphantly. "An envelope taped underneath the drawer. Someone didn't want anybody to find this."

"Is there a name on it?"

"It says, 'For D. W. To be opened only in the event of my death. M. W.'"

"D. W.? Deiter Weyandt?"

"Or Douglas Wyman. From M. W. Maxwell Wyman."

"Hurry. Open it," urged Alice Marie.

Helm carefully loosened the flap on the slim white envelope and removed a sheet of tissue-thin paper. As he opened the paper, a small brass key fell out in his hand.

Alice Marie drew close. "What did you find, Helm?"

"Not what I was looking for."

"What? Tell me."

"Only this paper and a strange little key."

"Another dead end?"

"Apparently so. Look. The writing is intriguing, but it makes no sense."

"Is it a letter?"

"No. It's a quote from some book—something familiar, but I can't place it."

"May I read it?"

"Be my guest."

She took the flimsy stationery and read the small, neat script:

It was the best of times, it was the worst of times, it was the age of wisdom, it was the age of foolishness, it was the epoch of belief, it was the epoch of incredulity, it was the season of Light, it was the season of Darkness, it was the spring of hope, it was the winter of despair, we had everything before us, we had nothing before us, we were all going direct to Heaven, we were all going direct the other way.

She looked at him. "This is a famous passage from literature."

He nodded. "Yes, I know, but so what?"

She grasped his wrist. "Maybe it's a clue—a secret message."

"Which means we're right back where we started. Trying to decipher codes."

She leaned on the edge of the desk. "Hurry. Let's figure it out."

"The passage describes the world today, and Germany during the war. But beyond that, I don't—"

"Wait." She closed her eyes and repeated the first lines. *It was the best of times, it was the worst of times.* I should know where that quote's from."

"Shakespeare?"

"No, not Shakespeare."

"Who then? Hawthorne? Hemingway?"

"No. It's—it's Dickens. Charles Dickens."

"All right. Which book? *David Copperfield? Oliver Twist?*"

"No, it's another one. *A Tale of Two Cities.*"

"You're sure?"

"Yes, I think so. Annie would be the real expert, of course."

Furrows plowed his forehead. "So what do we have now? A book title. It's pointless. We're going in circles."

She knew he was right. They were grasping at straws. "Maybe—maybe Max hid some information in the pages of a book."

Helm brightened. "In a book called *A Tale of Two Cities?*"

"Why not? It could be in this very room."

Helm strode over to the shelves of leather-bound volumes. "He has everything here—classics, poetry, reference works—"

"Does he have *A Tale of Two Cities?*" she asked, fingering the spines of *The Old Curiosity Shop* and *A Christmas Carol.*

"I don't see it," said Helm. He paused and glanced toward the door, then put his finger to his lips. "Someone's coming," he whispered.

Alice Marie listened. Yes, she heard it too. Footsteps outside the door. She held her breath and waited, then sighed with relief when the sound faded down the hall.

After a minute, Helm said with a note of excitement, "Look! There it is. On the top shelf, out of reach and hardly visible beside that set of encyclopedias."

He pushed the desk chair over, stepped up on it, and grasped the thick, leather-bound book. He took it over to the writing desk where the lamplight was brightest. Alice Marie leaned close, her heart racing. "Hurry," she whispered. "Open it."

"I'm trying," he told her, tugging at the cover. He lifted the book to the light and inspected it. "Look, it's not a book at all. It only looks like one."

She shivered. "There's a lock on it, Helm."

He smiled knowingly at her. "And I think I have the key."

The key turned effortlessly in the lock and the cover opened to reveal a secret compartment, about eight by ten inches, containing a manila envelope. Helm looked at her, a light of triumph in his eyes, and said, "We've struck gold." He opened the envelope and spread the pages out on the writing desk. His voice was tremulous. "We've found it, Alice Marie—the lists of German names with their S.S. titles and their new names and addresses in North and South America."

Her mouth went dry. "Everything you suspected is true."

"Yes, it's all right here. In black and white. And look, there's more. Accounting sheets with lists of figures. It shows how the money Max collected has been spent—and it wasn't on innocent orphans. More accurately, on Nazi war criminals!"

"Take it and let's get out of here, Helm."

"Wait." He picked up several sheets of bank stationery. "Look at these notations. If I read them correctly, Max has been siphoning off funds from his own bank."

A cold chill streaked down her spine. "Oh, Helm, if Max Wyman knew we found these—!"

A deep male voice came from the doorway. "Yes, Miss Reed? If Max Wyman knew you found *what*?"

Alice Marie wheeled around, her heart in her throat, and stared into the malevolent, ice-blue eyes of Max Wyman.

26

Max Wyman stood in the doorway looking smug, unruffled, one hand in his tuxedo pocket, the other on the doorknob. "Such a shame, Miss Reed. You were so absorbed in your task you didn't even hear me come in." He crossed the room to the desk, but Helm had already gathered up the papers and stuffed them back into the envelope.

"I'll take those, Mr. Schwarz," said Max, holding out his hand.

Helm stepped back, slipping the envelope under his jacket. "No, Sir, you won't."

Max smiled patiently. "Suit yourself, Mr. Schwarz, but you won't be leaving this room with them."

"That's where you're wrong, Mr. Wyman. I'm walking out that door, and if you try to stop me, I'll make enough noise to bring every party guest running to this room."

"Don't force me to call the police, Mr. Schwarz."

"Call them," said Helm. "They might find it interesting that the president of the local bank bankrolls the resettlement of Nazi thugs in decent communities like Willowbrook."

"It's all a matter of opinion," said Max, his breathing heavier, his emotions rising. He stepped closer to Alice Marie and seized her wrist. His face was florid, his cobalt eyes bulging slightly. "My lovely songbird, perhaps you can persuade your Mr. Schwarz to relinquish my papers."

"Never!"

"Don't be a fool, Mr. Wyman," warned Helm. "Let go of her!"

"Not until I've had my say," said Max, his eyes glinting with animosity. "Mr. Schwarz, you look upon my countrymen as Nazi thugs; I see them as valued comrades who were swept up into something quite unfortunate. But why should they pay with their lives for something a madman like Hitler foisted upon them? Men like my brother, Douglas—or Deiter, as my mother named him—were simply obeying orders. If they had not followed Hitler's commands, they themselves would have been imprisoned or killed. Can you blame them for doing what was forced upon them, for observing the laws of the State?"

"That's a convenient excuse," said Helm with a tremor of rage, "but it's full of holes. Nothing you say can justify the mass murders, the gassings, the mountains of corpses, the starvation marches, the sadism, the sheer enormity of the killing."

"There were no winners, Mr. Schwarz," said Max solemnly, tightening his grip on Alice Marie's wrist. "My brother lost everything after the war. He could have lost his life. His wife and children were left homeless; they could have died—they who never lifted a finger against any Jew. I could not allow that."

"So you made your own kind of justice that lets murderers go free," said Helm accusingly.

"Surely you can understand family loyalty and kindred love, Mr. Schwarz. You feel it for your father, don't you? You will defend him to the death. And I feel the same. I will protect my brother against all enemies. Even you, Mr. Schwarz, and you, Miss Reed."

"We're not your enemies, Max." Alice Marie struggled to wrench her wrist free from Max's grasp, but he held her firm. "Please let us go," she pleaded.

"Let go of her, Maxwell," Helm warned again. "We're walking out of this house. Don't try to stop us."

"If my brother will not stop you, Herr Schwarz, I will," said a thickly accented voice. Alice Marie's startled gaze flew to the doorway. Dear God in heaven, they would never be free now! Deiter Weyandt stood holding a pistol, not an ordinary American gun, but what looked like a German Luger, a semiautomatic weapon.

He strolled into the room, looking natty and professorial in his tweed suit and bow tie, but his gray eyes were cold and steely as ball bearings. "You are a hard man to discourage, Herr Schwarz. A car crash does not stop you. Nor robbery." He leveled his gun at Alice Marie. "What will it take to stop you, Herr Schwarz?"

"He found the papers," Max told his brother, relinquishing his grip on Alice Marie. "He has them under his jacket."

"He will return them, of course," said Deiter, approaching Helm, gun in hand.

"I will not return them," Helm retorted. "They prove what I suspected all along. Your brother Maxwell has been resettling Nazi fugitives for years. And you, Herr Weyandt, are the man I have been looking for since the war. You were my father's guard at Auschwitz. He recognized you tonight just as he knew you when you broke into my apartment."

"I did not remember the old man," said Deiter, "until tonight. These days he does not have the look of death about him that he had then."

"You gave him that look, Herr Weyandt. You will pay for what you did to him."

Deiter stepped closer to Helm. "Maxwell tells me you are an evangelist. Does not every man, even a Nazi, deserve redemption, Herr Schwarz?"

Helm averted his gaze. "Redemption is in God's hands, not mine. I am looking for justice."

Deiter's gunmetal eyes narrowed. "If God gave to mankind justice instead of mercy, would we not all die, Herr Schwarz?"

"God may forgive you, Herr Weyandt, but I never shall."

"Then, as an evangelist, you would not show me the way to heaven?" Deiter taunted, his thin lips curling.

Helm's charcoal eyes flamed. "I would gladly escort you to the gates of hades!"

"Where is God's love, Herr Schwarz, the love that covers a multitude of sins?"

Helm advanced toward Deiter, ignoring the gun. "Where was compassion when you flogged my father and left him for dead? Where was your humanity when you tortured him and kicked him with your iron-toed boots? Where was mercy when my fiancée and my mother and aunts and uncles and cousins were murdered?"

Deiter nudged Helm's chin with the barrel of his pistol and mocked, "Even Jesus said, 'Father, forgive them, for they know not what they do.'"

Helm lunged forward and with one broad swipe knocked the gun from Deiter's hand and seized his throat. "You Nazi devils knew exactly what you were doing!" Helm's strong fingers closed around the soft flesh of Weyandt's neck. "I could kill you with my bare hands!"

"Let my brother go!" shouted Max.

"Stop it, Helm!" cried Alice Marie. "Don't be like him!"

Helm moved as if in slow motion, choking Weyandt, the muscles of his face contorting, mirroring Deiter's twisted features. Deiter's arms flailed and his fingers clawed the air.

Alice Marie ran to Helm and clutched his arm, his shoulder, shaking him even as Helm shook Weyandt. "No, Helm!" she begged. "Let God be his judge, not you!"

Helm froze; then, as if rousing from some hypnotic reverie, he released Deiter and shoved him against the wall. Deiter rebounded and stumbled against the desk, coughing, holding his throat. He sank down in the arm-chair, gasping as Max Wyman stooped down swiftly and grabbed up the pistol.

Max aimed the weapon at Helm, his hand trembling. "Stay where you are, Mr. Schwarz," he demanded breathlessly, his face flushed, a pur-plish vein bulging along his temple. "We're going to wrap this up promptly now, because I have a party going on downstairs." Maxwell looked over at his brother and said something in German. Deiter answered in German, still rubbing his throat.

Alice Marie went into Helm's arms. He held her close, his body turned to face the pistol.

"Now we are going to do things my way," said Max darkly, approaching them. He held out his free hand. "You will give me the papers, Mr. Schwarz. Then you and Miss Reed will leave the party and go home. You will forget everything you have seen and heard in this room." He paused to catch his breath. "If you try to make trouble, or if you go to the police or any other authorities, you will risk your lives."

"Do you think that will stop us?" Helm shot back.

"Perhaps not. But I know something that will." Maxwell's heavy-lidded eyes narrowed. "If you insist on causing trouble, I know of a little Jewish baby that will never make it home from the hospital."

Alice Marie's blood ran cold. Her knees gave out and she clung to Helm for support. "Not my baby! You wouldn't! You can't!"

Max flashed a grim smile. "You have nothing to fear as long as I have nothing to fear, Miss Reed."

Deiter, his neck veins throbbing and his eyes malicious slits, charged toward Helm and grabbed his lapel. "Did you hear my brother? The papers, Herr Schwarz! Give them to me!"

Helm sidestepped Deiter and jumped back, pulling Alice Marie with him toward the open doorway.

"Stay where you are," Max ordered.

Helm took another step backward, halfway out the door now, then stopped abruptly at the sound of a cheery masculine voice in the hall. "So here you are, Alice Marie! I've been looking high and low for you!"

Dirk Wyman ambled into the room, an affable smile fixed on Alice Marie. He stopped and glanced around, his puzzled gaze taking in his father and uncle and the gun in his father's hand. His expression turned to alarm. "What's going on here? Dad? What's wrong?"

"Just a little difference of opinion, Son," said Max. "Go back to the party. We will all be down soon."

Dirk shook his head. "No, Dad, I'm not leaving, not if you're in some kind of trouble here."

Through clenched teeth Max said, "There's no trouble I can't handle, Dirk. Go back to the party. Keep our guests entertained."

Dirk stood his ground. "No, Dad. I want to know what's going on. What on earth are you doing with a gun?"

"Tell him, Maxwell," urged Helm. "Tell your son what you have done."

Max stepped forward, his nostrils flaring. "I said, get out of here, Son!"

Dirk held out his hand, palm forward. "Please, Dad, put the gun away. Someone could get hurt."

"No one will get hurt, Son, if you just go back to the party and let me handle this."

"Handle what? What's Alice Marie got to do with this?"

"Don't you know, Dirk?" challenged Alice Marie tremulously. "Your father hasn't told you?"

"Told me what?"

"Stay out of this, Dirk," said Max. "This is none of your business."

"If Alice Marie's involved, then so am I. I love her, Dad. You know that. And you're scaring her. Are you out of your mind, waving that gun around?"

"On the contrary," said Max. "It's Mr. Schwarz who is out of his mind."

Deiter broke in. "Your father is only protecting himself, Dirk. This man—Herr Schwarz—he has made outrageous accusations. He is a liar and a thief."

Dirk looked at Alice Marie. "In the name of heaven, somebody tell me what this is all about!"

Her voice trembled. "You really don't know?"

"I haven't a clue."

"Ask your father," she rasped.

Dirk took a step toward his father. "Dad? There must be some horrible misunderstanding. Give me the gun. This has gone far enough."

Max took a step backward, his pistol still aimed at Helm. "Not until Mr. Schwarz returns the papers he stole from me."

Dirk looked at Helm. "What papers?"

"Papers that prove your father has been financing the resettlement of Nazi fugitives in North and South America," Helm explained, tight-lipped.

Dirk laughed incredulously. "Nazi fugitives? Come on! You must be—"

"Starting with your uncle, Deiter Weyandt, my father's prison guard at Auschwitz."

"Auschwitz?" Dirk stared open-mouthed at his father. "What is he saying, Dad? Tell me! That my uncle is a Nazi? That you are helping Nazis?"

"Stay out of it, Son," said Max. "I have done everything in my power to protect you, to keep your hands clean. It's for your own good that you know nothing of this."

"Nothing of what?" challenged Dirk. "This man accuses you and my uncle of unspeakable things, and neither of you deny them?"

"It's true, Dirk," said Alice Marie shakily. "Helm and I have proof."

Dirk gripped the back of an armchair, his face glistening with a ruddy intensity. "Tell me, Dad! The truth!"

Something shifted in Maxwell Wyman's face; his eyes bulged in their sockets and a muscle by the side of his mouth twitched noticeably. In a halting, toneless voice he said, "Your uncle was a good soldier; he did his job well; he did what he was told, and for that they wanted to punish him."

"All right, I know Uncle Douglas had a hard time of it," said Dirk. "But what does that have to do with us?"

"Your uncle turned to me for help, and I helped him," said Max. "Then others insisted that I help them too. So I did."

Dirk nodded. "I know all about that. Everyone knows, Dad. You've dedicated your life to helping Europe's displaced persons."

"Not displaced persons," protested Helm. "Nazis! Death camp murderers! Hitler's henchmen!"

Dirk pulled off his silk bow tie and loosened his starched collar. His complexion had blanched to a pale gray. "Good heavens, Dad, tell me it's not true—you've been helping . . . Nazi war criminals?"

Maxwell's expression hardened. "I had no choice, Son."

"Of course you had a choice!" shouted Dirk. "What were you thinking of, Dad?"

"I did what I had to do. Don't condemn what you don't understand."

"But why, Dad? We're a decent, God-fearing family," argued Dirk, his voice heavy with emotion. "You're a pillar in this community, for Pete's sake. Why would you risk everything for something vile like this?"

Maxwell kept his weapon fixed on Helm. "I told you. I did it for my family. For my brother. Even for you."

"No, not for me! There has to be more to it than that!"

"There is more. I was told if I didn't cooperate someone would reveal how I had helped your Uncle Douglas—Deiter. I would have lost everything—my reputation, my home, my career. So I helped my fellow countrymen to begin new lives in new places. Is that so terrible? I am one small link in a vast chain. Our own American government has helped to relocate Nazis accused of war crimes. So do not blame me for doing what statesmen in high places have done."

Anguish raged in Dirk's voice. "How could this have gone on all these years and I never knew?"

"Because I was scrupulously careful," replied Max. "I never wanted you to know. If something went wrong, I wanted you to be blameless. I never wanted you to suffer for my actions."

Dirk raked his fingers through his fine blond hair. "Now it's over. You've been found out. You have the devil to pay!"

Deiter approached Max and the two spoke in German, their voices clipped, edged with anger. Then Max said to Dirk, "I'm sorry. I didn't plan it this way, Son. This wasn't my choice. But now you're involved."

"Involved? How?"

"It's your turn to protect our family. Take the papers Mr. Schwarz has in his jacket. Give them to me."

"Do as your father says," Deiter told him.

Dirk looked from Helm back to his father. "And if I don't?"

"I'm sorry, Dirk. I know how you feel about Miss Reed, but she and Mr. Schwarz are in a great deal of trouble. Until I have those papers in my hand—"

"If you think I'd let you harm the woman I love—"

"And if you think I'd let them destroy all I've worked for!" Maxwell took a step toward Alice Marie. The gun was pointed directly at her now. She saw Max's finger on the trigger and heard a click.

Dirk pivoted and faced Alice Marie, agony etched in his ruddy features. He sprang between her and his father, between her and the pistol. "Get out of here, Allie, you and Helm both!"

Before Alice Marie could react, Dirk lunged for the gun. "Go, Alice Marie, go!"

In the urgency of escape, with all her senses honed to the point of pain, Alice Marie bolted through the doorway and ran, clutching her long skirt to her knees, her three-inch pumps digging into the Oriental carpet. Helm sprinted behind her, his heavy shoes pummeling the carpet, his fingertips at her back, urging her on.

A shot rang out, echoing in the corridor. She looked back, a fractional glance catching the image of someone falling into the hallway and slumping on the floor.

Dirk Wyman.

Shot by his own father.

Something was wrong with Helm, had been since the night of the concert and Max Wyman's party. He was acting remote, distant, refusing to take Alice Marie's phone calls. It had been nearly a week now and she had hardly seen him since that terrible, fateful night.

He had stopped by briefly the next day to collect the papers hidden behind Catherine's painting. But he was like a stranger, brisk, businesslike, preoccupied. He said he was on his way to see the authorities, to talk with the police, the State Department, the Department of Justice, whoever would listen to him and start an investigation.

The police had already begun their investigation into the shooting and the allegations of bank fraud. Both Maxwell Wyman—who on coming to America years before had changed his name from Weyandt—and his brother, Deiter, were being held for questioning, but so far no action had been taken, no arrests made. Max Wyman kept insisting he shot his son accidentally, and Dirk, from his hospital bed, suffering only a shoulder wound, refused to contradict his father's claim. To mollify Helm, an officer contacted the Chicago police to look into a possible connection between Deiter Weyandt and Simon Golding's death, but it would likely be weeks before a report would be filed.

After the trauma of that night, Alice Marie felt too fragile emotionally to try to second-guess Helm's erratic behavior. If he didn't desire her company, so be it. He had taken his father home to his apartment and perhaps the two of them needed time alone to heal.

Meanwhile, Alice Marie hoped desperately to regain some normalcy in her own life. Besides enduring the nightmarish events at the Wyman mansion, she had experienced so many other upheavals this past year—finding and losing Cary, having Cary's baby and almost losing him, and now she was about to lose Helm, the man she loved most of all. She had never felt so vulnerable, so at risk.

Mama and Annie and the rest of the family tried to assure her she and her baby were safe now, but no matter how much she believed it intellectually, she still didn't feel safe in her heart. She found herself facing fretful days and sleepless nights. Even when she did manage to drift off, her slumber was filled with macabre dreams and grisly flashbacks to those horrifying moments in the Wyman library. She longed for Helm's consoling arms, but since he apparently wanted nothing more to do with her, she kept her yearnings to herself.

She spent her days at the hospital, making frequent visits to Dirk's room to cheer him up, followed by long hours in the nursery, rocking and feeding and playing with her baby. But she seemed to be running on nervous energy. She wasn't eating well and the nurses warned her that she wasn't getting enough rest; she needed to keep up her strength so that her son would receive sufficient nourishment. "Your baby has lost a couple of ounces this week," the pediatrician told her during his Friday morning rounds. "He should be gaining, not losing. He needs another half pound before I'll release him to go home."

"It's all my fault," she lamented. "I don't have enough milk. I've been a nervous wreck since . . ." She let her words drift off; she didn't have to tell him; everyone knew what had happened at the Wyman mansion. The newspapers were filled with the shocking headlines, and every day there were new stories, lurid rumors, and plenty of editorial conjecture. No wonder Helm was keeping a low profile these days.

"Don't worry about your baby's feedings," the pediatrician urged. "We can give him supplements if we need to. Meanwhile, you get some rest and try to relax."

Easier said than done.

During her hours in the hospital nursery Alice Marie rocked Chip and crooned simple hymns and choruses, hoping to soothe her own spirits as well as Chip's. As she rocked him she gazed out the window at the mid-April sunshine warming the earth, swathing bare limbs with bright leaves, and turning the lush grass emerald green. Silently she carried on long conversations with God; He was the only one who would understand the dark apprehensions of her soul. Only He could comfort her.

At night when she couldn't sleep she sat in the rosebud room, in her rocker by the window, the empty cradle beside her that Papa Schwarz had built. She rocked languidly, her open Bible on her lap, and memorized consoling passages from the Psalms, repeating the words aloud. *Yea, though I walk through the valley of the shadow of death, I will fear no evil: for thou art with me; . . . The sorrows of death compassed me, and the floods of ungodly men made me afraid. . . . Though I walk in the midst of trouble, thou wilt revive me: thou shalt stretch forth thine hand against the wrath of mine enemies, and thy right hand shall save me.*

The Scriptures drew her closer to God, giving her a precious companionship with His Spirit she had never known before. But she still struggled with recurring anxieties. It was as if something remained undone, unfinished, allowing a nagging unease to take root. Why wouldn't the fears go away? With the verdant glories of springtime in full bloom, why did she still feel a coldness of spirit, a chill in her bones? Perhaps she would feel better when Chip came home and the two of them headed to Chicago for a change of scene.

On the last Saturday of April, the pediatrician phoned and told Alice Marie she could come take her son home. "His weight's where we want it; he's a lusty, healthy boy, and he's raring to go home with his mommy."

Alice Marie's emotions reeled between ecstasy and panic. *I've got to call Helm,* she thought. *He always wanted to be with me when I brought Chip home.* But did he still feel that way? Did he have any interest anymore in her or her son? She phoned Helm with a measure of trepidation, half expecting Papa Schwarz to tell her what he usually said these days—Helm was busy, or out, or sleeping. And then he would add softly in his thick accent, "I tell Helmut talk to you, but he tell me nein. Is Dummkopf, ja?"

But this time Helm answered the phone, and for an instant Alice Marie was speechless. Finally she managed to blurt, "I'm bringing Chip home today. Do you want to go with me?" She hated herself for adding, "I'll understand if you're busy."

"No, I'm not busy," he said, sounding almost like the old Helm. He paused for a long moment, then said mysteriously, "Actually, I wanted to come over anyway. I have something I want to show you."

"Swell," she replied, trying not to sound too eager. "Come over whenever you wish."

"Fine. I'll be there in an hour."

An hour! She hung up the phone and flew up the stairs. How could she possibly bathe, style her hair, do her face, and find something suitable to wear in an hour?

Somehow she managed it, with even a minute or two to spare. She scrutinized herself in her full-length mirror and decided she liked what she saw. Her blonde hair was pinned back with tortoise-shell combs and hung in loose curls around her shoulders; a touch of rouge gave color to her cheeks, and she was wearing a lime green silk dress with a V-neckline and pencil-slim skirt that enhanced her slightly rounded figure.

Helm must have liked what he saw too; he gazed at her for a full minute before realizing he was staring. He apologized, his face reddening, and handed her a gold-wrapped package. "For you," he said. With a self-conscious little laugh she accepted the gift, invited him in, and offered him some of Mama's apple pie, which Mama served in the parlor with frosty glasses of iced tea.

"It's not my birthday," she said, opening the present.

He sat forward in the Queen Anne chair, rubbing his hands together nervously. "I know. This isn't really a gift. It was silly of me. I probably shouldn't have wrapped it. But I told Knowl I wanted to be the first one to show it to you."

She removed the paper and gazed down at a shiny hardbound book— Helm's book. Tears sprang to her eyes. "Oh, Helm, it's here at last— your book! It looks wonderful!" She turned it over in her hands, examining the spine and flipping gently through the pages. "Oh, it feels so solid, so important. And look at your name in big letters for all the world to see. I love it!" She looked at him. "Do you like it? Is it what you expected?"

He nodded, his eyes glistening. "It's strange, seeing my words, my thoughts right there in those pages, as if I were Shakespeare, or Sophocles, or Dante—some solemn historical figure. Not that I could ever write as well as they. But someone could pick my book up fifty years from now and share my thoughts. Someone halfway around the world in some remote village I've never heard of could read my words and be touched or changed."

"It is marvelous to think about," she agreed.

"Did you read the inscription?" he asked, sounding like an eager little boy.

"No, I didn't realize you'd signed it." She opened to the first page and her eyes scanned Helm's vigorous scrawl: *To Alice Marie, with love that goes beyond words. Always, Helm.*

"It's lovely," she said, her eyes filling.

"You helped make it happen. You and Annie and Knowl. I'll be forever indebted to you all for making my dream a reality."

"But it was your vision, Helm, your message, your passion."

They lapsed into a long silence. There was more to say, so much more, and so many tempestuous emotions beyond the words. But where to begin? She looked at Helm and saw that he was struggling too. He sighed deeply and pummeled his fist against his palm.

"You must wonder why I haven't seen you since . . ."

"Yes, I have wondered. I told myself you needed time alone, or maybe time away from me."

He ran his fingers through his thick chestnut hair. "I needed time to pray, to confront myself, and God. I needed answers."

She fingered the doily on the arm of her chair. "And did you get your answers?"

"Yes, but they weren't the answers I wanted."

She allowed her gaze to penetrate his deep sepia-brown eyes. "Tell me the answers, Helm."

He massaged his knuckles, his expression grim. "I learned some things about myself I didn't want to know."

"What things?" she asked quietly. Would he tell her there could never be anything between them, that he could never love her the way she needed to be loved? Would he tell her he was going away, and she would never see him again?

"It's about what I learned the night I tried to kill Deiter Weyandt."

"You weren't trying to kill him, Helm. Our lives were at stake. You were only—"

"Don't make excuses for me. I tried to kill the man." He rubbed his jaw, his lips tight and pallid, as if he were reliving the moment. Finally he went on, his voice wavering. "Alice Marie, I caught a glimpse that night of my own flawed humanity. I always believed a vast gulf existed between a man like Deiter Weyandt and myself. I always considered myself an honorable man, a man of principles and compassion, a man who hungered to salvage lost souls for Christ's kingdom."

"That's all true, Helm."

"But when I confronted that Nazi thug, I sank to his level. I became like him. I responded out of rage and bitterness. I felt the same loathing for Deiter Weyandt the Nazis must have felt toward my people—anger and hatred strong enough to provoke one to murder. I could have killed that man; I felt the power, that desperate, uncontrollable urge. I was no better than he—I, a man who claims to be motivated by the love of God. I was ready to kill, wanted to kill. Every fiber within me yearned to experience revenge."

She reached over and clasped his hand. "Please, Helm. Don't compare yourself to a monster like Deiter Weyandt."

"But don't you see, Alice Marie? I was reminded that whatever good is in me is there only by the grace of God. If I were placed in certain circumstances, as I was the other night, I could be as vile and unforgiving as Deiter Weyandt."

"But isn't that what we've always known about the human condition, Helm? There is none righteous, not one. We have no goodness in us, except Christ's. You taught me that."

He smiled faintly. "You're a good student, dear girl." He sat back in his chair and arched his shoulders. "At any rate, I want you to know there will be no more Nazi hunting. I will leave that to my colleagues and the authorities."

"Then what are you going to do now?" she asked, trying not to sound as if her life depended on his answer.

"I'm going to get on with the calling God has given him, to win souls to Christ. After days of agonized soul-searching and prayer, I am free of the chains Deiter Weyandt had on me; my hatred is gone. I feel cleansed inside, stripped of illusions, empty. But it is an empty spirit that Christ can fill with His love. I am ready now to pick up my life and go on."

"Wonderful, because I'm ready to get on with my life too," said Alice Marie, too brightly, blinking back tears. "So you will go to Israel with your father. And I will go to the hospital to get my son. And then, who knows? Willowbrook? Chicago? The world!"

When they had finished their pie, Helm drove Alice Marie to the hospital and walked with her to the premature nursery. "Your son's been waiting for you," said the nurse with a beaming smile. Alice Marie watched

272 CAROLE GIFT PAGE

nervously as the nurse dressed her baby in a cotton shirt, diaper, and flannel kimono. Chip was wide awake, his gray eyes moving around the room, his rosebud lips blowing tiny bubbles, his tiny round fists chopping the air.

"I brought an afghan to put him in," said Alice Marie. "It's one my mother crocheted for me when I was a baby."

"Then I'm sure your son will love it," said the nurse. When she had wrapped him snugly she lifted the tiny bundle to her shoulders. "Hospital regulations say I must carry your son out to the car. But after that he's all yours."

Alice Marie drew in a deep breath and smiled. "I'm ready."

All the way home in the car, as she held her son in her arms, Alice Marie whispered sweet endearments and hummed little lullabies. Helm looked over at her and smiled. "You're going to be a wonderful mother. Chip's a lucky little guy."

She brushed her finger against her son's downy-soft cheek. "Then why do I feel so scared?"

"All new mothers must feel that way," he said, turning onto Honeysuckle Lane. "But you'll do fine. I'm sure of it."

"I wish I could be so sure. If I can just get through these next few days."

"You'll have plenty of help and support from your family. Your mother can't wait to get her hands on her new grandson." They both laughed, then Helm said, "By the way, I heard something about a big welcome-home dinner for Chip tonight."

"Oh, you know Mama. She's putting on a big fried chicken dinner with all the trimmings. Every relative in town will be there." She looked over at him. "You and Papa are invited, you know. Mama wouldn't have a party without your father there."

Helm smiled, his gaze on the road. "I know. Papa wouldn't miss it. He's quite taken with your mother."

She chuckled. "The feeling is mutual. I haven't seen such a gleam in Mama's eyes in years."

Helm pulled up the winding driveway and parked. "Well, the house looks pretty quiet so far."

"I told Mama I didn't want any fanfare when we first got home. I want to keep things peaceful until Chip's settled in."

Helm took the baby from her arms as she got out of the car and carried him into the house. Mama bustled out from the kitchen long enough to coo over her grandson, shed a few tears, and kiss his rosy cheek. "Oh, Daughter, he's the spitting image of my Chilton. It's as if I've got my boy back again."

"I know, Mama. He reminds me of Chilton too. Listen, I'd better take him upstairs now, so he can nap before dinner."

"Yes," said Mama, her pale blue eyes glistening as she handed the baby back. "We want that young man to be bright-eyed and bushy-tailed, so he can have a proper introduction tonight to all of his family."

Alice Marie turned to Helm. "Would you like to come with me upstairs and lay Chip in his new cradle?"

"I'd be glad to do the honors."

They climbed the stairs to the rosebud room and Helm gently placed the baby in the handmade cradle. The wide-eyed infant looked around curiously for a moment, then closed his eyes, stuck his fist in his mouth and sucked vigorously.

"He loves his new cradle," said Alice Marie, bending down and tucking the crocheted afghan around him. "It's wonderful."

"Like his mother." Helm took her hand as she straightened up. They remained gazing at each other for a long moment, her hand still in his. Neither spoke. He pressed her hand to his lips and kissed her open palm, her wrist, then pulled her against him and brought his mouth down on hers.

Alice Marie wasn't sure whether the kiss lasted for moments or forever; she knew only that she was swept away to a rapturous world of gilded dreams and delight. She was in the arms of the man she had longed for all of her life.

When Helm released her he was as shaken as she was. He stumbled backward, bumping the writing desk. "I'd better go," he stammered, "and get ready for your mother's party."

He was nearly to the door when Alice Marie called him back. "Wait, Helm, don't go. I can't let you leave like this."

He came back to her and put his arms around her waist. "I must go," he said solemnly. "When I'm with you like this I can't think straight."

She searched his eyes. "Darling, how long will we keep running away from each other?"

Helm's dusky eyes clouded and a strange desolation crept into his voice. "What else can we do, dearest girl? We're going different ways. We have different destinies."

She ran her fingertips along his temple. "It doesn't have to be that way, Helm."

"What are you saying?"

"I'm saying I want to go with you."

"Go with me? Where?"

"To Israel or wherever God calls you." She cupped his face in her hands. "I want to be by your side, Helm. It's crazy, I know. I've made my plans. I have my life, my son, my career. But in my heart God is telling me—whispering in my soul—to go with you and be with you whatever you do. We belong together; it's as if God is saying we can serve Him better together than apart."

"It sounds wonderful, Alice Marie, but you don't know what you're saying—"

"Yes, I do, Helm. Listen to me. It's all so clear—don't you see it? We love each other, we love Chip, and we love God." She studied him intently. "You do love me, don't you? Your kiss said it more than any words could."

He chuckled wryly. "Yes, silly girl, I adore you."

"And I love you with all my heart!" She wound her arms around his neck and pressed her cheek against his chest. "Helm, there's a verse in the book of Ruth—I can't recall the exact words—but it says, Let me go with you. Where you dwell I shall dwell. Your people shall be my people and your God my God."

He cradled her head under his chin and smoothed her long tresses. "I know that passage well," he murmured against her hair. "'Entreat me not to leave thee, or to return from following after thee: for whither thou goest, I will go; and where thou lodgest, I will lodge; thy people shall be my people, and thy God my God: Where thou diest, will I die, and there will I be buried: the Lord do so to me, and more also, if aught but death part thee and me.'"

She gazed up at him. "That's how I feel, Helm. Let nothing but death ever separate us."

He held her in a long embrace. "It won't be easy, Darling. I don't know where God will call us or what life will bring, but I want you and Chip beside me always." He held her at arm's length and smiled tantalizingly. "What would your mother say if we told her she's not just throwing a welcome home party for Chip tonight, but an engagement party for her daughter and future son-in-law?"

Alice Marie laughed. "I'd say she'll be delighted to welcome you— and your father!—to the family."

He took her arm, his russet eyes dancing. "Shall we go downstairs and find out?"

"Yes, I'd love to. Just give me a moment."

He squeezed her hand meaningfully. "I'll give you forever."

"I'll hold you to that," she said with a lingering smile.

She stooped down and kissed her infant son on the forehead, then rose and gazed fondly around the rosebud room, feeling the loving warmth and tender memories of generations of Reeds and Herricks surrounding her, their presence as fanciful and delicate as the filigreed flowers in Mama's lacework.

THE END

ABOUT THE AUTHOR

Carole Gift Page, an award-winning novelist, is presently under contract for her fortieth book. Writing professionally for more than twenty-five years, she is a frequent speaker at conferences, schools, churches, and women's ministries. Carole has taught creative writing at Biola University and is founder of the Inland Empire Christian Writer's Guild.

She is the author of the first three books in the Heartland Memories Series—*The House on Honeysuckle Lane, Home to Willowbrook,* and *The Hope of Herrick House*—and of *In Search of Her Own* and *Decidedly Married,* among the first romances from Harlequin's Steeple Hill line. Carole and her husband, Bill, have three children and live in Moreno Valley, California.

Look for the first three books in the Heartland Memories series

The House on Honeysuckle Lane

The first in the series, this novel takes place in the 1930s, where best friends Annie Reed and Cath Herrick share their dreams of the future at Annie's beautiful house on Honeysuckle Lane. But never in their dreams could they have imagined how troubles in the world around them would reach into their lives and change so much.

0-8407-6777-3 • Trade Paperback • 286 pages

Home to Willowbrook

This moving sequel to *The House on Honeysuckle Lane* takes place after Cath Herrick awakens from a coma and must rebuild her shattered life. And though her best friend Annie wants desperately to help, Cath knows she must make the choice to let go of bitterness and learn to forgive.

0-8407-6778-1 • Trade Paperback • 240 pages

The Hope of Herrick House

After a fire kills her mother and destroys her home, Bethany Rose Henry comes to live with her half-sister Catherine Herrick. Resentful and frightened, she must now contend with a new world as she gets to know the family she never knew she had and soon learns that her mother's death was not accidental. As clues point to one of Catherine's family members, will she speak up? Or push everyone away, including the handsome young minister who has fallen in love with her?

0-8407-6780-3 • Trade Paperback • 280 pages